Windwalker

a Novel

Author ~ Donna Sundblad

Epress-online.com
An Imprint of Writopia, Inc.
Norfolk, VA U.S.A.
ISBN: 0-9772224-8-9

Editors: Joan McNulty-Pulver, Joy Hardin, Debi Markee
Afterword by Jack Herrmann
Cover Art by Mel Landon
Book Design by Nadene Carter

First printing, 2006

Dedication

To the All Knowing One

With Gratitude

I wish to acknowledge the contributions of the following people:

To my sweetheart and husband, Rick, for the space and time he freely gives for me to write, and for his invaluable feedback. Windwalker wouldn't exist without his willingness to go the extra mile with chores around the house, and his patience as I cart around the laptop as a frequent companion.

To my grandson, Jeremiah, for listening to Windwalker chapters and asking me what happens next.

To my granddaughter, Taylor, for our walks and talks about the characters that come alive in this book, and the tears in her eyes that show the story touched her heart.

To my good friend and cover artist, Mel Landon, for putting up with changes to the cover without batting an eye, and for her willingness to offer an expert opinion along with creative input.

To my son-in-law, Kraig, for his technical help saving my files when my hard drive crashed and for answering my questions no matter how foolish.

To my daughter, Heather, for taking care of household chores while I lived within the pages of Windwalker's many stages.

To my editors Joan McNulty-Pulver, Joy Hardin, and Debi Markee for helping Windwalker become what it is today.

To my editor-in-chief, Margaret Carr, for believing in me.

Chapter 1
The Telling

She dipped her fingertip into the mud
and painted a circle on her forehead representing the eternal hope.

Fires burned in the bellies of small stone statues forming a circle within the Kiva. An orange glow warmed the chamber to the center of the gathering. In the back of the crowded cave, Awena sat against the wall resting her arm across her stomach. The baby kicked. Soon, her life with Cedrick would change. What kind of world would their child find? Cedrick's talk of fulfilled prophecies and the cycle of death scared her.

Steady beats of a drum echoed within the chamber. Cedrick stepped to the center of the circle. He sat upon the teaching stone and the drumming stopped.

"Ojal pulled her poncho tighter and steadied her steps with the twisted staff," Cedrick started. He glanced at the intense faces, young and old. "The chilled mountain breeze tugged wisps of steel gray hair free from thick braids draped over her shoulders. She stopped, leaning against the sheer rock wall. Cold seeped through the thick, hand-painted animal skin, but it felt good; this trek was almost more than her old bones could endure. She flexed her foot and secretly cursed the malformation."

A nearby group of girls huddled and whispered. "She was the last of the Augurs," the oldest said.

"There will be another," the girl beside her piped up, "chosen from among the Windwalkers."

Trinak, Awena's aunt, leaned forward and tapped the girl. "Hush!" She settled back into the shadows. "Listen and learn."

Cedrick cast a glance in their direction and smiled at Awena. His dark hair gleamed in the firelight as he turned his attention to the other side of the room. "The joints in Ojal's fingers burned," he said, "her age-spotted hand clutched the staff that served more as a cane than an amulet."

A murmur spread through the crowd.

Cedrick stood. "The time for discussion follows the telling." The missing Augur's staff remained a popular debate throughout the land. Each head bowed in respect awaiting their Potent's permission to look up. The Potent glanced at his Jonnick guests. The Jonnick healer shouldered a hump on the left side of his back, yet bowed out of respect. His brother Philander also honored Stygian ways. If only all Jonnick behaved like them. Cedrick walked the circle and touched the head of each man. They glanced up at their Potent and in turn touched the heads of their women and children. One by one, heads rose.

Philander's blind eye glowed in the firelight as he looked up into the Stygian leader's face. Cedrik paused with his hand on the Philander's thinning white hair. Time would reveal if he was the one. He stepped backward to the teaching stone without turning his back on his listeners and took his place.

"Rivulets of melting snow trickled in zigzag patterns, diverted by the spiny-leafed shrubs that grew at that altitude," he continued. "A cluster of delicate yellow flowers with white centers sprung from the rock wall and caught her attention. What do we call these flowers today?"

"Ojal's Hint," the people answered in unison.

Cedrick smiled and nodded. "Ojal's gnarled fingers reached toward the delicate petals while she inhaled the light scent. It took her mind off her discomfort and released her to think of Kynan. The young Potent led the tribe well. She loved him as a son."

One among the group of girls stood.

Cedrick tipped his head in the girl's direction as he got to his feet. "You have a question, Guese?"

"Yes, Potent. Did Augur Ojal have to take her mind off herself to walk on the wind?"

Guese fiddled with the end of the long dark braid draped over her shoulder.

Cedrick sat again and waited for the girl to approach and take her place at his feet. "Augurs travel upon the physical plane with much discomfort. Born of a Windwalker, a true Augur is marked by a bumble foot. Throughout the ages, people debate why Ojal didn't wear the body of one of her metots. We don't know the answer. It's not part of the telling. Some say that if she took the form of a bird, an archer might have shot her through, and she'd be no more." Cedrick smiled at the girl. "What we hear in the telling is what we need to know. Ojal's trek to the site where she could see Kynan was most difficult. Remember, an Augur, while in human form, must see the person she plans to visit or have an invitation to join them.

"Guese, take your seat." He glanced around the crowded cavern. "Please withhold anymore questions until the time of the telling is complete."

Awena shifted her weight, and folded her hands across her stomach.

Cedrick perched one hip against the teaching stone at the center of the Kiva. "Ojal leaned against the mountain pointing her staff toward Kynan in the distance. Sunlight glistened on the three small stones on the pendant hanging against her chest. Each stone marked a symbol. The characters etched in the silver outlined steps that opened her eyes to know the future. As the wind carries sparks from a fire, Ojal's gift carried her to the cliff jutting precariously toward the sea. A stiff sea breeze clawed at the hide draped across her shoulders. She stepped beside the young Potent, resting her hand on his shoulder.

"'Kynan, the ships of which I foretold will be here soon,' she said.

"He nodded and turned toward the old woman. His dark eyes studied her. 'We've expected them for decades. You told my father's father of this visit … this merging. It is the time of the thaw.' His attention drifted to the rolling waves of the sea below. 'This may be the year.'

"She ambled closer to the edge of the overhang and leaned on her staff."

Within the Kiva, Guese bent toward her companion mumbling about the unknown whereabouts of the staff.

Cedrick sat straight glancing in her direction.

"Forgive me, Potent." She tucked her chin to her chest. The girl's father reached out and placed his palm on her head. When she looked up, he placed his finger to his lips. She bit her bottom lip and nodded.

Cedrick continued. "Ojal said, 'It is different this year, Kynan. I'm not here to tell you it may happen, or that it will take place in the month of the thaw twenty-four moons from now. The time is now. Four moons ago I saw them in a vision. Men, women and children filled four great ships. Hunger and disease chased the Jonnick from their homeland but a lingering menace travels with them. Be cautious of the magic of the Mage, yet show them hospitality, for the skies and seas have dealt a harsh journey.'

"Kynan had heard this familiar telling from childhood. 'They don't sound dangerous,' he said, 'but in need of help. The land can support them as well as us. It would be wrong to turn them away.'"

Cedrick watched the humpback Healer and his half-blind brother from his peripheral vision. They nodded with the others.

"'Yes, it would be wrong,' Ojal said. She propped her weight on the sturdy staff. 'The difficult path.' She smiled. 'They search for new beginnings.' Her dark eyes searched the horizon where the blue sea melded with the sky in an indiscernible line. 'They arrive on these shores soon.'

"Ojal pointed toward the crashing waves at the base of the mountain. Dark sandy shores lined with boulders stretched to the right for as far as they could see. 'The land' she said, 'will sustain them in spite of their ways.' Visions of stockade walls flashed through her head. In her mind, noisy crowds spilled onto the tiny outcropping where she now stood with Kynan, but in another time; a future time. The unsettling faces of the future scared her. She massaged her temple. 'Their alien customs shall change the land. In their tongue, they call the land *Ranaan*.'

"'Ranaan.' The foreign word rolled awkwardly from his tongue. Kynan stepped directly beside her. 'They've named the land,' he repeated flatly, 'as if they own it.' He shook his head. 'So, they do not understand the relationship?'

"With the tip of her staff firmly planted, she turned to look at him. 'Correct. They do not understand,' she said. 'The Jonnick clan will stake claims.'

"Kynan stood straight. 'Don't lose hope. I will teach them to live in harmony with the land. They can migrate with our clan or join another. They will—'

"Ojal raised her palm to interrupt him. 'You will be a good teacher.' She nodded and stared at the sea. 'Do your part, Kynan. Teach them to let go of the hatred; have faith that the joining brings unity. You have been prepared for this day.'

"Kynan adjusted his poncho. 'Ojal.' He cocked his head slightly. 'Does this mean that you will make the journey to meet your forefathers?'

"She nodded and tucked a loose strand of gray hair behind her ear. 'I travel to a place of rest until the Cycle of Death. At that time I'll return to the land, called to guide, while another takes my place.' Tears brimmed along her lower lashes and quietly followed the creases of her wrinkled cheek. 'Trouble, Kynan. Trouble before the joining.' She swallowed hard. 'And a time of silence.'

"'But that's not in my lifetime, Ojal.' Kynan shrugged one shoulder. 'I can only teach them our ways. I'll welcome them and offer the new beginning they seek. The land will provide. I cannot be responsible for choices others make.'

"'You are right,' Ojal said. 'During your lifetime Jonnick and Stygian shall live in harmony, working together. However, Stygian life in the land shall wax worse and worse until the time of silence.' A smile lifted the folds of time on her face. 'Do your part, Kynan. Write down what you've been taught. For it is from your loins the Arich shall come, and one day rid the land of the division about to be forged. The eye will guide the ones who want to see.'"

Cedrick glanced at the two Jonnick seated among his clan. Philander's blinded eye shined like a silver orb in the firelight.

"Warmth from Ojal's palm rested on Kynan's shoulder," Cedrick reached out and plucked a twig from the fire in the closest statue, "her touch grew hotter, burning his skin." He waved the burning stick through the air. The red ember streaked through the darkness until he pressed the glowing tip against the rock floor crushing it to ash.

"Kynan pulled away and rubbed his shoulder. Sometimes Ojal's powers unnerved him, but he didn't tell her so. Roaring waves slammed the base of the mountain drawing his attention to the sea and out to the horizon.

"'What does that mean?' he asked. 'The eye?' He turned, didn't see her, and twisted in the opposite direction. 'When will that … be?' He threw his hands in the air. She'd disappeared again. He massaged the sting of her touch."

The crowd within the Kiva laid one arm atop the other in front of their chests slapping their forearms in applause. Philander glanced at the Healer and leaned close enough to whisper something in his ear.

Cedrick stood, lifted his water skin and shot a stream of water into his mouth. "Add fuel to the fires, for within tonight's telling a new revelation shall unfold."

Muted sounds of excitement mingled with the stirring of bodies settling down to hear more. He smiled and resumed his seat.

"Back on the mountain trail, Ojal leaned forward and inhaled the light floral scent of the yellow blossoms. The aroma caressed her troubled soul. She turned to see Kynan in the distance standing on the cliff. The wind lifted his dark hair away from his face like the mane of a stampeding stallion. He watched for the ships. In time, he would see the mark of the eye and understand his place in history. The birth of fulfillment of the words of the ancients had come to pass and the seed of his loins would save the Stygian race from extinction. This Arich would bear the same mark.

"Water dripped from the scraggy branch of a shrub growing from the side of the mountain and formed a pool near her foot. She mixed the light brown dirt with the toe of her deformed foot. In her visions she walked without a limp, could even run, jump and fly. Would it be so while she awaited the joining? She dipped her fingertip into the mud and painted a circle on her forehead representing the eternal hope.

"A sigh whispered past her lips. She'd never bore a child, had missed the pleasure of a man's touch." Cedrick cast a glance in Awena's direction. "People flocked to Ojal as Augur but a deep-seeded loneliness served as her companion. She'd surrendered these pleasures for long life. All these years, people thought it didn't bother her and soon it wouldn't. She'd witnessed her end to this existence and that of many others. It arrived with the ships and the sickness stowed like cargo. No different than Kynan, she had choices to make.

"Using the tip of her mud-coated finger, she painted the line of life from the Spirit circle down the bridge of her nose. 'Life is the breath,' she said."

Cedrick stood. The crowd did the same, slapping their forearms furiously. "Tonight," Cedrick announced above the noise, "we have an honored guest to give forth a telling. A Teller with a tale never told within this clan." The applause died. People glanced at one another wide-eyed. Cedrick gestured with his arm for the one-eyed Jonnick to join him at the teaching rock.

Cedrick motioned for the people to sit. A handful of men hesitated, but sat one at a time when they saw they stood alone. "Most of you know this man," Cedrick said. "Philander of Chock comes from the clan that arrived on those ships. Tonight, he presents a telling of the Jonnick's arrival to the land. A telling Jonnick, today, ignore." Cedrick stepped to the side and pointed for Philander to sit upon the teaching stone.

He sat in the seat of honor, bowed his head to the Potent, and turned toward the crowd. In a gesture of humility, he looked down, honoring his brother and others while clutching a brown leather book to his chest. "Thank you, Potent, for this opportunity. My forefathers owe their lives to your ancestors. I have their stories here." He lifted the book to face them.

Murmurs and low-voiced chatting peppered the crowd. Cedrick's voice boomed within the Kiva. "I expect you to show our guest the same respect you offer me."

Conversations ended abruptly.

"He doesn't have to present a telling. If you prefer to remain ignorant, I will not require you to stay." One by one, the people lowered their heads. Cedrick walked the circle, touching each man's scalp. From oldest to youngest, the people sat united. Cedrick bowed toward Philander, walked to the back of the circle to touch Awena's head and that of her elderly aunt, Trinak. He crouched and took his seat beside his wife.

Chapter 2
Telling of the Jonnick

"The crew's saying it's the spirits; that we're all going to die."

Philander cleared his throat. "I've lived my life as a goatherd not a speaker like this." He glanced toward his brother, Nilenam, who smiled nervously. Philander turned his good eye toward Cedrick. The Potent signaled for him to begin. "The captain of the Jonnick ships served much like a Potent. I wanted to explain this before the telling."

Cedrick nodded; Philander took a deep breath, let it out slowly, and sat upon the teaching stone.

"Captain Donnel Brophy leaned against the railing and stared into the dark water from the deck of his ship. He'd lost three more people on the Adara, but not until after he'd quarantined them with the others on the Vanya.

"His thoughts troubled him knowing that if they didn't find land soon, they'd all be doomed to this blasted disease. He fingered the egg size lump on his neck. Visions of his mother-in-law spitting a curse in his face flashed through his mind. 'As a blade divides bone from marrow, so shall you carry the seed to divide the land where your feet come to rest.' She'd cursed him for taking her daughter and unborn grandchild across the sea, yet in her selfishness she refused to come along. The spiteful woman never accepted the ordinary mortal.

"He yanked the collar of his uniform higher to hide the swelling, and raked his fingers through his blonde waves. He grabbed a fist full of hair and yanked in frustration. If that curse were real, would it be fair to take his family to a new land? He knew what she wanted. She expected him to turn around, return to Jonnick and grovel at her feet for the cure, but he set his face toward the new land. He'd rather die than have his child grow under the influence of the Mage.

"'Sir?'

"Donnel spun around, slipped his hat into place and stood face to face with his cousin and first mate Evan Davis. 'Yes, Davis?'"

Philander sat upon the teaching stone playing with the neck of his tunic mimicking the Captain's moves. "Captain Brophy fiddled with his collar."

"His cousin, Evan Davis, had bright blue eyes that stood in stark contrast to his sun reddened face. They'd set sail in the month of Yeppa as winter set in. Not a choice time to sail, but the sickness would overtake them if they stayed. People on the harbored ships started to drop from the sickness. No one neared the ships. The sickness spread throughout Jonnick like wildfire. Donnel Brophy, Evan Davis and the others threw the dead overboard and confiscated four empty ships. Now, ghosts of the dead cursed them with the sickness.

"'Well, Sir. It's the Vanya.' Davis stared at his cousin eye to eye, his hands folded at the small of his back. 'It's gone.'

"'Gone?' Donnel Brophy stood straight. His mind raced to take in the ramifications of a missing ship. 'What do you mean gone?'

"Evan took a step closer. 'The crew's saying it's the spirits; that we're all going to die.'"

The Stygian within the Kiva stared at Philander without a sound. Cedrick took Awena's hand in his own and squeezed it. A smile flickered across her lips and the two turned their attention back to the telling.

"The captain shoved his palm against the first mate's chest. 'Don't be absurd.' Fear of the Mage's power filled him with panic. Could her powers reach this far? He searched the rolling waves. The Adara drifted off their bow, sails almost slack while the Namo trailed behind them by at least a half a mile. He turned left to scan the horizon, spun and searched the vast emptiness to his right. Queasiness grabbed his innards and squeezed. His fingers fumbled with the telescope in the pouch at his waist.

"*It can't be*, he thought, *I have one hundred thirty sick people aboard that ship.* The cool metallic eyepiece rested against his weathered skin. Methodically, a sector at a time, he scrutinized the sea for debris or a survivor. A thick rolling fog retreated in the distance. He rubbed his eye and looked again. The fog had cleared leaving behind clear seas.

"'Maybe they went mad from the sickness and sunk the ship,' Evan said. He stepped back and waited for the Captain's reply.

"Donnel sucked in a deep breath and let it out slowly. 'That makes more sense than spirits. There's nothing out here to cause a wreck.' He nibbled peeling blisters on his sun-dried lips. Could his mother-in-law's icy control still touch lives around him? He would not accept it.

"'Land, ho!' a seaman shouted from the crow's nest.

"'Land?' The Captain lifted the telescope to his eye one more time. 'I didn't see ?'

"'We're saved, Donnel.' Evan clapped his cousin on the back. 'We've made it. I didn't think you could do it, but you did.'

"Distant mountains obscured by purple haze looked like sleeping giants on the horizon. 'I see it.' Donnel handed the telescope to Evan. 'We actually made it!'

"The smile on Evan Davis' face disappeared as he handed the telescope to the Captain. 'Too bad we all couldn't have made it.'

"Donnel stared at the deck and nodded. Should he tell Evan the truth? Warn him? He shirked the idea and barked orders. He'd get the rest of his people to the shores of Ranaan if it took his last breath. His hand moved to the swelling knot in his neck. A warm trickle leaked from .his right nostril. He blotted it with his knuckle, stared at the blood and prayed for the wind to pick up.

"*I'd like to feel dry land beneath my feet before I die,* he thought. He wiped the blood on his dark blue trousers and moved to the bridge. He pushed thoughts of his wife Amelia and their unborn child to the back of his mind. First things first, preparations needed to be made in order to disembark the crew and their families."

Philander stood and Cedrick's clan filled the Kiva with arm-slapping applause.

* * * *

Across the Valley of Rocks a mammoth castle loomed above the southern ridge.From the spire of the eastern tower, Queen Riona poised on the balcony in her royal robes. Staring north into the valley, as the shadows of twilight crept from one rock formation to another, she considered the Stygian prophecies.A few lazy clouds drifted in the violet sky where stars appeared as twinkling pinpoints of light in the moonless sky.

Piece by piece, she'd taken these prophecies apart seeking opportunities to make it impossible to fulfill them. Yet, uncertainties lingered. Had she overlooked something as Senta suggested? Thanks to her mother's planning, the castle stood as the only large stone structure within the valley. If the Stygian expected to rally and take the land by stealth from a Fortress of Stone, it would be here and she would be ready for them.

Her Scribe, Senta, stirred doubts in her confidence. Why hadn't these

details been brought to her attention years ago? It reminded her of
Philander. Anger churned in the pit of her stomach as she slipped into
the warmth of the throne room. The sting of rejection lingered as fresh
as the day it happened. She cast a glance at the mirrored wall, and for
a brief moment wondered what she'd look like if the fulfillment of the
times removed the spell of youth.

"Have you corroborated the details surrounding the birth of the
Arich?" she asked.

Senta stood beside her throne nodding, adjusting her cape as she took
her place.

Her stiff posture pressed against the ornate straight back of the
throne trimmed in gold and precious stones. She leaned on one elbow,
massaging her chiseled chin. Her attention drifted to her reflection. The
jewels in her crown glittered in the firelight.

The spell committed to memory a lifetime ago ran through her
mind:

Immutable youth, control to keep
Cleansing of Ranaan, Stygian sleep
Frozen within the dragon's lair
The cage of ice imprison there
Arcane powers make them mine
Transform, protect, Ranaan refine
Carry me to the Fortress of Stone
Entrust the kingdom to me alone

Without warning, she thrust from her throne in a blur of velvet
and satin. Senta skittered back a few paces. She swept the length of
the polished stone floor with long deliberate strides. The sound of her
footsteps echoed and came to an abrupt halt. Her cape draped across her
back as the balloon of air beneath it deflated.

She turned and looked at the short, round man standing beside her
throne. "How sure are you, Senta?"

Senta studied the floor and glanced at the queen without raising his
head. "I'm sorry, Queen Riona, but the wise ones say the prophecy is due
to unfold when the moon is but a crescent and a star lays beneath it."

"Fools!" She walked toward Senta. Her lip cured into a sneer. "*That*
prophecy tells of the coming of the Arich to power, not his birth." Her
memories shot to the past and the lessons she learned from Philander in

her youth. If only he'd agreed to join her as Conscript....

"If they can't determine signs in the skies what use are they to me? Fools serve me as Wise Men."

Senta backed toward the door and trembled. "I ... I'm sorry, Queen Riona, I only tell my lady the words spoken to me."

Riona lifted her chin. Her haughty blue eyes fixed on the messenger. "My dear, Senta," she drew in a breath, exhaling slowly, "if we snuff the life of the Arich at birth, we'll have no concern to watch for a crescent moon or a star."

Senta stood straighter. "May the Queen extend her grace that I may speak my mind?" He bowed and waited.

"What is it, Senta?" Riona let out an exasperated breath.

"We have more than one birth to watch for, my dear Queen. If we eliminate either child, mentioned in the prophecies, we overturn the power of fulfillment."

Riona hurried across the room toward Senta standing beside her throne. He stepped back pressing his eyes shut. Riona's hands clasped his face and squeezed his cheeks. "You're a genius, Senta. Do you know what it says?" She shook his head. "The exact words? We must know exactly?" She stared into his eyes as they opened.

"Yes, my Queen."

She let go of his face, spun and sat on her throne. "Tell me." Her face inches from his; she leaned on the arm of her throne.

Senta rubbed his cheek. "The interpretation may—"

"Tell me!" Blood pumped in her ears and heated her face. "I want to know the exact words."

He stood straight and stared ahead avoiding the queen's gaze. "Birth of the Augur hidden, surrounded by a sea of strangers from which the Arich will emerge."

"Fool! It tells us nothing about *when* this Augur will be born."

Senta closed his eyes. "Yes, my Queen, but an Augur is born with a deformed foot. A female child, coming from the line of Windwalkers, but more powerful." He opened one eye peeking at the queen. "If we kill every child born with a deformed foot," he said, "no Augur will meet the Arich. If that relationship doesn't occur, it eliminates the chance for the Augur to assist the Arich in ushering the Stygian forces to occupy the land." Senta winced and waited for her orders.

"Ranaan belongs to me!" Queen Riona slapped her hand against the armrest. She clicked her fingers. "Write this for me."

Senta rushed to the desk, dipped his quill in the bottle of pigment and scratched the words across the parchment.

"I decree it against the law to speak of this Arich or teach the ways of the Stygian people. Let the citizens of Ranaan destroy Stygian works to eliminate their sympathizers."

Senta scribbled furiously and marked the end of the document, took in a deep breath and blew to dry the ink.

"Secondly, to every midwife, healer or citizen…"

The Scribe spread the parchment across his desk, dipped his quill and frantically scratched each word.

"…report the birth of any child born on a moonless night whether in the past or present."

Senta glanced up. "Moonless?"

"Write it!" Riona didn't necessarily believe all this superstition, but it wouldn't hurt to keep her eye on any child presenting a threat. Her fear rested on the possibility that her people might honor a new leader based on the timing of their birth.

Senta looked up from his task. "How do you expect the barbarian Stygian to honor our laws? They won't understand."

"Careful, Senta. You border on sympathizing with the Stygian. I should hate it if you forced me to take the sight of your left eye."

Senta shot his attention to the parchment and avoided her stare. "Yes, Queen Riona. I only meant they could not be trusted."

She stepped from her throne and walked to his side. With the palm of her hand, she petted his thinning hair like a dog. "That's better, Senta. Tickle my ears with what I like to hear, and you shall serve at my side as long as you live."

He glanced up. "I am blessed to serve."

A deep chuckle escaped her throat and she turned away. "Even Stygian use midwives and healers. I'll reward anyone offering information."

Her mistrust for Senta flared. "Add this." She avoided looking his direction. "Every soulless child, born on a moonless night shall be put to death at birth and reported to the throne. Likewise, any child born with a deformity of the foot, a Bumble Foot, shall be put to death at birth and reported to the throne."

She spun around and grabbed the parchment from her assistant. The quill dragged across the paper smearing a black line to the edge of the parchment. Her eyes scanned the blotchy scribbles. She raised her chin and glanced at Senta with half closed lids. If she placed her seal on this decree it became law, and she had to trust him to tell her what it said. "Would you say this is adequate?"

Senta bowed his head. "Yes, my Queen. It thwarts the Stygian problem before it takes root."

"Well said, Senta." Riona thrust the parchment toward her Scribe. "Read it to me. I want to hear the sound of it falling from your lips."

"Queen of Ranaan, Riona of Jonnick, issues the following decrees:

"First, when the Stygian return from their wanderings following what they call the cycles of life and enter the great valley and surrounding mountains, they will honor Jonnick law or be forbidden to live in Ranaan."

Riona propped her thumb beneath her chin, the remainder of her fingertips tapping her ageless cheek. Eventually, she'd rid Ranaan of the Stygian. Nothing would give her greater pleasure.

"Second, it is forbidden to speak of an Arich or teach the ways of Stygian people. In obedience to this decree, let the great citizens of Ranaan destroy Stygian works.

"Third, each midwife, healer or citizen must report knowledge of any birth taking place on a moonless night in the past or present. Furthermore, every soulless child, born on such a night shall be put to death and reported to the throne. Likewise, any child born with a deformity of the foot, a Bumble Foot, shall be put to death at birth and reported to the throne."

A smile spread across Riona's lips. She swiped the quill from Senta's hand, made her mark and blotted her seal at the bottom of the page. She held the parchment in the air to dry. Her hand trembled as Senta plucked it from her grasp. "Deliver that to the Captain," she said.

Senta bowed from the waist several times as he backed out the door. Beyond the threshold, he straightened his back and smiled. "Thank you, my dear Queen. That's exactly what I'm going to do." He slapped the rolled parchment against his palm, turned and headed down the hall with his cape fluttering behind him.

Chapter 3
The Births

*"Tonight I travel to the Fortress of Stone to prepare for the great gathering.
My ancestors call for me to join them at the gate to the new land."*

Only by the power of Cedrick's position within the clan, did this outsider sit upon the teaching stone. Hearing about the unborn child of the Jonnick leader tugged at the father-to-be's heart. His focus rested on Awena's stomach, swollen with life. He turned his attention back to the slender, white-haired teller standing before his people, still clasping the brown book to his chest. He bowed toward Cedrick who walked to the center of the circle.

Two men scurried with bundles of fuel, feeding fires in the bellies of the statues. Light flickered to life, brightening the center of the circle where the teaching stone stood. Elongated shadows danced across the cavern walls.

"Thank you." Cedrick clapped Philander's shoulder. "You have filled a gap in the telling we've never known." He motioned toward the empty seat beside the Healer. Philander shuffled from the center of the circle to sit with his brother.

The fire keepers hurried to sit with family members in the crowd while Philander settled in. Cedrick sat upon the scooped out center of the large smooth stone. Flickering light danced across the faces of his listeners.

Cedrick stepped to the teaching stone. "Droves of narrow, shallow boats cut through mild seas paddling toward the three ships anchored in the bay off the coast." Kynan stood on the shore and awaited the arrival of the fair-haired Jonnick foretold of in the prophecies. He closed his eyes and breathed in a breath of salty sea air. He'd been warned for decades, now the survival of his people rested on him.

"Sunshine warmed his shoulders. He loosened the animal hide draped over his back and moved into the shade of a tamarack tree. The flutter of wings rustled the leaves above his head. A shiny, black raven cawed from the low-hanging branch. Terror seized him. For an instant, he longed for simpler times when he didn't understand the signs, when he didn't know the iridescent shimmer of the raven's feathers carried a message of death.

"A signal from the ships grabbed his attention. A Stygian elder waved a flaming torch back and forth from the deck of the closest ship. Black smoke poured from the flame, drifted skyward and feathered above the ship in the light breeze.

"The crew jumped from the ship. Arms windmilled, slicing through the sea toward our boats. Fair heads bobbed like milk melons in the tranquil water while others splashed toward shore.

"Kynan admonished himself. He wanted to be with the others doing something more than standing at the lookout. He preferred leading by example."

"This is my favorite part," a boy sitting beside his father within the telling circle cried out. His father gave him a stern look; the boy glanced around, smiled and bowed his head until his father reached out with the touch of forgiveness.

"The breeze kicked up," Cedrick continued. One of his favorite parts as a child, he enjoyed this part of the telling. "Sand peppered his ankles. He shifted his stance. Something tickled his ankle and wrapped around his leg. He reached down peeling a transparent snakeskin from his limb. What were the spirits telling him? Ojal's words rang in his mind. *'It's a sign. Learn to read the signs.'*

"Shouts from the burning ships sounded far away. Cargo splashed into the indigo deep as crew and Stygian hurled barrels overboard. Fire devoured canvas sails and crawled up the three masts as the first wave of Stygian and Jonnick worked toward shore. Hazy black smoke hung over the water like a sinister cloud. The ship furthest from shore leaned, smoldered and slipped into the sea. Without those ships, the Jonnick were here to stay.

"Giggles disrupted Kynan's thoughts. He turned and caught a glimpse of the dark haired child cowering behind the boulders near the path. 'Ikki, what did I tell you?' He glanced over his shoulder at the burning ships. 'Wait with your mother at the camp.'

"Ikki bowed his head, turned and scurried down the trail. Kynan shook his head. His son, the curious one. A smile lifted the left side of his mouth as the boy disappeared around the bend. The breeze tugged the snakeskin in his hand. He smoothed it between his fingers and folded it once.

"'Birth,' he doubled the discarded skin a second time, 'life,' he folded, 'death...' He creased it one last time sticking it in the pouch at his waist. He stared out at the haze rolling above the water. '...and rebirth.' It was a sign of hope. Ojal would be proud.

"'Yes, rebirth.' Ojal spoke to his left.

"Kynan's heart fluttered; his nostrils flared. 'I wish you'd warn me before you speak. One moment I am alone, and the next I have an old woman telling me what I already know.'

"Ojal looked different. Her dark eyes lacked luster. 'The Jonnick's arrival marks the cycle of life; followed by death. Remember, it is only slumber until the time of the Arich which ushers in the time of rebirth.'

"Kynan searched the horizon; the last ship leaned to the left engulfed in flames. 'I know death follows life, but how can this be a time of life if the ships carry death?'

"'A cycle within a cycle,' Ojal said, 'death is part of life. As Potent you must remain strong, Kynan. Hardship washes ashore.' She rested her gnarled fingers on his well-muscled arm. 'You're right. These ships bring death and something worse than death,' she nodded toward the crowd gathering on the beach, 'but many will survive. Look beyond; use the wisdom of the Seeing Eye. The loss will make you stronger and draw you close to the Jonnick forging the bond of unity.'

"'Can't you tell me plainly, Ojal? I want to know what to do, how to lead our people.'

"A spark of fight flashed in her eyes. 'As Potent think for yourself and pass on what you learn. As Augur, I guide. I've done my part to prepare you.' She shook a gnarled finger in his direction. 'You must go to your people and teach them to follow the path leading to unity. The cycle of death foretold by the ancients obliterates our people if the Arich does not do his part, for the Arich's role has bearing on our destiny. His dreams influence his actions and his actions alter reality. You lay a foundation. When he builds upon your foundation, death will be naught but sleep. However, this will not come to pass if you neglect to hand down what you've learned. You are the keeper of the gift. Write it in stone. Preserve it. Others will do the same. Teach your son and your son's son.'"

Cedrick stood. "Now," he said, "I'd like to ask our guest to come and finish his part of the telling." He gestured toward Philander.

The white haired man stood, bowed his head and stepped to the center of the circle.

Cedrick rested his arm across Philander's shoulder. "We follow the path that leads to unity," he said. He gestured for Philander to take his seat.

"Thank you, Potent."

Cedrick rejoined Awena and her aunt as Philander sat upon the teaching stone. He opened his book and glanced at the pages in the flickering light, closed it and resumed his telling.

"Davis' knees rested beside the pallet where his cousin lay burning with fever. *What will I do if you don't make it, Donnel?* he asked himself. He stared at Donnel's pale flushed face. *What of Amelia?*

"Donnel's eyelids fluttered. His skin shined in the firelight, coated with an oily layer of perspiration. A fly lit at the corner of his mouth. Evan chased the insect with a wave of his hand. Donnel opened his eyes, but stared blankly at the ceiling of the small cave.

"'Donnel? Donnel, we made it.' Evan whisked the persistent bug from his cousin's face. 'We're in Ranaan!'"

The Stygian crowd shifted nervously at the mention of the name. Philander bowed his head. "I'm sorry I mention the name, but it is part of the Jonnick telling. Perhaps, it will help you understand; it means new land."

The crowd glanced at each other and absorbed the information. Surprised expressions marked each face. Cedrick nodded for him to continue.

Philander drew in a deep breath. "Donnel Brophy vacantly stared at his cousin. Shallow fetid gasps washed across Evan's face as Donnel fought to live.

"'Amelia?' Donnel whispered his wife's name. His blue eyes grew wide. The muscles in his neck strained. His head lifted a few inches but fell to the ground. 'Amelia?'

"Evan placed his palm under Donnel's head. 'Amelia is waiting outside,' he said. A lump the size of an egg at the base of his cousin's head startled Evan. For the first time he noticed the swollen knob on the side of his neck half hidden by Donnel's beard.

"'Rest.' He eased his cousin's head to the floor. 'You need to save your strength. It's better if she doesn't come in here, Donnel. In her condition you don't want to chance passing the sickness.' He waited. 'Did you hear me? Donnel? When you get better, she'll be at your side.'

"Donnel strained to sit up. 'Amelia!' He propped onto his elbows, frantic eyes staring at nothing.

"Evan gently forced Donnel Brophy's body onto the cool stone. 'Rest.'

"He nervously fingered his mustache wondering what the Jonnick would do if the Captain died.

"Donnel turned his head to the side. Fresh blood trickled from his left nostril. Evan lifted his cousin's limp arm and placed it across his chest. Without warning, Donnel's hand shot through the air as if new life pulsed through his veins. His fingers clutched Evan's lapel, twisting it in his grasp and pulling Evan inches from his face.

"'Throw it into the sea.' He panted. "Baby...,' he gasped, 'curse.' He coughed. Spittle sprayed Evan's face. Donnel's breath smelled of death. 'First born. Three gen...' He fell back on his makeshift bed. His half spoken words died on his lips. The thud of his head hitting the rock made Evan wonder if the blow knocked him out.

"Donnel's teeth chattered, but his eyes stayed closed. A trickle of blood leaked from his right nostril. His clammy hand stayed clamped around Evan's lapel like a child clinging to his mother.

"With each labored breath Evan felt more helpless. He stared at the rise and fall of Donnel's chest. His cousin was like a brother. His delirious babbling made no sense. Throw the baby into the sea? It hurt to see him struggling to hang onto life without being able to help. Evan peeled Donnel's cold fingers from his jacket and laid his cousin's hand across his panting chest. Evan shivered. For just a moment, Donnel's pale lips and ashen pallor made him look more like a dead man than Evan cared to see. He glanced outside the tiny cave.

"Amelia, Donnel's wife, sat awkwardly on a stone slab with her legs spread to accommodate her swollen abdomen. The baby had dropped. She showed a white stone to one of the raven-haired native women. Soft feminine voices drifted into the cave as the two of them attempted to communicate.

"Evan patted his cousin's unshaven cheek. 'Come on, Donnel. You've made it. Your family's here.' He dragged his fingers through his light wavy hair.

"The rustle of leather fabric drew his attention to the mouth of the small cave. The Stygian woman who spoke with Amelia bent to slip through the opening with a small painted bowl balanced in her slender fingers. Steam curled sending a savory aroma throughout the tiny enclosure. It reminded him of matelote back home.

"She gestured toward Evan and extended the bowl toward him." Philander extended his hand toward his Stygian listeners. "He held up his palm, pointed to Donnel and gestured with his hand to his mouth in an eating motion. 'He needs to eat something. Maybe it would help.'

"Tiny lines gathered between her brows. She shook her head. Setting the bowl of clear liquid on the ground, the young Stygian woman untied the sash around her waist and crouched beside the Captain of the great ships. Her slim fingers dipped the end of the sash into the steaming liquid and gently massaged the blood from Donnel Brophy's mustache and beard. Crusty dried flakes dissolved leaving behind a pink stain on his fair hair. She rinsed the cloth in the golden broth and daubed beads of perspiration collecting along his hairline.

"Evan sat back on his haunches. Donnel's breathing eased into a rhythmic pattern. The woman glanced at Evan and smiled. A reluctant grin tugged at the corner of his mouth while he scratched the back of his neck. He stole a quick sideward glimpse of the attractive dark woman, touched by her willingness to care for Donnel and Amelia. His stomach growled.

"He put his hand to his chest. 'I'm Evan.'

"She nodded; rung liquid from the strip of cloth in her hand and plastered it across Donnel's forehead. 'Salus,' she said using her index finger to point toward herself.

"'Thank you, Salus,' Evan said. A shiver ran down his spine. His body ached. So much had happened on this first day in Ranaan. 'I need to sleep.' He eased back on the bare stone and let out a deep breath. Fleeting thoughts of his feather bed back home gave way to the logic of why he'd left. If he'd stayed, he would probably be dead. He glanced at his cousin and back at the woman nursing him.

"'Ev-an?' Salus said. Her leather trousers creaked as she scooted to the narrow area between the two men. She placed her palm against his chest.

"'I'm well,' he let out a sigh, 'just exhausted ... and worried.' He closed his eyes and rubbed his eyelids with his thumb and index finger.

"'Salus, it is time,' an older woman's voice sounded within the confined area.

"Evan opened his eyes and blinked at the silhouette of an old woman darkening the door. How was it that he could understand her? Salus sat back on her heels, looked at the woman and bowed her head. The old woman leaned on her twisted walking stick. 'Take this.' She extended her hand, an amulet dangled by a thin leather strap draped across her gnarled fingers. 'Wear this; it will protect you from the sickness.'

"Salus stared at the round silver piece. Two silver arrows connected a leather strip to the flat silver metal. A third arrow dangled from the bottom of the pendant. Small jewels glistened in the dim firelight. Green, white and red gems each centered within foreign symbols. 'I can't take that.'

"Evan looked from Salus to the old woman. *Am I dreaming?* he wondered. *Why do I understand?*

"The white haired woman pointed a shaky finger toward Salus. 'Birth of the Augur hidden, surrounded by a sea of strangers from which the Arich will emerge,' she said. 'Listen to me young one. You are chosen among the Windwalkers.' She glanced at Evan. 'This man is the one.'

"Evan looked from Salus to the old woman wondering what it meant.

"'Tonight I travel to the Fortress of Stone to prepare for the great gathering. My ancestors call for me to join them at the gate to the new land.' Heavy eyelids drooped over the woman's dark eyes. Even in the dim light, Evan wondered about the markings painted across her face. She pointed with a shaky finger toward the necklace. 'It is yours now, guard it.' She chuckled. 'I won't need it anymore. Keep it safe. For one day an Augur with a heart of love shall use it to serve the Arich.'

"Salus tucked a dark strand of hair behind her ear and clasped the amulet in her fist. The small silver disk fit in the palm of her hand while silver arrows poked through the space between her fingers and the leather strip dangled next to her arm.

"Evan glanced at the door, but the old woman with the painted face had disappeared.

"'I can't believe she's chosen me.' Salus slipped the leather strap over her head and around her neck. Silver shined in the dim light against her chest."

Within the Kiva, Cedrick stood and joined Philander at the center of the circle and sat beside him on the teaching stone.

"Salus brushed her fingers against Evan's cheek," Philander said as he nodded to the Potent beside him. "A tingle shot through her hand and made his jaw quiver. A blinding light flashed. Salus' arms felt heavy as if she pushed them through water. The amulet around her neck reflected light onto Evan's face. She turned toward the sleeping one, reached out but darkness settled across his mind. She recoiled. His sickness carried him beyond her ability to help." Philander closed the book and looked to Cedrick. "Thus ends the telling."

The two men stood at the teaching stone. Applause filled the Kiva before Stygian young and old stopped to thank them for the telling.

Cedrick spoke with the two Jonnick men at length. He'd learned much from the half-blind man's telling. Stygian searched for centuries for the Augur's amulet and debated at length as to the whereabouts of the walking stick. Without it there would be no heir to the Augur power. Philander's telling corroborated the Stygian telling. Although they didn't know where it was, perhaps now they could trace family ancestries to find the line of Salus, locate the necklace and hopefully the Augur's staff.

The mountain of Ryu Belay rumbled across the way. Smoke smoldered from the snow-capped peak spreading a hazy layer along the causeway linking the two mountains.

Philander stood at the entrance of the cave mesmerized by the slumbering volcano while the Healer spoke with Awena and her aunt.

"It's getting late," Philander said. He pointed to antelope playing near the lake on the mesa stretching between the two mountains. "They're amazing, fearless and sure footed."

Cedrick's eyebrows arched in mild surprise. "The antelope's message is one of sensibility. Their actions benefit the community. From the telling, I'd say some of the early Jonnick settlers possessed antelope energy. Spending time with you, I've learned some still do."

Philander looked at Cedrick with his good eye. "We've enjoyed our time among your people, but the Healer and I should be heading back to Chock."

"I wish all Stygian and Jonnick would share in the tellings," the Healer said as he stepped from the mouth of the cave. "It could mend the breech forged by time and hatred."

"Time heals," Cedrick said. "Hatred divides."

A splash of water sounded from the shadows of the Kiva. "Cedrick," Awena called. "It's time. The baby comes."

Cedrick froze. "Now?" He cast his eyes to the moonless sky and hurried to his wife's side.

Chapter 4
It Comes to Pass

"It's a time of great difficulty. Survival of his people depends upon Stygian faith to enter the cycle of death while believing that at the proper time the Arich will release them from the Cage of Ice."

The Healer wiped his brow with his sleeve. "You've a healthy son, Potent. Do you have a name for him?"

"The naming ceremony shall be held in three days." Cedrick walked away without another word.

The Healer looked to Trinak. "Did I say something wrong?"

Trinak waved it off. "Pay no heed to him. He's a moody one. A thinker."

Awena slept on the Healer's cloak with the infant at her side. "Come," Trinak said, "you have dealt kindly with my niece and great nephew. I'll take you to the Waters of Nen to refresh yourself."

Cedrick ran his fingers though his hair and rubbed tired eyes.

Trinak glanced over her shoulder at Cedrick. He nodded his approval.

The Healer looked from Trinak to Cedrick. "Are you sure? I don't mean to do anything that might offend."

"You delivered my child," Cedrick said. "If I can trust you with his life, I believe I can trust you with the secrets of the Yoke of Inspiration."

"Very well." The Healer gathered his herbs into his sack. "Do you want to come along, Philander?"

"No, Nilenam, I'll stay here." He watched his stooped brother shuffle behind the older woman down a passageway at the opposite end of the cave.

"Come let us sit in the cool of the morning." Cedrick gestured toward the mouth of the cave to the grassy plain connecting the two mountains.

Outside, the first signs of sunlight mingled with the smoldering haze cast off by the low rumbles of Ryu Belay across the way. Cedrick squatted amid the tall grass, and Philander perched on a large stone beside him. Pastel hues brightened as dawn crept across the horizon. "My bones don't like sitting on the ground much these days," he said with a smile.

Cedrick plucked a long blade of grass twirling it between his thumb and index finger. "Among the tellings, we learn of a new land where the people live united. Young and old alike possess the agility and energy of youth."

"I suppose I'd have two good eyes in the new land?" Philander's fingers brushed his blinded eye. He glanced down at Cedrick.

"I believe you would." A smile flickered across his lips but disappeared. "Philander, do you mind if I ask a few questions?"

The Potent's serious expression sent a wave of uneasiness through Philander. Had he offended the Stygian leader in some way? "What do you want to know?"

Cedrick plucked a second blade of grass and studied it in the diminished light. "Do you have any children?"

Philander shook his head. "No, the stars didn't hold that privilege for me."

Cedrick nodded and sat quietly for a moment. He pointed to Philander's face. "What about your eye? How did you lose your sight?"

Philander let out a deep breath and leaned back a little straighter. "That is a bit complicated…." He meditated on the sky.

"Was it taken from you, or did you give it freely?"

"That's an interesting question." Philander rubbed his eye. "When I was a young man, Riona's mother showed an interest in adding me to her daughter's collection of Conscripts."

"Wait," Cedrick held up his hand. "Do you mean Queen Riona?"

Philander nodded. "She and I knew each other before she … before her coronation."

"What is," Cedrick frowned, "a Conscript?"

"Instead of one spouse, or mate," Philander said, "the Queen has many men, Conscripts." Philander's good eye glazed over as he stared at nothing in the distance. "The Queen follows her whims. Not many men met with approval by her widowed mother. She found me desirable because of my *pure* bloodline. In the telling earlier," he pointed into the darkness beyond the cave entrance, "when I spoke of the Captain's unborn child?"

"Yes?"

"My family line comes from that child, the same as the Queen's family.

The Jonnick looked upon Amelia, the Captain's wife, as a leader after the death of her husband. Her daughter had a child by Ikki, Kynan's first born, but after a rift she left and took the child with her. The Jonnick split. Evan stayed and made Salus his wife. So, although Donnel Brophy and Evan Davis came from the same family, once they reached these shores they became two separate clans. Amelia's heirs split. Among Jonnick today, I'm not sure how anyone can claim a pure bloodline, or what difference it makes.

"My family settled in Chock. Nilenam, my brother, is the village Healer. He's a bit older than me, and escaped the Queen's purview. It's a sad story really. In the day, he was a bit smitten with her, but she acted as if he were invisible. Wealth, stability and my age made me a perfect candidate to father a child for the Queen. An heir. Except for one thing. I didn't hate the Stygian, and I desired a companion for life. When she was younger, Riona had a heart. Now, she's nothing but a … a power wielding, harlot wearing a crown.

"My father didn't openly support the Stygian, but I remember as a child watching Stygian settle on our land where my brother and I herded goats. If I accepted the honor of becoming Riona's Conscript before she became Queen my reward would be a place of prestige among the Conscripts, but first she required that I admit that termination was the answer to the *Stygian problem*. I tried to teach her that most disputes stemmed from a clash in cultures. I hoped to turn her views to a more understanding outlook than that of her parents and explained we could possibly remedy the problem if we learned to communicate."

He touched his unseeing eye. "Instead of prestige, she rewarded me with the loss of my sight. This marked me as not only a Stygian lover but an unsuitable mate." He shrugged one shoulder. "Actually, I decided it best not to have a family. I wouldn't want them looked upon as desirable breeding stock."

Music drifted from the cave. Philander gestured with his head, "My brother and his music. It's been his companion since our youth. He says it's healing to the soul."

"Does the Queen have children?" Cedrick asked.

Philander shook his head. "She's barren. Perhaps I gave up my eye for nothing."

"No." Cedrick moved to his knees, settling his rump against his heels. "Actually loosing your sight is a sign to me."

"A sign?" Philander's stomach flip-flopped. He didn't like the sounds of that; he only wanted people to learn to get along.

"My son," tears brimmed in Cedrick's eyes, "born on a moonless night," he pointed to the sky now coming to light, "within the Yoke of Inspiration, among strangers...." He wiped his eyes. "Please, excuse my tears. This is difficult. I've grown up expecting the Arich. I just didn't expect him to be my son."

"The Arich?" Philander stood. "Your son? That's all ... real?"

Cedrick paused. "Of course it's real. Have you learned nothing from the telling?"

"Well, yes, but what does this mean? I've heard daunting details about the time of the Arich." Philander reached into the pouch slung across his shoulder, clasped the leather book and shook it in the air.

"Evan Davis' writings speak of the Arich, about times of great flooding and destruction. Death crouches at the door to consume those who ignore the warnings."

Cedrick stood and brushed the seat of his trousers. "What does he tell you of the Arich's upbringing?"

"Upbringing? I don't recall anything about that?"

"It's a time of great difficulty. Survival of his people depends upon Stygian faith to enter the cycle of death while believing that at the proper time the Arich will release them from the Cage of Ice.

"You've been entrusted with pieces of the prophecy until now hidden from us. It's no coincidence your brother brought us together. I need to learn all I can from you, because, if I'm reading the signs correctly, the responsibility of leading the remnant through the cycle of death rests upon me." He rubbed his forehead and stopped to massage his left temple. "Time is short."

"Are you sure, your son is the Arich?"

"As much as I'd like to say, 'no,' many of the prophecies regarding the Arich's birth have been fulfilled tonight including the one-eyed stranger looking on."

Firelight glowed brighter from within the cavern behind them. "I hate to admit it," Philander said, "now that you've pointed out those prophecies; the journal puts other signs in place as well."

"Like what?" Cedrick grabbed the front of Philander's shirt. "Please, I need to know ... everything."

Philander licked his dry lips. "The Arich's coming is marked by the control of a seedless child born of a dowager. That would be Riona."

Cedrick nodded. "But what of the Augur? There hasn't been a bumble foot child born among our people since Ojal released her power to Salus."

"Perhaps the child is yet to be born. Certainly, you cannot know every Stygian child born."

"True enough," Cedrick rubbed the back of his neck, "but a bumble foot would be announced throughout every clan. It's an honor and a sign of the coming, but it's against the law to allow the child to live."

"My brother travels throughout the valley tending to the people. He befriends many. We can ask him to watch out for a bumble foot child."

"Perhaps," Cedrick said. "This one sign remains unfulfilled tonight. If it is lacking, we will look for another."

"Only one sign Cedrick? Surely he is the one if only one sign is lacking."

"No, my friend, if one sign remains unfulfilled he is not the one. This shows the importance of knowing the complete telling."

"Cedrick!" Awena's aunt called from inside the Kiva. "Awena's calling for you."

He glanced behind him to see her silhouette at the mouth of the cave.

"I'll be there in a moment, Trinak." He looked at Philander. "Let's not talk of these things until we have time to think."

Philander nodded and followed Cedrick into the Kiva where the Healer's music drifted happily about the cavern.

* * * *

Within the Valley of Rocks in the village of Theya, Adish grabbed fists full of reddish blond hair on each side of his head and glanced at his brother. "What's taking so long?" He leaned forward with his elbows propped on the polished table. "I wish the Healer was here."

The shadow of a stout woman stretched from the door of the bedroom into the dimly lit living room. "She's asking for you," Yram said. The midwife's silhouette blocked flickering light flowing from the other room.

Adish pushed to his feet and hurried to follow the old woman to his wife's side. Yram shuffled to the bed and rested her hand on Estel's rounded stomach. The midwife's ample hips blocked Adish's way, causing him to awkwardly sidestep. She moved right as he moved right. Her slate blue skirt swayed back and forth like a broom sweeping the floor.

"Sorry." Adish stepped to the left, but again she mirrored his movements. They froze in place. His gaze locked onto hers. She didn't smile or offer a hint of levity despite the silly dance. Instead, she shook her head and stepped aside.

Estel's fair face lacked its usual color; her linen nightgown soaked with perspiration clung to her swollen abdomen emphasizing the fact that the baby had not come.

"Estel." He brushed matted hair from her forehead and cupped her hand in his. "Estel, do you hear me?"

Estel's eyelids fluttered. Her staccato breathing eased to a more rhythmic pace. She licked her dry lips and a smile flickered across her face and died. "Adish, I'm sorry this is taking so long." She winced. The muscles in her stomach contracted. Her face contorted, but she bore the pain without a sound. Finally, she let out a breath. "It will be worth the wait. We'll finally have our child."

"Yes." He swallowed hard.

"Adish?" Her breathing grew shallow as her pain eased.

"Yes," he stooped with his ear next to her lips. "If anything happens..." she winced again, and a small moan escaped her lips. "If anything happens, promise me..." Her fingers twisted the sheets as her stomach hardened.

The midwife shushed him from her bedside. "I'm sorry," she tugged his arm, "this is no place for a man." She pushed him from behind. "Her time is near. I'll call you as soon as the baby arrives."

"Wait," Estel begged.

Adish bent and kissed Estel's forehead. His lips lingered above her clammy skin. "I love you." His calloused hand gently stroked her cheek. "When I come back in here, we'll be a family." He pretended to smile, but inside he wanted to cry out. He and Estel had longed for a child for years. Many thought them beyond child bearing. His brothers had three to five children each and they were younger than him. He wrapped his hand around hers. Something slipped into his palm.

"A gift for our baby. Promise me you'll give it to her for her seventeenth birthday if I'm not here."

He glanced at the strange markings etched into the silver. As a metal smith, he'd seen better craftsmanship. He flipped it over in his large palm. "Your necklace?" She wore the family heirloom when they met.

She wet her lips. "Please promise me you'll give it to her."

Adish stood and straightened his back. He pretended to laugh. "You seem pretty sure we have a daughter on the way."

Estel's hazel eyes shimmered with tears. "Promise?"

"I promise." He dropped the trinket into his breast pocket lifted her hand and kissed it. "You'll be able to give it to her yourself. *If* it's a girl," he tried to jest, and hoped his face didn't betray his heart. He glanced toward Yram. With a flick of her head, the midwife gestured toward the door.

Adish nodded. His rough fingers gently placed Estel's hand on the birthing rod, but her arm fell limp on the bed. Her chest rose and fell in tiny gasps. Terror rushed him. He trundled toward the door, paused at the threshold and stole one last glance as birth pangs squeezed Estel's body.

His brother, Laul, stood when Adish walked into the outer room. "How is she?" Adish's youngest brother, normally a joker now looked as pale as Estel. "Is she going to be all right? Why hasn't the baby come?"

Adish sucked in a lung full of air and let it out slowly, wiping the back of his neck with his handkerchief. He shook his head and collapsed into the wooden curve-backed chair. "I don't think she's going to make it." His shoulders drooped as he leaned forward resting his elbows on his knees. "Why us?" He buried his face in his hands for a moment, wiped his face and straightened to sit in the chair.

Laul studied his feet, glanced at his older brother and shrugged. "I don't have the answer. She may be fine when the baby arrives. Not everyone is meant to bear children."

Adish nodded. "If we make it through this, I don't think I'll risk having another."

Laul raised one eyebrow. "You? Celibate for the rest of your life?"

"Oh, be quiet." He plucked the rag from his back pocket and threw it at his younger brother.

"Adish," Yram called from the bedroom door. "Estel would like you to meet someone."

He thrust to his feet sending the chair clattering across the floor. In a few quick strides, he walked through the door and paused. He ran his thick fingers through his unruly hair, and stared at Estel now beneath a blanket on the bed. Dim candlelight cast a warm glow across the sparse furnishings. Estel rested on the birthing bed with a small pile of rags wrapped around the still form clutched to her breast. Adish's heart sank. *Is something wrong with the baby?*

Estel's eyelids fluttered and opened. With glazed eyes, she stared in her husband's direction. "We have a daughter." She pinched a corner of the swaddling and moved it enough to see the baby's face. The infant squirmed and nestled against Estel's breast. "I told you it would be a girl." Estel looked from her husband to the sleeping infant. "Jalil, meet the most wonderful man in the world. Your Papa."

Adish placed the tip of his index finger next to the baby's minute hand and slipped the silver necklace from his pocket dangling it like a toy above the child's face. His dirty fingernails and skinned knuckles stood in contrast to the baby's tender skin. "Hi, Jalil. I'm your Papa. We've been waiting for you for a long time." He touched the tip of his finger to the baby's hand and dropped the necklace onto Estel's stomach. "You can give it to her yourself."

Estel slipped the leather strap around her neck, unbuttoned her gown and placed Jalil at her breast. "She wasn't so small an hour ago." A smile tugged her thin lips. The child suckled without prompting. Adish stroked his wife's fair hair.

"She's blonde; our worries are over," he said. "Even if her eyes are brown, no one will know. Her fair skin and blond hair will pass as full blooded Jonnick."

"Adish, would you love her even if she were dark haired?"

The burly man paused. "I don't have to answer that. She's as blond as you are." His face heated with embarrassment.

"But would you love her?"

"Of course I'd love her. She's my daughter."

"If she had dark hair it wouldn't be her fault." Estel stroked the fine fuzz covering Jalil's head. The baby fell asleep at her breast. "You and I are responsible for her coming into this world. She can't help her ancestry any more than you or me.

"Jalil Orenda. Sounds like she's been part of the family for years." A smile played across Estel's lips. "She's beautiful."

"When will we know the color of her eyes?" Adish worried for the future. He cared for the sake of not only his child but that of his wife. They'd hidden her mixed ancestry well.

A scowl creased Estel's forehead. "Adish! How can you worry about such trivial things? I almost died! Let's think on the things we can be thankful for. I'm alive and we have a baby." Tears quivered along her lower lids and spilled onto her pale cheeks. "What's important is that you love her as you love me," Estel sighed, "just as I am." Her eyes searched his face. "Promise me that you'll love her just as you love me. Without conditions."

He picked up her hand and patted it. "Now, now, there's no need for frivolous promises. You know that I love her."

One more tear leaked from the corner of Estel's eye. "It's not frivolous." She peeled back the baby's wrapping to expose their little girl. Adish smiled. The baby yawned and stretched. "Five fingers on each hand and...." He froze. The baby's left foot turned in as if someone snapped it at the ankle and reattached it haphazardly.

"...a bumble foot," Estel finished. "Our baby is a bumble foot."

Chapter 5
Secrets

Estel slipped the doll from her grasp and loosened the stitches along its back beneath the dress just enough to stash the necklace inside.

Adish backed away, raking his fingers through his unruly mane. "I've only heard of it. I never…" He took in a deep breath and let it out slowly. "You know the law."

"Adish, we can't. Please promise me." She grasped the edge of his sleeve. "We can hide it. People don't need to know. We may never have another child."

Adish pulled away and paced the small room. Estel motioned weakly for him to return to her side.

He rubbed the back of his neck and accepted her cold clammy hand, caressing it between his palms. "Estel," he played with his mustache, "if people see we have a bumble foot, do you know what they'll think? Only Stygian bear bumble foot offspring. They'll call her Stygian and … and witch."

"Adish." The muscles in her neck tensed as she lifted her head from the pillow. "Promise me!" Her strained voice remained determined. "It's not her fault. Look at her. She's just a baby. She hasn't done anything wrong. You couldn't live with yourself if you killed your child to hide your family's past."

Adish eyed the tiny pink infant. She scrunched her face and drew her knees up to her chest while cuddling against her mother's abdomen. Her dark eyes opened a slit. Adish's hardened heart melted. This was his little girl. Her eyelids drifted shut.

Adish nodded. "My family." He rubbed his forehead. "My family could be done. I don't just mean us, Estel. My brothers and their wives and children. All the hard work would be for naught. The village would know. I can't do that to them."

"Adish, many Jonnick have Stygian blood somewhere in their past and don't admit it. The time of the Beginnings—"

"Shhhhh," Adish placed his finger across her lips. "We are not to speak of such things." He glanced toward the door to the outer room where Yram and Laul spoke in indiscernible low tones.

"Estel," he removed his finger, "you don't realize the ramifications. It's not just about the baby. To produce a bumble foot means both you and me have Stygian blood running through our veins. My family prides itself on a pure bloodline. They will not accept it." He faced the wall. "They will say the child is not mine." He didn't dare to look at her. "Is she mine?" The words almost caught in his throat.

Estel gasped, clutched the baby and whimpered.

Adish turned. "I'm sorry. This is all too much. Of all things, a bumble foot. Why couldn't we have a normal baby?" Emotions battled for his loyalty. He'd waited through months of pregnancy, after years of hoping for a baby. His heart wanted to love the child, but she could ruin his position in Tehya. If he accepted the child as his, it would mark him a half-breed. The Queen conducted business with pureblooded Jonnick and encouraged her people to do the same. His family's mining business would dry up, and the loyal citizens in Tehya would travel to another village to find a smith.

Remorse fingered into his thoughts. Estel would never give herself to another. They'd been through so much together. The child exposed an uncomfortable truth. Somewhere in his lineage ... some Stygian ... probably raped an Orenda. Now he had to live with the consequences.

He'd heard the lore. The power of a Stygian bumble foot outweighed that of the ancient Windwalkers. Until now, it was nothing more than a childhood fable. This was life or death, not only for the baby but for all of them. If they allowed her to live and word leaked of a bumble foot child, it meant death to all of them.

He rested his arms across his round stomach. "We'll keep her in hiding." He studied the floor and shrugged his muscular shoulders. "I'll tell people the baby died. There's no need to mention the bumble foot. We'll convert the root cellar into a nursery."

The corner of Estel's mouth quivered. "Thank you. I promise, no one will know she's here."

Adish stepped into the outer room. Yram stood with Laul. Adish shook his head. "The baby didn't make it." The old woman's heavy lids lifted slightly as their eyes met. Fear gripped Adish. *She saw the bumble foot.*

* * * *

A knock at the door of her small home interrupted Yram's troubled thoughts. Should she report the bumble foot birth? She shuffled to the door. "Yes?" she called through the door.

"Yram?" A quiet male voice answered through the thick wood.

"Nilenam?" Her fingers fumbled with the latch to open the door. "What brings you here? I didn't expect you until the waxing moon." She tugged his tunic. "Come," she shut the door behind him, "I have something to tell you."

Yram lowered the flame on the lamp and the two of them spoke in hurried, hushed tones.

Nilenam listened intently, nodding his gray head with every word."Events I once thought mythical now come to pass in my lifetime."

Yram drew in a breath."Then you believe?"

"Yes," he stood, "I'm afraid I do.I only wish I understood all that I know." Nilenam walked to the door and stopped.His bushy white brows drew together above his meaty nose as he paused at the threshold. "Don't mention this to anyone. Do you understand?"

She nodded, and closed the door behind him. Regret kindled a hint of fear in her heart. It was too late for that. Why couldn't she learn to hold her tongue? Maybe she should go with Nilenam. Leave this place and take the secret with her.

He knocked.

"Did you forget something, you old goat?" She opened the door. Her smile vanished.

"What are you doing here?"

* * * *

Laul stepped onto the small porch of his brother's house, slipping his hat from his head. He mustered his nerve, knocked on the door and waited. The small mound of freshly turned dirt in the side yard brought home the reality of his brother's loss.

Soft footsteps fell across the floor on the other side of the door. He missed the days when Adish and Estel came over to enjoy the children and share a meal.

Estel cracked the door open and peeked out. The hinges creaked quietly as she opened the thick wooden door a little more.

"Laul?" Dark circles rimmed Estel's hazel eyes.

"Hi Estel." He shifted from one foot to the other. "Is Adish here?"

"No, he's at the shop." She cast a glance at the floorboards near his feet. "Since the baby … well he's working more these days." She looked back up at his face and for a moment, he felt like they connected.

"Is something wrong?" she asked.

Laul nodded. His bright blue eyes teeming with tears. "I know you don't need any more bad news, but I thought you'd rather hear it from family. Yram is dead." Laul swallowed hard, searching for the right words. "The two of you spent a lot of time together..." he shuffled one foot back and forth. "The village didn't have a better midwife."

Estel gasped and closed the door without another word. Laul stood outside the door wondering what to do. In the days since the baby died, his brother worked at the shop nonstop and Estel withdrew from life. Adish wouldn't talk about it, and Estel wouldn't allow him past the threshold. He slipped his brown felt hat onto his head and turned to head to the shop.

Stepping from the porch, Laul noted people gathered down the street to mourn the old woman. She'd been dead for days before they found her. From the little he saw of Estel, she wouldn't be far behind; her pale features no longer pretty but gaunt and drawn.

He took in a deep breath. The fresh mountain air mingled with the perfume of gardenias growing alongside the house. Snowcaps topped the tallest mountains in the distance, but that would change quickly enough. The sunny warm climate told him it was almost time to journey to the Village of Chock to make the annual trek. So much had changed in a year.

Anger churned in the pit of his gut. He resented it. He thrust his hands in his pockets and took off toward his brother's shop.

Humid heat hung in the air as Laul walked into the shop. The sour odor of his hard working brother filled the air. Not that long ago he'd have kidded Adish about smelling like a mule, but now he didn't dare. His brother acted like a different person since the baby, always on edge. He stood at the threshold and waited for Adish to hammer the last nail into a mare's shoe. When he released his hold on the horse's leg, he looked up and mopped his forehead with his sleeve.

"Hi, Laul. What brings you here?" He patted the horse's rear flank and stepped out and around from behind the animal and walked toward his brother.

Laul pulled his hat from his head and twisted it in his hands. "Well, I don't see you much at home these days. I stopped by the house...."

Adish froze. "You were at the house?" He pulled a rag from his apron pocket and wiped the back of his neck.

Laul nodded. "I'm worried about Estel." He paused and looked into his brother's eyes.

Adish looked away, stared at the floor and swiped the back of his neck a second time with the cloth. He nodded. "She's not well." He glanced at his brother. "I don't know that she'll ever recover. She needs time." He glanced toward the table near the front of the shop. "Did the two of you talk?"

"She didn't let me past the door." Laul stuffed his hat into his back pocket. "From what I saw of her, Adish, I'd say she needs to see the Healer."

"I think you're right." Adish pointed to the table. "You want a drink? Water or ale?"

Laul waved his palm back and forth from the wrist to ward off the offer, but moved to the table in the corner. "I'd just like to talk." The chair screeched across the wooden floor as he scooted it away from the table and turned it around. He straddled the seat and sat on the chair backwards, propping his arms along the top of the straight back. He leaned his chin on his knuckles and watched his brother wash his hands at the pump. "Did you hear the news?"

Adish paused. "News?" Water sprinkled the floor as he shook his hands to dry them before wiping them across the seat of his trousers.

"Yram is dead."

Adish closed his eyes. The image of the old woman eyeing him after Jalil's birth wormed into his thoughts. "She's lived a good life full of years," he said. The secret would go to the grave with Yram and it almost made him happy. Adish avoided looking at his brother and pumped a canister of water.

"She was murdered."

"Murdered! I don't want Estel to know." He carried the canister to the table and sloshed a bit over the side as he sat in the chair to the left of his brother.

Laul stared at the tabletop. "I'm afraid it's too late. I've already told her. Not that she was murdered, but that she's dead. Bad news moves through the village like lightning. I thought she should know."

"How did she take it?"

Laul raised his hands, palms to the ceiling and shrugged. "I have no idea. Adish, I'm not exaggerating. I don't cross the threshold of your house these days. Estel peeks between the doorframe and the door like she's keeping out Sting Flies."

He leaned his elbows on the back of the chair. "Did you hear about the Queen?"

"No. What about her?" Adish thanked the stars Laul wanted to change the subject. He pressed his spine against the uncomfortable chair, sitting up straight, spreading his legs to accommodate his stomach.

"The Stygian have migrated north. They've left the valley like they do every year at this time, but the Queen forbids their return. The possession of Stygian literature and the telling of their stories are forbidden." He dipped his fingertip in the spilled water and doodled.

"What about half-breeds?" Adish took a sip from his canister eyeing his brother over the rim of his mug.

"Half-breeds?" Laul shrugged one shoulder. "Hadn't given them much thought. I suppose they migrated with the Stygian. If not, the Queen will take care of them soon enough." He laughed quietly. "Guess they'll be surprised when they try to venture back into the valley. They'll find no place to rest their heads." He slapped the tabletop. "It's a good thing. I hate the way they'd come onto our land and hunt and live like they own it. Now, we'll be able to tell them to leave with the Queen's authority."

Adish nodded. "Yeah, but how can it be enforced?" He sipped water.

"Adish, this is good." Laul reached over and clapped his brother on the back. "I have more news. The Queen wants us to manufacture explosives. Our reputation brought us to her attention. We'll be supplying black powder. It's perfect. We have access to the sulfur and coal at the mines. The grinding and mixing process can be done here." He cut a broad sweeping gesture with his arm. "She wants us!" A wide smile spread across his face.

Adish's mind raced. "Interesting. That will change the scope of things." He felt trapped. The family business needed him. His brother would never understand if he decided to leave.

Laul rested his hand on his brother's muscular forearm. "We'll be rich."

The flutter of wings drew Adish's attention to a crow on the sill of the open window. It cocked its head and peeked into the room.

Adish smiled. "That bird's been hanging around here like a pet."

Laul leaned forward. "Adish?"

"Yeah?"

"I'm worried about you. Something's not right. I know you lost the baby, but you need to put it behind you. This is what we've always dreamed about. The elimination of the Stygian problem, our family couldn't be more in the Queen's grace, and we're going to be rich!" He clapped his hands and extended his arms. "I thought this would cheer you up, and maybe help Estel snap out of it. Instead, you want to talk about ... about birds?"

* * * *

Estel hurried into the cellar. The flame of the oil lamp lighting the hideaway flickered as she rushed by. She snatched the necklace from her neck. "Where can I hide it?" she asked herself. Her eyes searched the sparse make-shift nursery, but her focus became sidetracked when it came to rest on the tiny sleeping form. Jalil lay peacefully in her cradle. Estel straightened the small blanket and covered her feet."If Yram told anyone of your bumble foot...." She swallowed the stress constricting her throat. If villagers knew of her daughter's bumble foot, they might suspect the use of magic in killing the old woman. "Why would anyone kill her?"

The necklace provided enough proof for any Jonnick knowledgeable in Stygian ways to take the baby and drown her. Part of Estel grieved for Yram, but her death eased her angst. It eliminated the likelihood that details surrounding Jalil's birth would slip into conversations and grow and spread like a disturbed anthill.

"No one will know," she whispered as she stroked Jalil's fair head. Even with the midwife dead, dread of Adish's heritage coming to light loomed over her.

She glanced at the necklace in her palm. Light reflected across the symbols etched in the silver. She didn't need the heirloom to walk on the wind. Her part was to pass it on. Now her daughter could be the one to fulfill what the legends foretold. If only it granted the wisdom her mother had told her about before she died. She'd know what to do.

She clasped the silver pendant in her hand and glanced at Jalil asleep in her cradle. A flash of light encompassed the two of them. Peace filled her as a vision unfolded within her mind. Wisdom granted her clearness of mind. She'd speak with the Healer the next time his circuit brought him to Tehya. The light dissolved. Estel blinked as her eyes adjusted to the dim light of the oil lamp.

She reached into the cradle to pick up the tiny rag doll she'd fashioned from one of her worn dresses. One of the doll's yellow yarn braids was clasped in Jalil's tight little fist. Estel slipped the doll from her grasp and loosened the stitches along its back beneath the dress just enough to stash the necklace inside.

* * * *

2 Years Later

Estel cradled her daughter at her breast within the stone walls tucked beneath the house. Jalil played with her mother's golden hair as she nursed.

Adish did his best to make the underground room comfortable, but Estel reminded him almost daily that she desired more for Jalil. "Perhaps we should move."

Dim lantern light cast sickly shadows across her face. She had never regained her color since giving birth. Staying cooped up in the cellar didn't help. He'd offered to stay with Jalil while Estel went to the market, but she usually asked him to buy what they needed.

Adish struggled with what to do. "I've lived here all my life," he said. "My family's here. Our livelihood, not just the mines and smithing, we're tied into that business with the Queen. We can't just pick up and leave." He stood and paced. "Where would we go?"

"Adish, sweetheart, do you want Jalil to live in this little dungeon her entire life? You've done a wonderful job providing a place for her to hide, but she needs sunshine." Estel coughed and placed the toddler at her feet.

Jalil clung onto her mother's skirt and pulled herself up, wobbling on her good foot.

Adish choked back his frustration. "Estel, it's almost time to go to Chock to celebrate the Dawn of the Beginnings. I'll talk to people there and see if they might need a smith. I could tell my brothers I'm expanding the family business. We can sell black powder from the shop once the Queen's decided she has all she needs."

"Oh, Adish that would be wonderful." She coughed again. "The Healer has a brother living there on the northern edge of the village. Perhaps you could talk with him. See if there's any news." Her color looked gray in the limited light.

"Estel, I know the Healer was your friend, but you must promise me you won't bring him up. We don't need to draw attention to ourselves by asking about the well-being of a murderer."

Estel's lips tightened into a thin line.

He turned his back to his wife. "We never see my family. It won't matter if we do move." A tug on his trouser leg grabbed his focus. His little girl pulled to her feet, holding the fabric on his leg to steady her footing. Golden curls framed her round face.

"Pa-Pa, hold me."

Adish drew the child into his arms, hugged her and closed his eyes. "It won't happen overnight," he warned. "You'll have to be patient."

Chapter 6
Walking on Wind

Estel squeezed her eyes shut searching for the light of the portal.
Heavy footsteps clomped along the corridor toward her.
"Hurry," Nilenam hissed under his breath. "Be gone."

Estel tucked Jalil beneath the handcrafted blanket humming the tune the Healer used to play on his flute. So much had changed since she'd sewn each stitch with love and anticipation. While great with child, she'd draped the blanket over her rounded stomach and dreamed of the wonders of motherhood like a child playing make-believe. Now, she stared at the reality. Her precious daughter in the cradle. A bumble foot trying to learn to walk, hidden away from the outside world. Life had become complicated.

Her thoughts drifted to her own childhood. As far back as she could remember her mother trusted her with the family secret. Today, no one living knew, not even Adish. The women in her family walked on the wind. Now the law forbade her to speak of it. She intended to tell him all along, but veiled the secret within her heart when she saw the intensity of his hatred for the Stygian. He almost didn't marry her when she'd confessed that Stygian blood tainted her family's line; he'd sworn her to never speak of it. If he learned she walked on the wind as a child, even after all these years, he'd probably disown her.

She'd been fortunate enough to know her grandmother and mother. Her daughter would know neither. A baby late in life missed out. Estel's troubled thoughts sifted through the latest news as she slipped her cloak around her shoulders. How could anyone think the Healer killed Yram? She'd never met a kinder soul. Her heart longed to talk with the old man. They'd formed a bond during her pregnancy, but she avoided his visits after Jalil's birth.

She had ignored the vision too long.

The song he played so often on his flute lingered in her mind. "The

Joining Song," he called it, played in honor of the child to come into the family. He reminded her of her father and now she regretted not seeing him when he stopped to visit. Two years had passed since Yram's death. The unthinkable news of his recent arrest had stunned her. Blamed for the midwife's murder, he'd been thrust into the Queen's dungeon.

Guilt for lying to him about the death of her baby weighed heavily on her mind. Did anyone leave the dungeon alive?

Eyes closed, her mind drifted toward the brightness, searching for the old man's essence. Her body gravitated toward the light. The breeze played with her hair, her cloak fluttering as she walked on the wind. Excitement mingled with fear; for the first time in her life, she would expose herself as a Windwalker to an outsider. Something in her propelled her past the fear. She had to see him.

The Valley of Rocks passed beneath her. Light, feathery clouds hovered in the sky casting shadows like a patchwork quilt across the foothills. Her eyes locked on the castle towers reaching like spears toward the sky in the distance. She'd heard tales of the Queen and the intimidating fortress her family constructed over the years, but seeing it evoked a sense of caution.

The Healer's presence lay deep within the great walls; she could feel him. If only she had an Augur's power, she'd let him know she was coming. Could her daughter be the Augur? She pushed the thought from her mind and concentrated on locating the Healer.

Estel circled the castle. Once her feet hit the ground, the transference would be complete. She'd become visible to the guards in the watchtower and Jalil would be alone in the nursery. Without hesitation, she slipped through the thick stone and mortar into a dark narrow corridor. A damp icy chill wrapped around her. Her feet brushed the floor. She stepped twice and found her footing as her eyes adjusted. The musty smell tickled her throat as her physical form took hold.

She felt the Healer close by. "Nilenam?" she called out in a hoarse whisper.

Dim light painted shadows of bars across the narrow passage where the shuffling of feet on the stone floor marked his whereabouts. "Who is it?"

She hurried to his cell. One small window high overhead allowed sun for light without the warmth.

"I had to see you," she said.

His stooped frame bent toward the bars separating them. He showed no surprise at her presence. "You shouldn't be here."

"My heart broke when I heard they'd taken you away. I know you didn't kill Yram. Why after two years would they say you are the murderer? Adish has connections." She searched his face for an answer. "Maybe he can clear your name."

A pang of guilt struck as she remembered Adish's words. He thought the Healer was the murderer.

Nilenam's white wispy hair brushed his shoulders as he shook his head.

Estel wanted to help. "What can I do?"

He pressed his finger to his lips. "Estel, you are in danger here." His hand shook as he clasped the rusty iron bar. "Yram and I ... we'd known each other many years. Your daughter, is she well?"

Estel nodded. The flush of embarrassment heated her face. "No one knows." She glanced around the dark dungeon. Tears blurred her vision of the empty cells lining the corridor. A rat scurried from one cell to the other.

"Take heed, Estel. Don't worry about me. I have what I need. We each serve a purpose. Go, care for your daughter. I believe she is the expected Augur. Prepare her for the day to come."

Estel's hand covered her mouth with a gasp. "*The* Augur?" Thoughts and questions tumbled through her mind. "Who killed Yram?" she asked. "Do they know of Jalil?"

"I don't know." Deep sadness clouded his eyes. "When I last saw Yram, she shared the news of the birth of your child. We agreed to keep the secret as we looked forward to the fulfillment of time. I've often wondered who would take her life and why. I had to admit my surprise when more than two years later, the Queen's Captain arrested me for her murder.

"I've given it thought. It's not about Yram. If they really thought I killed her, they would have arrested me when they found her. It's more a matter of revenge. Ever since my brother declined the Queen's offer to become her Conscript, she does what she can to hurt him. Locking me up in here," he waved at the small enclosure, "gives her a sense of pleasure. She probably came across an old bit of information. The Captain said that someone saw me leave Yram's home that night. It's a logical conclusion."

"Your brother and the Queen?" Estel's thoughts raced to keep up. "He's so old—"

"Things are not always as they seem, Estel. The Queen stands as young today as she did when I looked her age. Do not be deceived. Her power is greater than the spell of youth."

An eerie unsettling washed through her. The hair on her neck prickled. "What am I to do?"

Nilenam's icy fingers wrapped around her wrist. "Don't come back here. It's too dangerous. If the Queen finds a Windwalker within the castle walls, she won't rest. I've seen her handiwork in the asylum. One by one, Windwalkers I've known find their way to the asylum. Part of their being ... their inner essence damaged," his eyes widened, "they are beyond healing.

"It's no secret that a bumble foot is foretold to come and guide the Arich at the time of the joining. She studies the tellings. A bumble foot can only be born of a Windwalker." He released his grasp and let his arm fall to his side. "You must go. The Queen searches the prophecies not for enlightenment, but for a way to thwart the joining. I've seen others in the Asylum."

A key clicked and tumblers turned at the end of the corridor. Estel gasped. A rush of panic swept through her. Lifting the hood to her cloak, she covered her head.

"Hurry," Nilenam said. "Flee, don't look back! Be off. Don't let her catch you!"

* * * *

Awena brushed a tear across her smooth olive cheek. Wisps of dark hair freed from the thick braid trailing between her shoulder blades danced around her face in the warm breeze. "I wish our people never allowed the Jonnick to settle here. None of this would be happening if we had turned them away."

Cedrick shifted the load across his shoulders. "That would make us no different than them. The land does not belong to us anymore than it belongs to them."

"But what good does it do to run?" She spoke quietly so the others would not overhear. "They violate the land. Their hunger for more is like the grave, never satisfied. They chase after us until we have no place to go. What will we do, Cedrick? "Her arm swept through the air in an exaggerated movement. "We are the last of the Stygian. There's no place else to go!"

"Awena...." He turned, held her shoulders and looked into her dark eyes. "I believe in the Arich. Think of the tellings. Did it ever occur to you that we are the remnant?" He exchanged glances with a few of the Stygian men threading up the trail toward the Yoke of Inspiration. "The prophecies tell us the time of fulfillment is near."

Awena stomped her foot and squirmed free. "Then why? Why did we leave Manelin behind?" She crumpled against Cedrick's chest. "Our son, our only child." She stepped back and wiped her face before anyone saw her crying. "If you truly believe the Arich's time is near why, by the stars, did we leave him with the one-eyed teller to live among the Jonnick? He needs to be with us to await the great awakening."

Cedrick grabbed Awena's lean, muscular arm and pulled her close not to be overheard. "Awena, the Arich will not be with us in the Cage of Ice."

Her dark eyes grew wide. She covered her ears. "I don't want to think about it. I don't want to enter the cycle of death, Cedrick. "Her eyes pleaded. "Our son is so young. What becomes of him while we are gone? Do you seriously believe he will thrive among the Jonnick? How is he to survive without the training of his father?"

"His needs differ from ours. I've spent many hours with Philander. Remember, I left him written copies of the tellings. We must let go of selfish desires and look beyond. Our son requires freedom," Cedrick's belief wavered, "if he is to come to us at the proper time."

Awena's dark eyes blinked once. She glanced at the pale blue cloudless sky and back at her husband. "You truly believe he is the Arich?" She pulled a single loose hair from her lip. "Our baby?" The light breeze caught the hair pinched in her fingers and whisked it away. "You can let him go so easily?"

"What have I told you, Awena?" Cedrick put his finger to his lips. "Of course I believe. How else *could* I leave him behind?" He squinted and stared into the distance. "We are not to name him," he let out a long breath and glanced at his wife, "just expect him. We cannot speak of it to the others. They may say, Manelin? Isn't he the son of Cedrick and Awena? How can he be the One. It could bruise their faith and make them falter." For a moment, he cherished the way the sunlight and shadow played across her face highlighting her high cheekbones.

"Come, we must move on," he said.

* * * *

Awena lifted her trembling hand to her lips, stifling her tears. She nodded as Cedrick shifted to the head of the clan.

Awena fell into step beside Trinak.

"I hate the Jonnick." Trinak stopped, easing herself onto a boulder like a chair. "They've complicated our lives." She rested the palm of her hand at the small of her back and stretched. Dark circles rimmed her eyes as she glanced back at the trail. "I'll never see the Valley of Rocks, again." She shook her head. "I won't survive."

Awena backtracked to the woman's side. The last of her mother's sisters, Trinak held a special place in Awena's life. "Come, Trinak, lean on me." She helped the woman to her feet, draping Trinak's arm across her shoulders for support. "Don't focus on the past. We can't change the past."

"Nor can we change the future, Awena. I recognize the times." Her focus drifted to the treetops. "I never thought it would happen in my lifetime, but now I'm living it. We each have a role to play. My life draws near the finish. Even now, I have my part. The Queen will pay dearly for her laws barring us from the Land."

Awena dismissed the old woman's rambling. "We'll stop and rest within the Yoke of Inspiration." Awena glanced at Trinak stooped and resting against her shoulder. "Can you make it?"

Trinak licked her lips. "I long for a drink from the Waters of Nen. The still waters quench the thirst. We are to look for answers there. Perhaps they could wash away my hatred." Wrinkles etched the old woman's face lifting to form deep creases as she smiled. "I'm sorry. I know I shouldn't hate the Jonnick, but I can't love them. They've ruined the Land and stripped away our way of life. If we all run, who remains to meet at the Fortress of Stone and eat at the Potent's Table?" She shook her head. "I'm too old to run, too tired."

Awena nodded. "Trinak, have you considered we are the remnant?" She repeated her husband's words with confidence.

Trinak stopped, and looked up into Awena's face. Her head nodded slightly. "Yes, Awena. I believe we are. Forgive this old woman." She turned, studying the trail behind them. "It's hard to let go."

The group filtered into the pine trees lining the foothills. Members of other small clans joined them as they cut through the Nefarious Forest toward the tunnel system carved within Mount Idisra. They'd follow the passageways through the Yoke of Inspiration and across the grassy causeway to Ryu Belay.

Potents clustered in a circle and discussed plans in hushed tones.

Trinak watched the leaders for a short time. "We give, we give, and we give. It's time to take a stand." She spat on the ground. "I'll run no further."

* * * *

Estel squeezed her eyes shut, searching for the light of the portal. Heavy footsteps clomped along the corridor toward her. "Hurry," Nilenam hissed under his breath. "Be gone."

Footsteps hurried, voices shouted—echoed—vanished for a moment. She slipped through the bars and floated above the Healer. Two men barked at him, asking who she was and where she'd gone.

Nilenam shook his head. "The Queen will not be well pleased to know you're tipping the ale while on duty."

The taller of the two men yanked on the sleeve of his companion. "Come, Olif, there's no sense talking with the old goat."

"No, I'll stay here. Go sound the alarm; get the Captain. Tell him the Healer's been visited by a Windwalker."

Estel eased through the wall and glided on the currents, higher, drifting above the castle toward Tehya. Instead of joy and freedom, she felt stripped, exposed. She wanted to scream for them to leave her alone. Let her live in peace with her bumble foot daughter. Instead of peace, she'd found trouble. The Valley of Rocks blurred beneath her. She wanted to cry but no tears could form as she walked on the wind

A warning tolled from the bell tower behind her. A disturbing sense of no escape followed her.

Chapter 7
Cycle of Death

An evil hatred ripped into her thoughts. Ojal slammed the door
to her mind shut with a gasp. Could the evil power of the Mage search out the Arich?

News of the Windwalker sighting sunk in. Riona's anger cooled. The
time of cleansing she'd waited for her entire adult life had arrived. A
wave of dizziness washed over her. "Out." She thrust her finger toward
the door.

The messenger bowed, turned on his heel, bumping into a statue
almost as tall as him. His attention shot from face to face of the odd
collection scattered about the room. He stared at the familiar stone face
standing nose to nose with him, glanced over his shoulder and ran from
the room.

Riona hurried to the breakfront against the west wall and reached to
the back. Her fingers struggled with the stiff panel. A click announced the
release of the secret she had thought about everyday since she accepted
her mother's gift of youth. The bell outside warned of the Windwalker's
escape. The concealed panel activated the hidden drawer. It slipped open
with a whisper.

A white stone nested on a dark red silken cloth. Without hesitation,
she clutched the Magestone in her palm. Euphoric tingling spread from
her chest to her arms. She'd used the stone's power over the decades
to extricate the ability of the Windwalkers, but had sacrificed so much
to meet her destiny. She glanced around the room at the statues of the
men who had stumbled upon her secret. A brief flash of apprehension
paralyzed her. Hatred for her controlling mother surfaced. The day she
forced Riona to hold the stone and accept eternal youth had sealed her
fate.

The muscles in her jaw clenched. Philander's face flashed in her mind,
refusing the offer as Conscript. "I want more for my life." His words
echoed in her mind. A fresh wave of bitterness erupted. His love for the

Stygian infuriated her. How could he choose them instead of life with her? His actions solidified her resolve.

She held the stone tight, recalling the cleansing spell handed down through the years. The power of the Mage would not be complete until she eliminated the last Windwalker.

"Transcendent power across the sea

Apotheosis, transform me

"Immutable youth, control to keep

Cleanse Ranaan, natives sleep."

She lusted for a cleansed land. Hatred of the Stygian intensified, consuming her emotions. Her focus rested on the day she'd rid the land of Stygian dross and with it the threat of a Windwalker taking what belonged to her.

"Otherworldly powers release

empower the form, the foretold beast."

Her body floated above the room. She stared at the crown on her blond tresses below. The mirror on the wall reflected blood red eyes staring from the head of a ghostly serpent. She opened her mouth. The snake did the same, revealing dripping fangs. Frost painted the mirror. *It is me.* Her attention rested briefly on her human body below. No one would know what she was about to do. Her serpentine essence moved to the balcony overlooking the valley.

"Frozen within the dragon's lair

The cage of ice imprison there."

Power surged through her lean, muscular body. No legs or arms, her strength grew with her size. She practiced swimming through the air. No one could stop her now. She thrilled at the rush of omnipotence.

"Arcane powers, make them mine

transform, protect, Ranaan refine."

A savory flavor filled the air. She thrust into the expanse outside the castle twisting and coiling over the valley. "Ssstygian." Her long tongue flicked tasting the vermin. Finally, true power to rid Ranaan of the stubborn pests coursed through her veins with fury. Strength exploded from within as she streaked through the air splintering trees in her wake.

* * * *

Trinak ran her sleeve across her chin. "Why should they benefit from their selfishness?" The ground rumbled beneath the old woman's feet. The vibration forced her to lose her footing. She let her arm slip from around Awena's neck. "Go," she said. "Hurry. The ashen monster moves faster than I can run, but be encouraged. The prophecy foretells: we'll strike by stealth from the Fortress of Stone."

"Ashen monster?" Awena stared at pinecones vibrating along the moss covered forest floor. She tugged Trinak's arm. "I thought you wanted to drink of the waters of Nen? Please," she checked over her shoulder, "hurry." Awena struggled to get the old woman to her feet.

"No, Awena. Leave me here." She yanked her hand free and waved her off. "Go now! Don't turn back." Pine cones sprinkled the ground around her like huge raindrops. "Support your husband. He's a good leader. I'm just not a good follower." She tipped her head back and laughed hysterically.

"Awena!" Cedrick called from up ahead. "Come."

Awena searched for a glimpse of Cedrick through the branches. She glanced at Trinak. "I've got to go." Worry tore her in two. "I belong with Cedrick."

"Yes, and I belong here." Trinak's laugh filtered into the deep woods.

A rush of wind shot through the forest. Small pieces of debris whipped through the air stinging Awena's skin. "I'm sorry." She squinted. Tears streamed in unpredictable patterns across her face. "I love you, Trinak," she yelled over the rushing wind. She turned and ran off through the bog, twisted one last time and looked back. The woman's hair flew wildly in the stormy fury drowning out her laughter.

"Awena!" Cedrick urged her to hurry.

"I'm coming." She glanced over her shoulder at the old woman. "I'm sorry," she whispered under her breath. The ground beneath her feet shook, and the sound of wind snapping branches warned her not to look back. Awena poured all her energy into sprinting through the woods toward her husband. She spotted him in the distance, standing at the maw of the cave. The boggy soil slowed her stride, but she battled her way up the incline, fighting the tangle of thick vines.

Hand over hand she used the rope-like vines to pull herself toward the mouth of the cave. A scream of agony penetrated the forest and chased Awena up the hillside. Vines strangled her ankles. Her feet slipped, a large branch crashed into the hillside beside her. The wind howled. Thoughts of Manelin flashed through her mind. Anger and fear propelled her toward her husband.

"Awena!" Cedrick wrapped his fingers around her wrist and pulled her into the cave. "Hurry, the curse is activated. If anyone had a doubt, this will erase it!" He spurred each Stygian into the inner recesses of The Yoke of Inspiration. "This way, keep moving. Follow the map. Drink from the Waters of Nen, but do not dally. Hurry through the Kiva and across the bridge. Our rest awaits in Ryu Belay."

* * * *

Tehya loomed on the horizon before Estel when an icy blast struck her from behind, sending her spiraling off course stealing her energy. Her mind raced. What was that? Why did she leave the sanctuary of her hideaway? Another icy blast pushed and pulled her off course taking a bite out of her soul. Instead of Tehya, she stared at ribbons of gold aspen winding through dark pines. One more shove of icy air hammered her, sending her tumbling into the trees. Branches broke her fall before she slammed into the boggy soil. The earth trembled beneath her. Pain shot through her. She scurried into a hollow tree and pulled her cloak tight around her.

Amid the howling wind, the sound of hysterical laughter peaked her curiosity. Estel peeked from her hiding place and spotted an old woman sitting on the forest floor laughing uncontrollably. Her hair mixed wildly in the wind. Trees crashed and splintered. A large shard pierced the old woman's chest. Blood seeped across her tunic. She stared silently at the crimson stain. With both hands, she grasped the spike, yanked it from her chest and fell to the ground.

Estel stared in horror while clutching her chest; searing pain chilled her body. A deafening crack from overhead sent her skittering backwards pressing against the back of the hollow. The top half of the tree above her crashed to the base of the tree in which she hid, fencing her off from the old woman. She beseeched the stars to keep her safe. The howling wind stopped. Estel peered through the fallen branches toward the injured woman.

Her hand flew to her mouth stifling a gasp. A monstrous serpent swam through the remaining trees, slithering in a circle above the debris focusing on the still body. Estel inched forward from the shadows of the hollow staring in disbelief at the ghost snake.

"Ssstygian Windwalker."

The voice of the apparition paralyzed Estel. It mistook the old woman for her. She moved to get a better view through the fallen branches. The snake's jaws spread to strike. Estel wanted to scream but fear closed her throat. Without warning, the old woman lunged forward pounding the bloodied stake into the serpent's underside.

"You'll never cleanse my blood from the land!" The old woman shouted. "Unless you die!" The stake disappeared into the snake's underbelly. The old woman slumped to the ground. "My blood mingles with yours," she said in a raspy voice. Her finger shook pointing at the embedded stake.

The snake recoiled and squirmed. It shimmered like a disturbed reflection. Estel backed into the hollow, positioning herself to see through the branches. The woman stared at her bloody hand and up at the snake hovering above her. "Oh yes, I recognize the hatred hardening your heart, Riona, for it mirrors my own." She stared at her blood soaked tunic and laughed. "The power of the Mage shall never overtake that of the Windwalker, for now you are contaminated."

In a flash, the serpent picked her up and held her tight within its jaws. The woman's laughter gurgled. "You devour me, and I," circling with its muscular body the snake squeezed, "become part..." The last bit of life rushed from her lungs in a final gasp. With a flip of its head, the snake swallowed the bottom half of the woman's limp body. After the second gulp, the woman no longer existed.

* * * *

Cedrick studied the milling crowd gathered in the cavern. Women collected children like hens garnering a brood of chicks. Husbands met in clusters of two and three making plans in case someone didn't survive the cycle of death. People moved slowly about the strange surroundings. Mineral water dripped from stalactite pointing like icy fingers toward damp puddles on the stone floor.

Every muscle in Cedrick's body ached. He forced himself to keep moving. Wind howled outside the cave as gusts tore down the mountainside whipping white caps on the lake below. The howl intensified to a shriek. Stygian crowded into the gathering place exchanging looks of concern. The ground shook knocking a few from their feet. Cedrick's strong voice echoed within the passageway.

"Go to the toans." He motioned toward the openings lining the walls of the cavern. "And don't let fear paralyze you. It was foretold that a time of trembling would mark the coming of the Arich." The crowd didn't move. Dark panic-filled eyes staring at him.

"If this is the right thing to do, why didn't you bring your son along?" A small, feminine fist shook above the heads of the gathered. "You've led us to our demise. We're all going to die." The hysterical woman pumped her defiant fist and collapsed to the floor crying. "We're all going to die," she repeated. Her husband rushed to her side to console her. He looked up at Cedrick. His powerless expression sent out a silent plea for help.

"Enough." Cedrick's voice grew stern. "This is no time for foolishness. Enter your toan. Now! If you do not, your blood is not on my hands." He pushed through the crowd, grabbed Awena's hand and pulled her to the door of their toan.

"You must stay in here. I'll be back as soon as I make sure the others are secure."

Awena grabbed her husband's sleeve. "Please hurry back. I do not want to awaken without you."

* * * *

Cedrick kissed his wife's forehead and slipped out the door. Awena stared at the sky outside the mouth of the cave. Across the way, Mount Idisra and the Kiva where they once gathered reminded her of happier times. Thoughts of Manelin's birth flooded her mind. A tear trickled down her cheek. A flutter within her womb reminded her of the secret she had not found opportunity to share with her husband. Manelin no longer would be their only child. Another would join their little family. *If ...* Gritty dust rained from the ceiling of the toan. *Will this baby see the light of day?*

The ground shook and threw her to the floor. Awena stared in horror at a white, ghost-like serpent swimming through the air. Its immense ashen body coiled around Idisra. Lush green plants climbing the mountainside transformed to brown, brittle vegetation and froze in a film of ice. Layers of steam hung in a haze around the mountaintop. She rested her hand against her stomach. Muscles in her throat tightened. Large icicles formed jagged teeth along the top ridge of the opening leading into the Kiva across the way. An understanding of the prophecies took hold. Could that be the Cavern of Ice? Her mind turned the familiar title over, as she pulled together remnants of the story told by her grandmother. She'd wondered as a child if the Cavern of Ice and Cage of Ice were the same place. Now she knew.

"Cedrick!" she screamed. "Hurry! The time of sleep is upon us!"

The ashen serpent turned icy hollow eyes toward Ryu Belay and shot through the air toward the hideaway. Its muscular body slammed against the causeway, crumbling the roadway in a thunderous avalanche. Blood dripped from the underside of the snake.

Awena stared in disbelief. In one swift move, the way out had vanished. "If we live, how will we leave here?" she asked herself. Why hadn't she listened to the tellings? She clung to what she did know.

The serpent's ghastly face turned toward the cave in Ryu Belay where Stygian families cowered in toans, trapped like bush rabbits in a snare with no escape. Whimpering and murmurs echoed through the chamber. Cedrick dove into his toan and grabbed his wife.

"It will be well, Awena." He pulled her against his chest and for a brief moment. "This is the place we are to wait."

Awena believed. They clung to one another. She cherished his scent and listened to the quickened beat of his heart.

The serpent hovered outside the entrance. Its tongue slithered into the cave freezing anything it touched.

Cedrick's voice reassured Awena as he stroked her hair. The child in her womb fluttered.

Outside, the serpent spread its jaws, exposing fangs taller than the opening in the mountainside.

Cedrick hugged Awena tighter. "We will surv...."

An icy squall blasted into the cavern, overpowering the Stygian remnant. Whimpering sounds of children disappeared. Conversations between adults cut off in mid sentence. Drops of water crystallized to ice. The remnant froze in place with their belief in the Arich unfulfilled.

Chapter 8
Dawn of the Beginnings

*"You will not speak of this place. It could separate us forever.
Do you understand? They would take me away."*

Sunlight leaked into the stagnant air within the fortress of stone. Energy flickered and took the form of a crow. The bird flittered to the table at the south end of the rectangular room and glided to the floor. Its wings lengthened, and its body grew taller expanding breadth and width, taking on human form. The form of Ojal, the ancient. Augur to Kynan. She glanced around the familiar surroundings and ambled to her walking stick. Her fingers brushed the dust from the smooth wood. On this side of death, she wouldn't be needing it—its magical abilities reserved for another. A young one. She sensed the girl's power.

Ojal stretched her arms. Physically, it exhilarated her to be back, but the emotional anguish sent her back two steps. She rested her hand on her head. After hundreds of years of peaceful waiting, it was almost more than she could bear. Thoughts of the young Potent hit her hardest. He'd done his part. Left his child in the care of the Jonnick overseer. She reached out to his mind.

Be at peace. You've put the pieces in place. I am here to guard the child.

Just as quickly as she'd experienced the flood of distress and fear, they disappeared. Although she felt the Potent's fear, she also sensed his determination. The door to the Potent's mind closed as the time of sleep fell upon them. She'd forgotten. Until the Stygian awoke, she'd be unable to communicate across the wind, except with the Jonnick hybrids. A deep loneliness crashed in on her. Everyone she'd known no longer existed in the land, but they'd gather at the joining. She clung to the hope while shuffling to the wall to study the petrographs. The image of the bumble foot stared back at her. She shook her head. If she failed to protect the Arich ... she pushed the thought to the back of her mind.

What would the world be like when she dared to step into it? Her fingers brushed dust from the images on the wall. She studied the petrography of the Arich, his Augur and the metot animals forming a circle around the three of them. How old would he be? Young for sure. She opened her mind to search for him.

An evil hatred ripped into her thoughts. Ojal slammed the door to her mind shut with a gasp. Could the evil power of the Mage search out the Arich?

She felt naked and alone. Her fingertips paused on each image forming a circle around the Arich and young Augur by his side. This feeling would pass as she learned to harness the power of the metot. Each animal served a different purpose. She touched the image of the dog. "The guardian," she shook her head, "but not yet."

She moved to the fox. "Observant and fast. Ready to take action at any time."

Her finger stopped on the falcon. She poked it. "Yes. Observe the situation, take initiative if necessary." A smile lifted the folds on her face. "And, a falcon always announces a special event."

She walked toward the center of the room and took in a deep breath. Even the dusty, old smell refreshed her. Hope within her revived. Her body flickered, transforming energy from human to falcon. For now, she'd be an observer. Not that many more years until the Arich came to age. Until then, she'd keep her eye on him and the others.

* * * *

Riona slumped on her throne nursing the wound in her side. The old woman's laughter haunted her mind. She pounded her fists against her head, trying to free herself of the mocking. Her crown clattered to the floor.

"May I enter, my Queen?"

Her breath caught in her throat and her eyes turned on Laul standing at the threshold of the throne room. His hat in hand, he looked toward the floor.

Riona eased from the throne and swiped her crown from the floor. She winced and stood straight. "Come in, Laul." She sensed no guile. He'd shown his loyalty by pointing the finger at the Healer. For a brief moment, frustration with Philander flooded her. She pushed it aside and focused on Laul.

"You've come to report?"

He shuffled across the room and stopped before her, bending one knee to the floor. "Yes, my Queen. We have prepared fifty barrels of powder as you requested." He peeked up at her. "What do you want us to do with them?"

* * * *

Philander boxed up the last of the parchments hidden under the floorboards in the bedroom of his brother's house. Manelin pulled his finger through the dust on the table. "Look Grandfather, I can write my name."

"Very good, Manelin." Philander blotted a tear with his knuckle. He'd given up hope of his brother's release. Three years had passed since they took Nilenam. Today the reality of Riona's grudge still hung over him like a boulder teetering on a cliff. He couldn't fight for his brother's freedom without drawing attention to the boy. Poor Nilenam, left to rot in the Queen's dungeon without an advocate.

Philander shuffled to the pantry and picked up two more vials of the purple concoction his brother had whipped up to lighten Manelin's hair. It wasn't as blond as Philander hoped for, but he passed for Jonnick and that's what mattered. He squeezed the vials into the box beside the parchments.

Philander hefted the box. "Hold on, Manelin."

Manelin clutched the end of Philander's rope belt and walked with him to the door. They stepped into the street and cut across to the thatched-roof house they called home. Philander missed his brother. The boy occupied his time, but he had no one to seek council from, reminisce of yesteryear or with whom he could toss ideas back and forth. From the shelf beside the hearth, he pulled the parchments penned by Cedrick and added them to the box. *I'm packing away my freedom*, Philander thought, *and the boy's future.*

Philander lifted the boy to his shoulders with a grunt. Soon he'd be too big for this. Manelin giggled, dangling his legs in front of his grandfather's chest. Finger pressed to his lips, Philander looked up with his good eye into Manelin's innocent face. "Shhhh."

Manelin sniggered, rocking back and forth. "Be my horse, Grandfather!"

"Manelin, once we step outdoors you *must* be quiet. This is not a game." The boy's weight slumped across Philander's shoulders. Once again, Philander considered all that the boy had given up. He didn't remember his parents, and he didn't know his heritage or position. It wouldn't be revealed for at least ten more years.

The boy clasped a handful of white hair in each small fist as Philander bent to extinguish the lamp. His heart thundered in his chest as he stepped into the cool spring night carrying the Stygian tellings. He cut through the orchard behind his house where he slipped through the seldom-used back gate and walked the narrow trail. His thoughts drifted to his youth as a goatherd when he traveled this trail often.

"Grandfather, why must we hide the tellings? What will we read?"

Philander stopped, placed the wooden crate on the uneven path and lifted Manelin from his shoulders. "Son, you must not speak of these books. The Queen issued a law…" he paused to find the right words, "she's banned books written by Stygian."

"Stygian?" Manelin's brow crinkled. "What's Stygian?"

Philander hefted the box onto his right shoulder. He longed to tell the boy the whole story, but he couldn't risk it. "They are … were people. People not of the Jonnick. Come, we have a distance to travel and must be home by daybreak."

"Why can't Stygian people write books?" Manelin hovered at Philander's side; his short legs pumped to keep up. "I don't understand."

"Neither do I." Philander shook his head. "Unfortunately, most of the people in Chock agree with her law. We'll hide these parchments until the law changes. It will be our secret."

Manelin grasped the rope tied around Philander's waist as taught since he'd learned to walk. The moon offered enough light to see the overgrown trail, while the scent of moon blossoms wafted in the night air. Philander paused, set the box on the ground and stretched his back.

An eerie howl bayed in the distance. Manelin scooted close to his grandfather, bumping into his leg. "What was that?"

"A wolf." Philander patted Manelin's back. "Don't let it frighten you. It's pretty far away. You know, we can learn from the wolf."

"Truly, or are you jesting?"

"Truly, Manelin. The tellings explain to look upon the wolf as a teacher. Wolves return to the pack to tell the others about new experiences and what they've learned." He considered his words. Cedrick would be proud of him. "The wolf passes on the power to become a teacher." Philander chuckled. "I could use some of that power."

He glanced at the boy with his good eye. A dark mood clouded his thoughts. Perhaps he should not teach the child the origin of the tellings. It could cause trouble for the boy and him.

Manelin yawned. "I'm tired." His dark liquid eyes reflected the moon's light.

Philander searched his memory. Cedrick had mentioned something about a dog. Would a dog be good or bad for the boy? Now that he had to keep the parchments secret, how would he find time to study? Hiding the manuscripts made caring for the boy more difficult. For now, he'd read the journal from cover to cover and see if it mentioned the dog.

"The sooner we finish, the sooner we'll be home in our beds," Philander said.

Pebbles crunched beneath their soles with a steady rhythm, joining the chorus of crickets along the path. Philander stopped. "Here we are. Stand right here."

Manelin stood to the far side of the path while Philander rummaged through thick, thorny branches in the moonlight. "This is where we will store them for now," his voice echoed from within the hollow in the hillside behind the branches, "but you are forbidden to return here until the law is repealed."

"Forbidden? But—"

Philander turned and put his finger on the boy's lips. At times like this, he questioned why he agreed to raise the child. "You will not speak of this place. It could separate us forever. Do you understand? They would take me away."

"Take you…" Manelin's eyes grew wide with nightmarish horror. He nodded silently and clutched the rope tighter. "I understand."

Philander hefted the box through the shrubs. Darkness from the forbidden cave swallowed the tellings. He'd played here as a child with his brother. Manelin's childhood lacked such freedom and friends.

Philander stood empty handed, brushing dust from his palms while the thorny shrubs snapped into place like a gate, hiding the entrance. He took Manelin's hand and headed toward the village. By the time they reached the back gate, Philander carried the sleeping child through the orchard and toward the house as dawn painted the first hint of pastels in the cloudless sky. His back ached and he looked forward to the comfort of his bed.

* * * *

Adish unfolded his map with cold, stiff fingers and checked his whereabouts. Why the Queen wanted to hide explosives on the far side of the Nefarious Forest rested beyond the facts to which he was privy. It took days for him to cross the Valley of Rocks, cut through the forest with his mule and work his way up to the tunnel system leading to this frozen rat's nest.

He'd never ventured into this part of Ranaan before working for the

Queen. In fact, as a child he'd been told stories of monsters living within the Nefarious Forest and beyond. Seeing the remnants of the swath of devastation that cut through the woods, belief in the stories resurfaced, lighting lingering fear, putting his nerves on edge.

He crouched within the secondary tunnel and stuffed the banded cluster of blasting logs with the horde of explosives lining the tunnel. How many would she expect him to carry and store here? The size of the banded logs only allowed him to carry two at a time. Why did she want to store them so far away? Maybe the queen thought them safe here in this frozen wasteland, but one quick blow from the fire-mountain across the way and the whole top of this mountain would disappear.

By the looks of the map, this tunnel system formed the shape of an ox yoke. He'd almost filled the western loop in two years.

For the first time he ventured beyond the narrow secondary tunnel. Centered in the heart of the yoke stood a pool of water. He followed the passageway into a large frozen cavern. Sunlight filtered through large icicles barring the mouth of the cave like a prison. A rainbow of colors highlighted the floor and walls, creating a frozen world of beauty. He thought of it as the Crystal Cavern and wished Estel could see it. Even more, he cared that she would desire enough to want to see it.

He steadied his steps by leaning on his mule, Jagger. His feet slipped, taking unsure steps across the icy floor.

The Queen called this system of tunnels "the Yoke of Inspiration." The only thing it inspired him to do was get home to be with his daughter. Estel had become a shell of the woman he loved. In his heart, he knew she needed help, and it concerned him to leave Jalil in her care, but what could he do? No one could know Jalil existed.

Vaporous puffs highlighted Adish's breath. "The Queen must be planning to blow this place to smithereens," he said to his mule. He didn't need to understand. Queen Riona rewarded him handsomely for each delivery and soon he'd have enough saved to put Estel in the asylum north of the Village of Chock. He'd move from Tehya to be near her, and when her mind was healed they could live as a family without the fear of being found out. Jalil could already walk better than he expected possible.

Poor Estel, he tried to remember her as she once looked, but her hollow stare haunted him. Her health steadily declined after the Healer had been imprisoned. Adish treated his wife with a helpless concern. In his heart, he felt her slipping away. She rarely spoke. Her spirit had withered and hung by a thread of motherly resolve to care for Jalil.

He pushed the thoughts from his mind and walked to the mouth of the cavern, overlooking the chasm filled with jagged shards of ice and stone piercing the depths of a frozen lake like sword blades brandished for battle.

Adish peeked between the bars of ice into the Valley of Blades and wondered if this place had always looked like this. Within the Crystal Cavern, the faint scent of smoke wafted on the breeze. Adish pulled his heavy cloak tight around his shivering shoulders. Frost painted his beard white around his lips. He dreaded the long journey home.

"This will be worth it," he reminded himself. He cupped his hands at his mouth, blew into them and rubbed them vigorously.

Across the Valley of Blades, a thick gray cloud of smoke lingered above the snowy cap of the fire-mountain. He glanced at his map. "Mount Ryu Belay." The smoldering mountain filled him with an unsettling dread. Each trip here made it more dangerous.

His mule brayed.

"You're right, Jagger. Our work here is done." Adish's words sprayed balloons of fog into the air. He grabbed the pack mule's reins and turned to head back through the "yoke." Sunlight bounced off a block of ice, and for a moment, it looked like a face.

He peered through the thick layers of ice and stared at carved detail of what looked to be a face. Similar icy blocks formed a circle around a large stone. Off to the side something sat in the shadows. It stood about waist high. He dropped the reins and walked into the dimness. It was a drum. People occupied this place at one time. *It must be Stygian.* For the first time since Jalil's birth, he wondered about his family line. Perhaps one of his ancestors had played this instrument.

He slapped the skin of the frozen drum. The sound echoed within the ice-covered chamber. He'd grown up hating the Stygian, but now he realized that without them he wouldn't exist. Part of him wanted to know more, but fear of losing all he cherished held his emotions in check. All that remained of the Stygian were artifacts like this drum.

Adish closed his eyes. He worked to bury his feelings so deep they'd never surface, but these long trips gave him quiet time to ponder life. His mule sidestepped as Adish grabbed the bridle and ducked into the warmth of the darkened tunnel system, leading back to the forest. He forced himself to think of the here and now. If that simmering mountain decided to blow, he didn't want to be anywhere near this place.

Chapter 9
The Calling

"...My father and my father's father passed these chronicles to me. They tell stories not many people remember today."

10 Years Later

Philander poured a thick ribbon of purple honey-like elixir from the vial onto Manelin's wet hair. Manelin hated this ritual, but Philander had little choice. Without the treatment, the young Stygian's true hair color would announce his heritage to the entire village. The empty vial slipped from his fingers, clattered and rolled across the floor. "It's almost time to make a visit to the Healer's house," Philander said. Worry colored his thoughts. The supply grew sparse. *Will it last another year?* What would he do when it ran out? Would that mark the coming of the Arich?

His mind drifted to the metalsmith's daughter. Her crippled foot left him on edge. Was she the bumble foot or a victim of an accident?

"I can do this myself." Manelin rubbed the mixture through his hair while he leaned over the large bowl of water. "I don't know why you insist on treating me like a child. I am almost of age."

"Allow an old man this bit of pleasure." He patted Manelin's soapy head. "You've become old enough that I don't do anything for you anymore. At least let me make sure you keep your hair clean. Someone's got to save you from smelling like those goats. Tomorrow you'll walk the Sacred Stairway to celebrate the Dawn of the Beginnings for the first time. I wouldn't want someone asking what that odor might be."

He laughed.

Manelin straightened his back; purple trickled along his cheek. He scowled. "My goats don't smell."

"And you don't think you need to wash your hair every night. I'm afraid you're wrong on both counts, Son." Philander threw the towel over his shoulder. "You wouldn't want that crusty condition you had as a child to come back." He crossed his arms. "Unless you are ready to lose your hair again."

"No," he bent from the waist and poured the pitcher of water over his head, "I just don't see you going through this every night." His voice sounded hollow as sudsy lavender water filled the bowl. "I don't even remember losing my hair." He cast a sideward glance toward his grandfather. "Sometimes I think you've made that story up just to get me to wash my hair."

Philander shuffled into the bedroom to avoid the discussion.

Manelin followed him into the bedroom drying his hair. He tossed the towel to the floor and walked to the ladder leading up to his bed. "Grandfather, you need to stop treating me like a child."

His long legs scaled the rungs to his bunk in two steps. He folded his body to nestled beneath the goat hair blanket. Philander watched him pull his knees toward his chest, tucking his lanky limbs to fit the short bed.

"When I'm out with the goats I don't wash my hair," Manelin said.

Philander picked up the towel, hung it over the bedpost at the foot of his bed and blew out the candle. The straw mattress crunched under his weight as he settled into bed. The stench from the glowing wick, drowning in melted wax, wafted toward the ceiling.

"All the more reason to wash your hair when you're home," Philander said. "I'll not sleep in the same room as a boy smelling of goat." He laughed quietly, hiding his fear. How much longer could he hide Manelin's identity? Even if the supply of hair lightener lasted, when his beard grew in the charade would be over.

"Grandfather?"

Philander rested one hand behind his head. The familiar smell of the tonic his brother concocted before the queen took him away clung to his hands. Manelin's voice sounded deeper each day. Eventually, the truth would be obvious.

"Yes, Manelin?"

"Where do we come from?"

"We?" Philander swallowed. A flush rushed across his body, heating him from head to toe. *He knows?*

The mattress creaked beneath Manelin as he turned to face Philander. "Yes, I've been thinking of the Dawn of the Beginnings. If we come from the other side of the sea, where is our homeland? Why don't we hear about it?"

Naked branches on the tree outside the window beside Philander's bed stirred in the delicate spring breeze.

"Why did we leave?"

Philander felt the boy staring at him from the threshold of manhood. In his endeavor to protect Manelin, he avoided the subject of history all together.

He chuckled, breaking the silence. Inwardly fear churned, clawing at his core. "Manelin, please, one question at a time. What do you think I am?" His laugh gradually distilled into rhythmic breathing. He searched for the right answers. Over the years, he'd done his best to sidetrack conversations headed in this direction.

"You have such an inquisitive mind. You remind me of your mother."

"My mother?"

Philander closed his eyes. He regretted the words as they slipped from his tongue. Cedrick had drawn a fine line. Keep the secret but prepare the child. Soon, Manelin's questions would cross the limit. He would have to tell him the truth and trust he was mature enough.

"A lethal sickness chased the Jonnick from their homeland." Philander hoped to misdirect the boy a little longer while honoring his parents' request. His sixteenth birthday would soon be upon them, and Philander dreaded the day he had to explain why the boy's parents purposely left him behind. Such a burden of responsibility for a young man.

"I remember hearing about that in school." Manelin let out a deep breath. "But there's something I don't understand."

The hoot of an owl drew Philander's attention to the window beside his bed. His eyes drifted to the crescent moon hanging low on the horizon in the ebony sky. Branches of the forked tree swayed. It stood as a perfect reminder of the division in Ranaan. *Two peoples that think they are right, and here I am like the trunk in the middle.*

Philander's heart thundered in his chest. The same questions he'd struggled with for years recycled. *What am I suppose to do if he asks questions before the time?* Emotion choked him as he thought back to the toddler he'd accepted as his own more than a decade ago. It seemed like yesterday when the young Stygian Potent spoke to him of caring for Manelin until they returned—if they returned.

Manelin continued the conversation from the other side of the murky room. "Our people were first spotted from the lookout where the shrine stands today, right?"

Philander relaxed and let out a breath. "Yes, that is right. The grotto and shrine honor The Beginnings. You'll see it for yourself tomorrow."

Quiet blanketed the room. Philander relaxed. Perhaps the boy would let it rest.

Manelin's voice cracked with a high-pitched squeak. "Grandfather," he cleared his throat, "if our people weren't here yet, then who spotted the Jonnick ships from the lookout?"

The old man sat up and fumbled for a match, striking it against the side of the table. A small flame sparked and lit up the room. Philander's hand trembled as he lit the wick. He blew out the match, stared at the lad and let out a long sigh. "I knew eventually you'd ask something like this. You never cease to amaze me." He made up his mind. The time had arrived.

"Come, I have something to show you."

Manelin hopped from his bunk, his bare feet slapped against the floor. "What is it?" He crossed his arms in front of his chest; his linen nightshirt clung to his spindly legs.

"Hush," Philander scolded. "Go." He waggled his finger toward the outer room. "Put a small log on the fire and sit at the table."

Philander slipped his feet into his sandals; thin bowed legs peeking from beneath his nightshirt as he stretched. With one palm resting on the mattress for support, he bent to reach under the bed. His weathered fingers worked a floorboard loose and shoved it to the side. He jerked a small brass box from the shadows of the hideaway.

"Here it is." He shuffled into the outer room where he slipped it onto the table. His fingers lifted the lid and let it fall. The shiny box snapped shut as Philander sat across the table from Manelin.

"What is it?" Manelin wrinkled his nose. "A book?"

"Yes, a book of history." Philander rubbed the back of his neck. My father and my father's father passed these chronicles to me. They tell stories not many people remember today."

"True stories? About the Dawn of the Beginnings?"

Philander nodded. His thin white hair stood out from his head as if he'd been licked by a nanny goat.

Had the time come? The tellings said a dog would come into the child's life, marking the time of enlightenment. According to Stygian lore, the animal served as a guardian to secret areas and ancient knowledge. He'd never keep all the animal signs straight, but learned to watch for the dog.

"Secret stories," Philander said as he stroked his beard.

"Secret?" Manelin's brown eyes grew wide.

"You understand what secret means?"

A frown took over Manelin's face. "Of course I do. I'm not a child." He crossed his arms. "I know how to hide the whereabouts of the herd. We haven't lost a kid yet from poachers." He shrugged one shoulder. "Just a wolf or two."

"I'm serious, Son, promise not to speak of these stories within the village."

"But—"

Philander slapped the table. "No exceptions, Manelin."

Manelin shot back in his chair, eyes wide.

"These stories are not popular." Philander's hand rested on the box. "They speak of history many pretend did not happen. In fact, today most people have never heard of these events. Seems the Queen wants it to stay that way. Her army has started confiscating books containing Stygian lore. Her laws work to wipe it out entirely."

"Stygian? Like the books we hid along the old goat trail?"

"Yes," Philander dipped his chin to the right, "and no." His head swayed to the left. He rubbed his tired eyes. "I'm surprised you remember that. You weren't more than five or six years old."

"You see." Manelin flashed a smile. "I can keep a secret."

Philander eased back into the chair. "The difference is that the writings we put away along the goat trail are Stygian writings." Philander lifted the lid of the brass box. Light from the candle flame bounced from the shiny brass sending a magical reflection across the ceiling. "This collection of writings, for the most part, was written by my ancestors." His fingers gently brushed the worn brown cover. "These Jonnick writings include Stygian history."

Philander's wrinkled hand rested on the book. "What you learn will change your thinking. We'll wait until after we celebrate the Dawn of the Beginnings to study them."

"Can we read it now?"

Philander yawned. "Not tonight, Son. I only tell you this tonight to put your questions to rest so we can get some sleep. Tomorrow, we make the journey up the Sacred Staircase. Tomorrow eve we'll learn of our true beginnings."

Chapter 10
Walking on Wind

"What's this?" A glittering silver point protruded from the doll's back.

Yeasty aromas mingled with pungent smells in the crowded village street. Sunshine warmed the spring day in spite of the breeze. Manelin's mind filled with questions as they headed through the village to the Sacred Stairway. His first trek. Finally old enough for grandfather to take him seriously, he wanted to run along the cobbled street and shout, but instead he patiently shuffled along with the crowd. He glanced at his grandfather by his side and stood a little straighter. Yes, he measured a hair taller than the older man, although Grandfather wouldn't admit to it.

The two of them flowed with the slow-moving string of pedestrians crawling toward the Sacred Stairway. "What's it like, Grandfather?" Manelin turned, walking backwards and looking directly into his grandfather's face.

"It's a long way up." He waggled his index finger toward their unseen destination. "But it's magnificent. From the shrine we can see the sea." He smiled. "We should go sometime without the crowd. Now turn around and watch where you're walking before you bump into someone."

"Tell me about the sea."

"It's water; for as far as you can see." Philander's hand swept in a large circular motion spreading away from his chest.

"I know that." Manelin spun on one foot and fell into step beside his Grandfather. "I mean, what's it like?"

"You'll see soon enough. Imagine, hundreds of years ago, four Jonnick ships setting sail to come here. When they landed on these shores, they thanked the stars for a new beginning. That's why many people leave a gift at the shrine. It's a reminder of our continued thankfulness for the opportunity to live in this land."

Manelin shoved his fist into the pouch at his side and fingered the four holes in the top of his oval flute. "I don't have a gift." He flipped the flute in his hand and rubbed his thumb over the two holes in the bottom. His music kept him company while he watched over the flocks. "Maybe I could offer a song."

"It's not really important," Philander said. "Thanksgiving is an attitude. Many in this crowd are selfish, greedy and never satisfied, yet they make this trek with a gift in hand." He sighed. "The true gift of thankfulness is carried in your heart each day and shared with others."

Manelin's attention drifted to pings of a hammer hitting steel from inside the shop on his left. A girl about his age, with golden shoulder length curls, stood watching the crowd from the open door. Grandfather had mentioned the new metalsmith when Manelin returned from tending his goats, but who was the girl?

She smiled, leaning one shoulder against the doorframe.

"Who's that?" Manelin gestured with his thumb toward the shop.

Philander glanced at the girl. Worry lines crisscrossed his forehead as he looked back at his grandson. "She's the daughter of the new metalsmith."

Manelin hopped on one foot from cobblestone to cobblestone while avoiding the cracks. "What about her?" Manelin gestured with his head toward the door. "Is she too young to go?" He guessed her to be a bit younger than himself. "To make the journey?"

Manelin walked a little straighter, lifting his chin.

His grandfather chuckled. "Manelin…" His smile wavered. "Physically you've been old enough for a few years. I didn't think you ready and chose to wait."

Manelin scowled, leaning toward his grandfather and keeping his voice low. "Grandfather, you have to stop coddling me. I'm not a baby. People already treat me like a spotted goat."

Philander gestured discreetly with his head toward the girl at the smith's shop. "She's old enough but won't make the trek." He paused. "This is not something to be talked about do you understand?"

Manelin rolled his eyes and nodded. His mind darted back to their talk last night about the book of his ancestors. Tonight they'd read. He itched to get started. And now, he would learn another secret. Growing older was exciting.

Philander raised one eyebrow. "I'm serious. I don't want you talking to anyone about this."

"Who am I going to talk to?" Manelin extended his arms at his sides.

"The goats?"

His grandfather's mouth lifted in a half smile that wavered and vanished. He gestured with his eyes toward the blacksmith's shop. "The girl will not make the trek because she cannot walk without assistance."

What did that mean? Manelin glanced in the girl's direction without turning his head. "She's lame?" The girl's skirt brushed the ground; he couldn't see her feet.

Philander put his finger to his lips. "Shhhhhh. Don't let her hear you. I'm sure she feels bad enough that she's not able to make the journey. It's an important festival not only to the villagers, but people travel from across the valley to make this journey. It's Jonnick tradition."

Manelin lingered, allowing the crowd to filter around him like a rock in the stream.

"Don't stare." Philander prodded the boy along with a gentle push. "She's crippled. She can't walk the stairs."

"Why can't someone carry her? She doesn't look too heavy. I could carry her on my back."

Philander chuckled. "That's a good question. It seems long ago the builders of the stairway made a rule that to be worthy of the trek, people must climb the Sacred Stairway on their own. Just as our ancestors each made their way to Ranaan, we journey the Sacred Stairway as individuals to celebrate our beginnings. I'll warn you ahead of time, my old bones will have to make a stop at the half way point."

"I don't mind." Manelin shrugged. "It's all new to me, and fun to do something different."

Philander's attention settled straight ahead over the heads of the throng. "The thing most don't realize is that people who look back too much don't look forward enough. Others don't look back at all. We should learn from the past and live for the future."

Manelin twisted from the waist and waved to the girl over his shoulder. She smiled and returned the gesture until a big man with bushy reddish blond hair filled the door beside her. He scowled at the sea of people flowing toward the Sacred Stairway. Manelin's arm dropped to his side. The man's large hand smothered the girl's shoulder, pulling her into the shadows of the shop and closing the bottom half of the divided door.

"Grandfather, do you know the new smith?"

"Yes, they arrived with the last snowfall; almost a month past. He tends to keep to himself." Philander ushered his grandson beyond the candle maker's shop and followed the upward slope of the street. The aroma of hot wax spilled into the crowd and followed them up the road, where it mingled with the scent of fresh baked bread wafting from the baker's shop.

"Couldn't someone change the rule?" Manelin pursed his lips. "Like the Queen?"

"What rule?" Philander scowled. "What are you talking about?"

"The crippled girl at the smith's shop." He nodded back in that direction. "Couldn't someone change the rule so she could be carried? It's not fair! Why should she stay in the village while the entire population celebrates? What about her father? Is he going?"

"Calm yourself." Philander patted Manelin's shoulder. "You've a good heart, Manelin. Someday perhaps you'll be the one to make that change. For now, it's best if we don't speak of such things."

"But—"

Philander stopped and pressed his bent finger against the boy's lips. He stared directly into Manelin's eyes. "Listen to me, Manelin. The time to speak freely of ideas is when we are in our home. You wouldn't want to take the chance that someone might think I'm not doing a good job raising you, now would you?"

A large woman bumped Philander's elbow, glared at him as if he'd run into her but shuffled past him. Philander grabbed Manelin's wrist and waited. "I'm serious. You don't want me to share my brother's fate." He yanked Manelin's arm gently. "Do you?"

Manelin blinked once, glanced toward the blacksmith's shop in the distance and back at his grandfather. He shook his head 'no' before studying his feet.

"I didn't think so." Philander stood straight, clasped Manelin's sleeve and tugged him toward the Sacred Stairway. The crowd grew thick as they funneled into the narrowing passage leading to the threadlike slabs of stone winding up the side of the mountain. Steep granite bulwarks walled each side of the Sacred Stairway.

Manelin peered at the chain of people snaking along the serpentine ascent, disappearing around a bend. He fell in line behind his grandfather and followed in his footsteps. His mind drifted to the girl at the smith's shop. "Do you know her name?"

"Manelin!" Philander turned and glared over his shoulder. His thin white hair blew in wisps as the wind kicked up. "Your mind is to be on The Beginnings."

"But it's not fair." Manelin jutted his jaw. She had no more control over her foot than he did over the color of his eyes. "She must be lonely."

"Her name is Jalil," Philander said quietly. "Now turn your mind to things that matter."

* * * *

Manelin questioned what mattered. His dark eyes and olive complexion left him with more friends among the goats than people in his village. *It's not fair that Jalil is left behind.* He watched his feet move from one step to the next and considered how fortunate he was to make this trip.

Impatience simmered as he waited for the crowd to file up the narrow stairway. "Grandfather, how did she become crippled?"

Philander didn't say a word. He paused on the stair, pulled in a deep breath and let it go before turning to look intently at Manelin with his good eye.

Manelin stared at the slab beneath his feet. "I'm sorry."

Philander pressed against the wall enclosing the stairway and pulled his grandson to the side. "Manelin, what have I told you about asking questions while we are away from home?"

"I said, 'I'm sorry.'" Manelin searched his grandfather's face for mercy.

Gusts tugged Philander's white beard, waving it about like a flag. "It's important." His focus narrowed as if looking at a speck on Manelin's nose. "You're old enough to make this trip, but if you can't control yourself, maybe you should return home until next year." His lips tightened into a thin line.

"No!"

People filing by with nosy curiosity.

"Very well, then." Philander nodded and merged into the line of villagers climbing the path to the shrine while Manelin fell into step behind him. He pulled the flute from his pocket and created a tune to pass the time. Notes floated up the crowded corridor, blending with peoples' voices. Stubby branches of sage tangled with vines climbing crags in the walls that stretched toward the warm spring sky.

Strong floral perfume filled the air. Manelin pulled the flute from his lips and inhaled. "What is that smell?"

"It's the gardenias people bring to the shrine."

"Where do they get gardenias at this time of year? The thaw fills the river, the grass is green, but flowers are barely in the bud."

Philander laughed quietly. "Seasons differ deeper in the valley. Most of the flowers come from Tehya. They grow them in groves to sell them here. It's become quite a business over the years."

They reached a narrow plateau wide enough for pilgrims to rest. People huddled in bunches talking to friends or sitting on benches while catching their breath. Philander moved through the crowd to mingle and take a seat while Manelin leaned against the side of the mountain and experimented with his new tune.

A crow fluttered overhead, landing on a thin branch swaying in the breeze from the rocky wall overhead. The crow cawed and Manelin played a note trying to copy the bird's tone.

People milled about the area. A glimpse of golden blonde curls caught his attention at the opposite side of the place of rest. The girl from the smith's shop! She peeked at him through the mass of people and smiled. His lips brushed the mouthpiece of his flute, blowing one last note. He glanced up at the bird, but it had flown away. He cupped his flute in his hand and hung it around his neck by the strap.

The girl cocked her head. Their eyes met. Pilgrims passed between them. He felt invisible. A family paused to greet a neighbor. When they moved on, Jalil no longer stood there.

* * * *

Adish packed his bag and slung it over his shoulder. "Honey, I'll be back." He held a cluster of white flowers in his hand. "I've got your offering. I'll leave it there in your name."

Jalil shuffled forward, closed her eyes and drank in the powerful scent. "They're lovely. Will you be leaving a gift for Mother as well?"

Sometimes she reminded him so much of Estel when she was well. He missed his wife's company terribly and the guilt for leaving her in the asylum gnawed at his conscience daily. Somehow, he should be able to help her snap out of it. Long ago, he saw glimmers of improvement, or so he thought. He'd put his hope in the asylum, but once he saw the beds filled with people, he didn't know what to think. Had he left her there to die?

"Father, will I ever make the journey?" Jalil asked. "I'd like to see the shrine."

Adish rested his hand on his daughter's shoulder. "Perhaps one day, but not this year." He kissed her forehead.

Her bottom lip protruded just enough to let him know her displeasure. "You say that every year."

He plucked a curl from her forehead and moved it to the side. "It's as true this year as last year. For now," he let out a sigh, "you cannot go."

Jalil looked at the floor. "At least this year I can sit outdoors. I'm glad we moved to Chock. In a way, it is my new beginning." Tears welled in her eyes. "But, I wish mother were here."

Adish nodded, staring at the flowers in his hand. He plucked one from the bouquet and tucked it behind his daughter's ear. She smiled and hugged his neck. "Thank you for setting me free."

"I need to start out if I'm to be back before dark. The village will be full of strangers. Don't sit outside on the bench today. I don't want to take chances while I'm gone."

"Okay." Her posture slumped.

"Promise?"

"I promise, Papa."

* * * *

"I trust you'll protect me while I'm gone," Riona said to the statues lining the walls of her sleeping chamber. She reached out and scraped her fingernail along the jaw line of the statue of a man not much taller than herself. "You fools." A throaty laugh worked from deep within her diaphragm. Steely coldness clouded her eyes and snuffed the laughter. "Traitors!" She shoved the statue sending it crashing. Bits and pieces powdered, the polished floor. A light breeze from the window scattered the dust throughout the room.

Her cape billowed behind her as she hurried to the stone's hiding place in the breakfront. She grasped it and sat on the chair at the center of the room. Above her body, the essence of her being gathered into a small compact form; she stretched her black wings. What better way to spy on the pilgrims making the sacred trek? Her wings carried her to the sill where she paused to turn and look at her royal body, frozen, clasping the Magestone. The power of the stone would protect her body until she returned.

As a raven, she took flight. Her keen eyes searched the sky for any hint of a Windwalker.

* * * *

Jalil hobbled up the stairs to her room and buried her face in her pillow. What difference did it make that they moved to Chock if she had to stay locked in their apartment? She pounded her fist against her mattress. The small rag doll her mother had sewn when she was a baby bounced to the floor with a clank.

What was that?

She stretched over the side of the bed, lifted her neglected doll by its yellow braid and lay back onto her pillow. It dangled by one braid over her face.

"What is this?" A glittering silver point protruded from the doll's back. She picked at the silver tip and pulled the necklace into view. "I remember this!" Visions of her mother wearing this necklace flooded her with an odd sensation. She sat up and laced it around her neck. A flash of light enveloped her with a weightless sensation. Something called her, drawing her through the light. She moved without a limp, almost floating inches above the ground.

Chapter 11
The Grotto

Jalil walked effortlessly through the bog surrounded by light.
Her curls formed a halo around her head.
"Thank you for inviting me. This is my first trek."
Light bounced off a silver amulet hanging against her chest.

Senta cowered behind the heavy tapestry hanging on the wall in the queen's bed chamber. Riona sat motionless in the chair at the center of the room. He edged into the open. She didn't move. An eerie sense of why she didn't allow him in here settled across his mind.

"Riona?" He took one step toward her. Dust from the broken statue ground beneath his boot. He paused studying the statue to his left. A sick feeling burned in the pit of his stomach. These statues. He knew the face of every one. Each had gone missing. It confirmed his suspicions. It was her doing.

He cast a nervous glance toward the window. Perhaps she caught them removing the stone from her hand. If he took the stone, would that steal her power? If he possessed the stone, perhaps it would give him the power to rule the land and put the queen into her dungeon. A smile flickered at the thought.

Senta rushed to the queen's corpse-like form, his fingers poised over the white stone. He rubbed his thumb across his fingertips. The faces frozen in agony stared at him. He couldn't back down now. For all he knew, she'd put a curse on these men for entering this room. The stone sat in her open palm for the taking. He swiped it, turned and took a step toward the door. His boot froze mid-stride. Horror filled him. He stared at the icy burn climbing his legs turning to stone. The Queen's stone fell from his hand and clattered across the floor. Cold crept through his loins and up his midsection. Inch by inch it stole the warmth of life.

The flutter of wings swooped through the room. He moved his eyes to the side watching the bird pick up the stone in its beak. Behind him, the flapping of wings moved to where the Queen sat. Senta wanted to scream, but his voice wouldn't work. His chest tightened.

The rustle of fabric behind him warned that Riona had returned to her human form. Her heels clicked against the floor as she circled him. "Senta, Senta," her tongue clicked, "and I thought I could trust you. Instead, your insubordinate actions called me home. Your timing is very poor."

His chest squeezed his heart. He couldn't breathe. His hearing dimmed....

* * * *

Manelin glanced to his left and right and hurried through the crowd to the other side of the plateau to search for the girl. *Where could she have gone?* People continuing the second half of the trek congregated in mass at the mouth of the crowded staircase waiting to take one step. People on the path beyond the plateau moved at a crawl like winter worms. He searched for a glimpse of Jalil's golden curls but didn't see her.

He pushed through the sea of people and surveyed the stairs leading up to the clearing. It writhed in an upward movement toward the shrine. People spilling onto the plateau from the village below added to the congestion. He stretched to see over the heads of the crowd. *There's no way she could be heading back to the village.* He scratched his head.

Cawing overhead caught his attention. A crow flew over the heads of the throng toward the shrine and disappeared into the blinding sun.

"Manelin." Philander's hand clasped his shoulder.

Startled from his thoughts, Manelin's heart raced in his chest, as he turned to face his grandfather.

"Are you ready to go?" Philander asked.

"Grandfather, I saw the girl." He pointed to the spot where she stood moments before. "The smith's girl."

"Jalil?" Tiny lines creased Philander's forehead. He glanced over his shoulder to where Manelin pointed and back to his grandson. "We'll talk about this later." He gently pushed the boy toward the second level of the trek, looked out over the crowd one more time, and turned to Manelin with his index finger pressed to his lips. His heavy lids raised just enough to expose the white around his good eye.

Manelin nodded.

The crowd pushed in and forced them to form a single file before stepping foot on the Sacred Stairway. Manelin waited while a mother, father and their son about Manelin's age climbed ahead of them. The family chattered among themselves, and the son wore a uniform like his father's.

Manelin's attention drifted to times past. He once knew that boy when he attended school in the village. His name was Delaine. Visions of the boy pushing him around and calling him "dung eyes" flooded to the forefront of Manelin's mind.

No, he didn't miss school or the likes of Delaine. Since the ache in Grandfather's back grew painful, he'd taken over herding the goats and grandfather accepted the roll of teacher. It was just as well. The students in school shunned Manelin because of his brown eyes. Grandfather not only trained him to read but also taught secret things. Forbidden things. He thought of that night so long ago when they'd hidden the Stygian writings within that cave along the old goat trail. *I wonder what those parchments tell.*

Delaine jerked his head to look at him as if he knew his thoughts. His icy blue eyes fixed on him as they waited to take the next step.

Old grievances churned. Manelin glared at Delaine daring him to say something.

Delaine turned his left eyelid inside out pretending to be blind in one eye. A dollop of spittle dribbled from his lip and landed on one of his shiny gold buttons.

Manelin drew his elbow back, his hand clenched in a fist.

Grandfather grabbed his shoulder and gently pushed him to the side stepping in front of him. Manelin gritted his teeth, falling into step behind his grandfather. He'd love to punch that freckled face nuisance some day. He unclenched his fist, pulled out his flute and played softly while he continued the climb. Music soothed his irritation and made a perfect companion to pass the time.

The line shuffled along at a steady pace. His mouth grew dry. "Grandfather, I'm thirsty."

Philander didn't stop. "We drink no water on this journey. It is to remind us of the hardship our ancestors endured to give us the opportunity for new beginnings."

"I see." Manelin slipped the flute into his pouch. "Grandfather, why do we climb these stairs to celebrate the new beginnings?"

The threadlike throng inched toward the left side of the staircase as the first pilgrims worked their way back from the shrine toward the village. "Because," Philander said, "it was from this point that the ships were first spotted. Our ancestors built a grotto made of cut stones to house the shrine."

Manelin's thoughts returned to their talk from the night before. "Who saw them?"

"Later, Manelin. Let an old man save his breath for the climb." He blotted perspiration from his forehead with his sleeve.

A steady stream filed down the staircase slowing their advance.

Heavy perfume wafted on the breeze as Manelin listened to the blend of voices around him. He wondered again what had happened to his parents. Did they celebrate the Dawn of Beginnings? Grandfather avoided the topic saying it was too painful.

"Just, beyond this next bend," Philander pointed, "is the shrine."

"That smell is so strong." Manelin wrinkled his nose.

"It's the gardenias." Philander puffed, his face reddened from the physical exertion. "All the women and even some of the men carry them as their gift of thanksgiving because they ward off evil spirits."

Manelin checked the sky "Evil spirits?"

"Legend says that the fourth Jonnick ship was lost to evil spirits. Other tales of long ago speak of creatures that lived in the land. They had the power to move from one place to another without being seen. The most powerful of these Windwalkers was the Augur. The scent of gardenias stayed their presence."

Manelin reached forward and held the back of his grandfather's tunic so the crowd wouldn't separate them. "Augurs?" He repeated the strange word.

They came to a standstill. His grandfather nodded.

Manelin's focus followed the uneven stone wall to his right. He spotted the crow high overhead on a dead branch reaching from the side of the mountain like an arthritic finger pointing the way. He looked to the other side. No signs of evil spirits. The flowers worked. He pursed his lips and whistled. The crow cocked its head as if to look at him.

The passageway widened as they neared the top. They stood waiting to enter the shrine and Manelin lingered beside his grandfather. The crowd in front of them thinned as pilgrims filed down the stairs back to the village.

"Why do we only come here one day out of the year?" Manelin asked. "Wouldn't it be better to give thanks more often? Instead of everyone squeezing up the Sacred Stairway at one time, we could take turns and stay up here to think."

"The queen expects her *loyal* citizens to attend each year. It's good for the economy and keeps Ranaan united."

Manelin cast a sideward glance toward his grandfather. "We wouldn't want to hurt the economy."

Grandfather nodded. They stepped from the last stair to the crowded cliff where the man-made grotto housed the shrine. One large tamarack tree shaded the area. Manelin stood on his toes and peeked at the sea beyond the body of Jonnick pilgrims. "It's awesome! Can we stand closer to the edge?"

"Let's wait until we have our turn in the grotto, or we could find ourselves at the end of this line."

Gradually fewer villagers stood between them and the alcove. People shoved and jostled for position to enter the sacred site. Delaine's father shouted for them to keep order and everyone quietly obeyed.

The line inched forward until finally Delaine's family stood next to enter. Delaine cast a smug look in Manelin's direction as his family entered the grotto.

Manelin leaned close to his grandfather. "Most of these people don't seem thankful," he mumbled under his breath.

Grandfather let out a brief chuckle as they stepped up to the door and waited. A light breeze stirred washing a whisper of relief from the heat of the noon sun.

Delaine's family stepped from the shadows of the grotto. "I'm a descendant of Captain Brophy," Delaine said as he pushed past Manelin bumping him with his shoulder. "There's no question about *my* bloodline. I've already been accepted into the queen's army."

Manelin ignored the boy's jab and stepped to the threshold. He peered into the dim recesses of the hallowed room. His heart slammed in his chest as his boot crossed the threshold.

"What is this?" Manelin squinted. He looked left and right, unimpressed with the tiny, sparsely furnished room. "It looks like rubbish."

Charred pieces of timber, an empty barrel, and a uniform jacket draped over a peg decorated the wall to the left. On a rough wooden shelf between the jacket and empty barrel sat a telescope.

A table piled high and overflowing with flowers hugged the wall to the right. The fragrance hung heavily in the small room.

A flutter of wings disturbed the silence. Manelin bumped into his grandfather as the crow lit upon his shoulder. "What?" He stared at the bird in disbelief. A stinging sensation spread across his shoulder. The bird flapped its wings, circled the room one time and slipped out the door as fast as it appeared. Manelin rubbed the sting.

"That was odd," Philander said. "Are you alright?"

Manelin nodded.

"That telescope's the one Captain Brophy used to first see our shores when he discovered Ranaan."

"If he discovered…" Manelin's tongue felt thick. Overpowering perfume sucked the oxygen from the air. The room closed in around him. His vision blurred. He shook his head. His sinuses swelled. He teetered and grabbed the edge of the table. Gardenias, spilled from the table to the floor. "Grandfather!" His voice seemed to catch in his throat. His eyes drifted to the telescope. Clusters of two and three of the potent white flowers decorated the shelf within the tiny shrine as the room spun. His head swam, his knees buckled and his shoulder burned.

"Manelin!" Philander grabbed for him.

Manelin reached out but collapsed before his hand felt the old man's touch. Darkness enveloped his consciousness as his body hit the floor.

"Maaaneliiin." A sweet, young voice called his name. "Maaaneliiin."

Manelin blinked. An opaque fog hovered around his body as he sat up. "How long have I been here?"

Jalil walked effortlessly through the bog surrounded by light. Her curls formed a halo around her head. "Thank you for inviting me. This is my first trek." Light bounced off a silver amulet hanging against her chest.

"What?" Manelin rubbed his eyes. "Invite you?"

She smiled. Her even white teeth captivated him. Manelin struggled to get up but his legs wouldn't move.

"I'm sorry, Manelin. You can't walk right now" She giggled.

"Jalil?" He put her name out as a test.

"Yes!" she curtsied, "I'm happy to make your acquaintance."

"What's happening? I don't understand."

"I longed to make this journey to the shrine. The entire village passed by our door on the way to the Sacred Stairway. I begged my father to let me make the trek, but he said I'd have to stay home. I went to my bed, but heard music and your voice calling." Her curls bounced as she shook her head. "I didn't know it was your voice, but somehow I'm here talking to you right now. I like it, but it's a little scary." She glanced around the room.

Heat radiated from the pain in Manelin's shoulder. He unlaced his shirt and pulled it to the side. His fingertips brushed his smarting flesh.

"What is that?" Jalil asked.

Manelin strained awkwardly twisting to look at the mark on his skin. "I don't know. My shoulder hurts. A rouge crow flew in here and landed on my shoulder and made off as quickly as it came in. Is there something on my skin?" With the tip of his index finger, he touched the sore spot checking for blood, but it felt dry.

Jalil stepped closer and bent in front of him. He gazed into her crystal blue eyes. "What is it?" he asked.

"It's an eye." She took a step back. Her delicate features pushed into a frown.

"An eye?" Manelin scrunched his nose and stretched his neck trying to check the mark.

"Not a real eye," she laughed nervously, "a picture of an eye. Does it hurt?" She reached toward the reddened skin.

Manelin fell back using his elbows to pull himself across the floor away from her reach. "No, it hurts. Don't..."

Her hand gently brushed the symbol. A soothing tingle washed away the burn.

Manelin grabbed her wrist. "What did you do?"

Jalil's eyes grew wide. "I ... I don't know. Let me go. I'm sorry." She squirmed.

"Don't be sorry. You made it stop hurting." He released his hold and touched his tender shoulder. Heat no longer radiated from the spot.

Jalil blinked. "I did?" She backed away. Her fingers wrapped the pendant in her hand. "I'm afraid."

"Why?"

"I don't understand what's happening. How did I get here?"

Manelin nodded. "I don't understand either, Jalil. Where are we? Are we still in the grotto?" Dim light from small rectangular openings high overhead fought through the fog. "What is this on my shoulder? And what did you just do to make it stop hurting?" He glanced toward Jalil's feet hidden in the fog. "How are you walking?"

She stepped back further glancing from left to right. "You know of my bumble foot?" Fog lifted from her feet and drifted across her torso. A tear trickled down her cheek. Her face disappeared in the cloud.

"Jalil! Jalil!" He laid his head on the floor and closed his eyes. *What am I going to do if I can't walk?* "I don't even know what a bumble foot is," he called after her.

A sharp slap against his cheek jarred his mind from the dilemma.

"Manelin!" Philander's voice called to him quietly. "Manelin, wake up."

He opened his eyes. The grotto closed in around him.

"Are you alright?" His grandfather's voice sounded strained.

Manelin sat up and glanced at the table full of flowers. "I think it's the flowers."

Philander helped him to his feet. "Come, I'll help you outside." He lifted Manelin's arm across his shoulders and shuffled across the stone floor a couple of steps and stopped. "Manelin, promise me you will not speak of this to others."

Manelin squinted at his grandfather's serious face in the dim lighting. "I just want to go home."

"Promise me." They moved forward another step. "Remember, the flowers ward off evil spirits."

Manelin pulled free. "I'm not..." He straightened his tunic and tied the lace at the collar. "I'm not an evil spirit." His mind drifted to Jalil. Fear gripped him. *Is she an evil spirit?*

Bright sunlight shot him back a step when he reached the door. He shielded his eyes with his forearm stepping to the threshold.

"What took you so long in there, Philander?" a thin man with a pointed nose asked. "It's not fair to the rest of us waiting. We want to get home sometime today."

"I'm sorry, Jorge. This is Manelin's first trek. He had many questions." He ushered Manelin past the impatient pilgrims.

Jorge mumbled a curse and pulled his wife with him into the grotto. Manelin stared at the gardenia in her hand.

"Come, Manelin." Philander tugged his arm.

"I can walk," Manelin said while rubbing his shoulder. He quietly followed his grandfather down the stairs and into the village. Instead of asking a hundred questions, he pondered his dream. *Why would I dream such a strange meeting with Jalil?* He didn't even know her.

They reached the bottom of the stairs where the crowd thinned enough for them to make it home quickly. Manelin stared at the door of the metalsmith shop as they walked by. Jalil did not stand at the entrance. He looked at his grandfather and for the first time noticed his pale color.

"Are you well, Grandfather?"

Philander shrugged. "Life has changed, Manelin. We can never go back to what we had for it is time to move forward." He turned his face toward home and stared into the distance.

Manelin had never seen him so serious or mysterious. The crunch of sandy grit on the cobblestones overlaid the indistinct threads of conversations from the waning crowd. *Never go back?* What did he mean? He swallowed hard and wished he would wake up. Maybe he was still unconscious in the grotto.

Chapter 12
Lessons

If he truly believed the boy's destiny,
he had to let go of his affections and move forward.

Philander shoved the five-inch double sided blade into the bread and sawed with all his strength. Crumbs scattered across the table. He'd known the time would come, but it was too soon. The boy wasn't ready.

What was he worrying about? Manelin hadn't confirmed anything more than passing out. Perhaps it was too much excitement. No, Manelin had said he saw the bumble foot girl.

He tossed the butchered bread onto a platter and scooped out two bowls of soup from the bubbling kettle. *How much time do we have?* He studied Manelin through the rising steam as he headed toward the table where the young man sat playing his flute.

Three last notes floated into the air and vanished. Manelin let the clay instrument dangle from the leather strap around his neck. He accepted the bowl from his grandfather and inhaled.

"Thank you."

Philander paused.

Manelin looked from Philander to the soup and back again. "What?"

"Are you feeling well?"

Philander didn't want to know. If only he could go back a day in time and choose to stay home instead of making the trek. He couldn't put it off forever. If he truly believed the boy's destiny, he had to let go of his affections and move forward.

Manelin stirred his soup thoughtfully. "I … I had a dream. You know, back in the grotto."

He plucked a thick mangled slice of yeasty brown bread from the basket. One eyebrow arched while eyeing the ragged slice. He shrugged and dipped it into the broth.

The spoon in Philander's hand shook. He scooped a spoonful to his lips and blew. His mind bolted, searching for the right words. "A good dream?"

Manelin's shoulders lifted and sagged. "I'm not sure. It wasn't good or bad, just strange. I couldn't walk. It was like I was awake. I felt trapped. I thought I was in the grotto, but it looked like someplace else. High over my head I saw what looked like windows." He massaged his shoulder. "It seemed real, not like a dream. Jalil was there."

Philander dropped his bread into the steamy broth. "Jalil?" He scooped the soggy crust from the bowl with his spoon. Like it or not, he saw the foretellings unfolding before his eyes.

Manelin nodded. "She didn't know how she got there, but said she heard me calling her."

Philander considered the curious vision. "What else did she say?"

Manelin let out a breath. "Was the crow real?"

Philander nodded. He shook his spoon toward Manelin as he spoke. "Now that was strange."

Manelin loosened the lace on his shirt. "After that bird landed on my shoulder, it burned like a spider bite. In the vision, it grew worse. Burned like fire. Jalil touched it and the pain disappeared. I can still feel the heat a little, but it doesn't hurt." He pulled the neck of his shirt to the side. "Do you see anything?" The collar of his tunic slipped from his bare shoulder. "Maybe a spider did bite me. That's why I passed out."

The symbol of an eye stared at the older man from Manelin's shoulder. Philander dropped the spoon in his hand and pointed. "It wasn't a dream." His throat grew tight. "It's a mark—a sign."

"That's what she said. What could it mean?" Manelin stood, tipped his chin and twisted to see the mark.

Philander pushed away his half-eaten dinner, slid his chair from the table, walked to the bedroom and returned with the brass box. He set it on the table next to Manelin's bowl.

Manelin trained his eyes on Philander's face. The old man gestured with his head toward the box. "Open it."

"Open it?" A frown pulled across Manelin's face. His hand rested on the lid.

Philander nodded.

He lifted the lid and peeked inside to see the old book and a rod carved with notches. His eyebrows lifted as he looked from the box to Philander with an unspoken question.

"Here," Philander slid the box from Manelin's grasp and used his sleeve to shine the lid. "Look," he said. "You can see your reflection." He pointed to the mirror like surface. "This will help." He moved the lantern closer. "Can you see it?" He pushed the box back toward his grandson.

Manelin turned the box toward his shoulder. An unblinking eye stared back at him. "It *is* an eye! Why? I've never had a birthmark. How did this happen? What does it mean?" He rubbed the brown mark.

Philander pulled the book from the chest. "The answer may be in here. I remember hearing about the mark, but my memory doesn't serve me as well as it once did. We'll see if it tells us anything."

"Right now?"

Philander shook his head lowering the book into the box. "For now we'll eat." His shaky hand closed the lid and moved the box to the side. "Eat." He waggled his finger at Manelin's dinner. "Everything will be fine, but for now I don't want you to tell anyone about this. Do you understand?"

Manelin nodded. "Don't worry. I'll not speak of it. I don't want anyone thinking I'm an evil spirit. Most of the people my age don't like me the way it is; I don't need to make it any worse."

"How many times do I have to tell you that isn't true? You just don't have close friends because you spend your time in the field with the goats."

"It's more than that, Grandfather. I'm seventeen. I *know* they don't like me. My skin is darker than most and I have brown eyes. Neither makes me popular. I chose to become a goatherd to get out of the village.

"Did you see the way Delaine treated me today? That's the kind of 'friends' I have here in the village. I actually prefer being in the field."

Philander let out a slow deliberate breath. "For now, eat."

Manelin sipped his soup. "Jalil said something I don't understand."

Philander pushed his bowl away and crossed his arms. "Tell me everything, Son. I want to know what happened."

"You know most of it," he said. "I asked how she could walk. It didn't make sense. She started to cry because I knew she was a … a bumble foot."

The color drained from Philander's face. His hand brushed the top of the brass chest. "It's time for you to learn of your people, and what is to come."

"Our ancestors? They could predict the future? Is that what's in the book?"

"It's a journal of the history of the time when the Jonnick and Stygian dwelled together."

"Together?" Manelin frowned. "I never knew they lived together. I thought the Stygian were our enemy."

"Manelin." Philander rubbed the back of his neck. His weathered fingers interlaced, resting his folded hands on the table. "The door to change has opened. I'm trusting you are old enough to keep a secret. I'd prefer to study the Stygian tellings, but this is a good place to start." He patted the box. "We'll begin tonight after dinner. If we read the journal together you can ask questions. Hopefully, I can answer them. One generation of Jonnick passed this journal to the next. I think it would pass the Queen's scrutiny unless someone decides to read it."

"Will we learn about this eye?" Manelin rested his hand on his shoulder. "Did anyone else in our family have this happen to them?"

"Truthfully, I haven't opened this book in years. My father gave it to me for safe keeping, and told me one day it would hold the answer to questions no one could answer."

Manelin smiled. "I'd like to know if it can tell me what happened today at the shrine. How did Jalil get there? What does this mark on my shoulder mean? Why could she walk and I couldn't? It doesn't make sense."

Philander chuckled. "I'd say those are questions that no one can answer. We'll have to see if my father was right." He picked up his spoon and mixed the vegetables in his soup. "This stays between me and you. Do you understand?"

Manelin nodded. "Trust me. I won't say a word. I'd end up in that asylum and never see the light of day."

"Once we read the teachings we may have to tell others what we've learned, but for now telling of your vision or that mark on your shoulder would only stir the villagers' imaginations. I don't want any trouble."

"I understand." Manelin tore a chunk of bread, stuffed his mouth and finished his meal without another word.

Philander picked up the book and leafed through the pages. "Here, see this?" He turned the book around and pushed it toward Manelin. The sketch of a tree spread across the page.

Manelin shrugged. "Is that supposed to mean something?"

"It's a forked tree." He traced his index finger along the sketch. "See how it splits in two directions?"

Manelin nodded. He looked into his grandfather's good eye, "What does it mean?"

"It has two meanings. The first is conflict within a person. Half of that person loves while the other half is capable of hatred. Both sides must learn to recognize one another and learn to become a whole balanced person. If not, it leads to death and destruction. It's what caused the problems in our homeland, or so my ancestors' writings tell me. It was never a popular view, but if I recall what my grandfather told me, the sickness that chased them from the land started as a curse."

"A curse?" Manelin glanced at the sketch on the page.

"The sorry thing about curses is that once they leave the lips there's nothing you can do." Philander looked at the page and nodded. "In the case of my homeland, hatred won. It all started over fishing rights. Some of the villagers fished at night and others claimed it depleted the fish population for the day fishermen. They thought the sea needed a time of rest.

"One old woman lost her son in a fight. He fell from the dock, hit his head and drowned. In her anger and grief, she cursed the night fishermen and their descendants but the curse spread sickness throughout the land because it touched descendants of any who fished at night—ever."

"You said this had two meanings." Manelin's index finger brushed the sketch. "What is the other?"

"It's a symbol of division among countries or clans. When a clan looks at other clans and decides they are…" he searched for the right word, "inferior or even unlawful, the tree symbolizes that clan."

Manelin scrunched his nose. "What?"

Philander tapped his finger on the page. "See how each side of the tree looks the same? Two parts of the same tree. We all reflect each other. People are the same. We are one tree, but we have to work at being united. Not everyone sees things the same way. Thus we have this," his finger stopped on the split in the tree, "division."

* * * *

The toll of a bell sounded in the distance marking the end of the sacred day. Adish swept the floor of his shop while Jalil sat on the wooden chest fiddling with her doll's braids. She'd held the doll since she woke from her strange dream. It left her with mixed feelings. The doll brought her comfort, probably because her mother gave it to her.

"Are you alright, honey?" Adish stopped and leaned on the handle of his broom. "You haven't played with that doll for years."

"Yes, Papa." She let out a sigh. "I'm not playing with her." Her fingers lingered over the opening in the doll's back where she'd stuffed the amulet.

"You seem awfully quiet tonight." Adish's ruddy face brightened. "I know it bothers you that you couldn't make the trek to the shrine, but don't let it. The Dawn of the Beginnings is celebrated in the heart. You don't really need to go to the shrine." A weak smile tugged at the corners of his mouth. "In fact, I heard someone say they saw you in the crowd today. No one will know that you weren't there."

She glanced at the doll's flowered print body and fiddled with the braid of yarn. *Does he know?* Jalil searched her father's face. *What would he say if I told him I visited the shrine today?* She looked at the doll on her lap and decided not to mention it. He wouldn't understand. She didn't understand. And he didn't care for that dark eyed boy. *I wish mother was here.*

How did the dream-like trip happen? Was it wishful thinking because he waved to her from the crowd? Her mother had told her stories about people who traveled on the wind. *What were they called? Windwalkers?* Her mind wandered to one story in particular about a Windwalker with a bumble foot. Among her people, she was known as an Augur. She was the most special of the Windwalkers. Jalil believed the stories to be fables, made up to entertain her and comfort her because of her deformity. Now, she craved to understand. *Mother, am I an Augur?*

Within her mind, a voice spoke. *"An Augur you are, Jalil."*

The voice sounded clear. But whose voice? Maybe her mind was succumbing to her mother's madness.

"Jalil?" Her father waved his hand in front of her face.

"I'm fine, Papa."

"Good," he propped the broom against the wall, "how about some dinner?"

Jalil smiled. "I'm hungry." She hobbled behind Adish to the stairs using the wooden railing to support the climb to the apartment above the shop. Her thoughts lingered on the freedom she'd experienced today. Jalil longed to move about unhindered again.

Adish stepped slowly two stairs above her, waiting for Jalil to keep up. Savory scents mingled with smells of the shop as they neared the door at the top of the stairs.

"Mmmmmmm, something smells great," he said.

"I made meat pie." She limped onto the top landing and through the door behind him.

"Yes, it smells great." He patted his ample stomach. "You'll make a fine wife someday. I don't know of another girl in the village who can cook like you."

Jalil looked at the floor. "You don't know the other girls in the village, Papa." *No one will want me for a wife*. Her shoulders slumped. She set her doll on the shelf under the window and hobbled to the oven to retrieve dinner.

Manelin's face flashed into her mind. He hadn't shied away from her. She treasured the thought and carried the pie to the table where Adish set two pewter plates he'd made for his wife for their second anniversary.

Jalil ate quietly, listening for the unfamiliar voice with mixed emotion. Did she really want to hear it?

Chapter 13
The Opening of the Book

"Tell the queen I'd be happy to serve, Father.
Tell her I may have found the girl she's searching for."

Philander sat in his upholstered chair near the fire with the brass chest on his lap. Firelight reflected and bounced off the lid onto the wall when he opened the box. Memories of the time his father read to him from the Book of History rushed in. His fingers brushed the tired cover, the letters long ago worn smooth and illegible.

In his mind's eye he saw his father's animated face telling stories of long ago. Things had changed since then. His great-great grandfather penned the original entries. Philander put the book away when Manelin joined him. If he didn't read it, he didn't chance changing the destiny of Ranaan because he misunderstood a prophecy or tried to force it to come to pass "his way."

His father knew most of the entries by heart, but for Philander they remained lingering disjointed memories. Fear of the knowledge of things to come almost paralyzed him because of his love for Manelin. The mishap at the shrine compounded his trepidation. He lifted the dog-eared leather book from the box and set the chest on the floor.

"Manelin," he called into their bedroom.

"Yes?" Manelin stopped at the threshold and leaned against the frame of the door as he dried his hair.

"Come have a seat." Philander patted the footstool in front of him. "This is a family tradition. My forefathers penned this journal and read from it to their sons when they reached the age of reason. It's different than the tellings—more personal. It is time for you to hear the words preserved for this time."

Muffled hoots from that owl outside the bedroom window leaked into the living room.

The fire in the hearth painted amber highlights in Manelin's wet hair as he sat on the stool. "I'd like to hear what it says. Are there more pictures? Like the tree?"

Philander nodded. "My great-great-great grandfather's cousin, Evan Davis, arrived on these shores at the Dawn of Beginnings." He opened the tattered brown cover. "He brought this journal from across the sea. In fact, the first entries were penned on the shores of Jonnick."

* * * *

Ojal's large wingspan carried her silently to perch on the branch outside the window of the home of the one-eyed Jonnick. Since her return, she'd watched the boy grow into a young man. Tonight, the old man sat teaching the Arich.

Excitement soared within her. She'd connected with the young Augur. The fulfillment of the times drew near. She longed for her lost ability to speak mind to mind with whomever she pleased and pour her insight into them. The young Augur was receptive. For now, fate trapped Ojal within her metot. She'd grown accustomed to the various animal forms making up her metot long ago. Birds were her favorite. Flying reminded her of walking on the wind. At night, she chose the owl metot to hear and see well.

The young Arich reminded her of Kynan. A trusting soul. The one-eyed Jonnick had raised him well. Sorrow colored her excitement. She studied the voice of the old man. He loved the Arich, as she loved Kynan—as a son. Like her, he had no children and had given his life to prepare for the gathering.

They rested on the cusp of change. Times of trouble crouched at the door. It wouldn't be long until the Arich was ripped from all that he knew and loved. Her heart broke for the one-eyed Jonnick.

* * * *

Philander turned to the first entry.

16th Yeppa, 1529

Cousin Donnel and I plan to commandeer the fleet of four ships stagnating in the harbor. Dead crews rot aboard ship while the plague spreads like fire within our borders. Harsh winter winds ravage from without while one by one our fair citizens fall to the sickness. Perilous seas promise an unsure future, but offer more hope than staying here awaiting death's tarriance.

For once, I don't regret my lack of family ties. If I were in Donnel's place, I don't know what I'd do. To think I bordered on jealousy when I learned Amelia carried their firstborn. Now, to stay in Jonnick puts them at great risk, and the jeopardy at sea may be even greater. We've agreed to depart under the blanket of darkness with the exception of Amelia's mother.

The hellish wench forbids her daughter to leave and threatened to place a curse on Donnel and his family if they flee. Who could have known the peril tied to marrying into the line of the Mage?

Poor Amelia's loyalties are torn. Her mother's abilities are known throughout Jonnick. Amelia worries that the power of the Mage will reach across the sea. If she chooses to stay, I'm not sure Donnel will leave. Without his guidance as Captain I'm uncertain we can leave. If he stays; I'll stay. But, I'm more than willing to relinquish my property in hopes to save my life. I'd rather own nothing and live than die a wealthy man.

As of this evening, we have enough able-bodied men to sail three ships and perhaps four. If all goes well, we'll set sail three days hence. Over these next few days we'll gather what food stores we can, in hopes it will be enough for the length of our journey.

Evan Davis

Philander stopped, rubbed his eyes and looked up from the book. His blind eye glowed in the firelight.

"What was the sickness?" Manelin asked. "It must have been terrible if it forced them to leave their home. I can't imagine leaving everything behind."

His grandfather nodded. "The sickness killed thousands. It's one of the reasons I stopped reading this book. It tells of difficult times back in our homeland and the struggles after the Dawn of the Beginnings ... it all can be depressing. These stories are the reason my brother became a Healer."

"Did they find the food they needed for the trip?"

Philander nodded. "We'll read again tomorrow," he said. "It's late and I'm tired. That trek up the Sacred Stairway has wearied my bones. If we read each night, we'll eventually read the whole thing."

The owl hooted.

Philander held up his finger. "Let me just look for one more thing."

Manelin waited, leaning forward, elbows propped on his knees, his hair almost dried.

"Here it is," Philander turned the book to face Manelin and pointed to an owl sketched in a circle of animals surrounding a woman. Light flickered across the image. "This is the symbol of magic and second sight."

"Second sight? What does that mean?"

"It's impossible to keep secrets from those who possess the energy of the owl."

A slight scowl crinkled Manelin's brow. "An owl?"

"Listen." Philander pulled the book back and held it toward the light as he read. "The owl is the essence of wisdom. It sees and hears things others cannot, and helps discover the truth and interpret the signs of fate. I remember reading about this in the tellings." Philander let the book drop to his lap.

"What about the woman?" Manelin pointed toward the page, "Look at her foot."

Philander smiled weakly. "Yes, the—let me see. The Augur. Ojal the Ancient. I heard about her in the Stygian tellings. These represent the eight animals to help her along the path of life." His finger traced the circle of smaller images.

"Animals?"

Philander pulled in a long breath. "I don't understand it. It doesn't tell us much here, just this drawing with the explanations of what each animal stands for."

Manelin smiled. "Maybe this is a sign that I can have a pet to help me along life's path." His finger pointed to the image of a dog.

Philander closed the book. "For now, you need to get to bed. It's sheering time. You'll be putting long hours in out in the field."

Manelin stood and stretched. "Yeah, and I won't have to wash my hair." He laughed. "I might even sheer my head. That would take care of the problem."

"Manelin!"

"Don't fret. I'm not about to shave my head." He ran his fingers back and forth through his coarse reddish-blonde locks. "And, you're right about the goats. It will be a lot of work, but their heavy coats will bring a good deal of money."

Embers in the hearth cast a red-orange glow across the small room. As Manelin walked into the bedroom, Philander lingered to clean up.

Manelin changed into his nightshirt and stood at the open window. A light breeze brushed his face. His attention moved to the owl in the tree. "So do you see and hear things others cannot?" He leaned his elbows on the sill. "Can you help me discover the truth and interpret signs of fate?" His nightshirt fell from his shoulder revealing the mark he received in the grotto.

The owl turned its head and stared at him. An unsettled feeling pumped through him. He eased to stand straight. "If you understand, give me a sign."

With a rush of wind, the owl flapped its great wings and lifted from the tree. The tip of its wing brushed Manelin's cheek. He stood mesmerized. His fingers lingering against his face marking the magic moment. The bird swooped, beat its wings and disappeared into the night sky. Manelin grabbed his shoulder. Fiery heat of the crow's touch rekindled and he backed away from the window wondering what it meant.

* * * *

The Captain hugged the shadows along the cobblestone street heading toward his home. A large owl swooped low over his head dropping him to his knees. He skidded across the pavement, rolled and scurried to his feet searching the sky for the big bird. Straightening his cloak, he hurried a few doors down to his house. He tried the locked latch and glanced over his shoulder. His knuckles frantically rapped on the thick door.

Firelight shined behind Delaine as he opened the door still dressed in his uniform.

"Father, you're home?"

The Captain pushed past his son. "Senta has disappeared. I'm afraid the queen may have learned of his plan." He slammed the door, slipping the bolt into place. "It's too risky. Our strategy has to change." He hurried to sit at the table.

"Why?" Delaine sat across from his father. "With Senta out of the way, if we eliminate this Arich and the queen, it will all be ours."

His father slipped his helmet from his head and ran his fingers through his matted hair. "I'm not sure, Delaine. Maybe we should back off. It's too dangerous. We're messing with things we don't understand."

Delaine nodded."The queen will trust us when you tell her we may have found the Bumble Foot. She'll reward you. You'll probably be promoted to take Senta's position." He slapped the table top. "I'll not give it up. We're close to holding the kingdom in our hands."

The Captain stared at his son. Greed for power had taken over the young man. He'd lost control. He buried his face in his hands trying to figure out what to do.

"Tell the queen I'd be happy to serve, Father. Tell her I may have found the girl she's searching for."

The Captain pushed to his feet. "Delaine, listen to me. It's too dangerous. The queen has powers we don't know about or understand."

Delaine set his jaw. "I've met the girl at her father's shop. I have to go back to check on the progress of the blast logs. If it makes you feel any better, we won't say anything until we know for sure. I think she's taken with me." A smile crept across his face. "She'll never suspect a thing."

* * * *

Philander slid the chest under his bed.

"Grandfather?" Manelin paused with his foot on the ladder to his bunk.

"Yes?" The bed creaked as Philander sat on the mattress and slipped his feet from his well-worn sandals.

"Never mind." Manelin climbed into the niche that served as his bed. Why hadn't his grandfather told him about the journal before now? *Something isn't right.* Fear edged his thoughts. The owl responded to him as if it understood. The symbol on his shoulder simmered and his mind turned to the grotto. Maybe Jalil could explain it.

Three soft hoots seeped through the open window. Manelin turned to his other side. His grandfather's deep rhythmic breathing told him the old man had already fallen asleep.

It'll be nice to get back to the flocks tomorrow, Manelin thought, *and get my mind off all this.* He fell asleep with his arms crossed in front of his chest, his hand pressed against the mark.

* * * *

Estel lay on the small cot motionless. Her mind drifted to her daughter and a great sadness pressed in on her. Part of her understood why Adish put her in this place. She searched the inner recesses of her heart but reached an emptiness—something missing. Dreams haunted her each night. A great ashen serpent gobbling her soul.

Since that day in the forest, she'd changed. The sad thing was she recognized it, but couldn't fix it. Part of her was—missing. It always came back to that. Adish thought it a sickness of her mind and perhaps he was right.

She rolled to her side listening to the sounds within the walls of the forgotten place. Cries and moans echoed throughout the corridor outside her door. She'd wandered those halls many nights looking for the answer, but returned to her bed still lacking. She remembered her daughter. Her bright smile, clear blue eyes and something else. She pounded her fists against her skull. Why couldn't she remember?

The hoot of an owl pulled her from the cycle of frustration. She looked to the opposite wall of the small room at an owl sitting on her sill. It stared at her. Something within her stirred. Was it because it broke the monotony of this place? No, it was something more. It touched the emptiness, offering a fragment of the missing piece.

Chapter 14
Potent's Table

A hint of light up ahead lured him onward. Light? Inside this big rock?

Manelin awoke at dawn. A rosy blush radiated across the hazy horizon painting the distant mountains a dark purple. The forked tree sat empty. Thoughts of the owl primed his mind with questions. What did it all mean? Manelin pondered Jalil's appearance in the grotto. Would she know or understand these things that confused him? She'd probably think him crazy. He shook off the thought. It was a dream. *But the mark on my shoulder. . . .* This circle of thought would drive him mad.

He slipped his poncho over his head, wrapped bread and cheese in a cloth and stuffed it into his pouch along with his flint and steel. The mark on his shoulder felt fine as Manelin slung the strap of his pouch across his back. Part of him couldn't wait to get back to his flock. Every fiber of his being wanted to leave the bizarre experience at the grotto behind him. The thought of evil spirits stirred an uneasiness that left Manelin a little on edge. He let out a breath. Could Jalil be an evil spirit?

Manelin grabbed his staff from the corner near the door, slipped the strap of his water skin over his head and across his chest and ducked into the early morning stillness without waking his grandfather. An early start would provide more time tonight to read the old book.

Beyond the village wall, songbirds greeted the sunrise as one called to another. A sense of freedom lifted his burden as he slipped through the gates. A coyote bayed in the distance starting a chain reaction. His mind drifted to the flock and the vulnerable young kids. He neared the bridge that crossed the swollen river and left the road traveling down the grassy bank to get a drink and fill his water skin.

Floodwaters overflowed and reached into the trees along the shore. At this rate, the spring thaw would put the rickety bridge under water in a couple of days.

Manelin knelt, his knees sinking into the mucky soil while he cupped rushing water in his hand and ladled it to his lips. A faint yelp caught his attention. He paused. A series of quick, high-pitched whines drifted above the splash and pull of the stiff current. His eyes searched the flooded tree line. Water spun through and around the trunks creating whirlpools of debris. Here and there, the current deposited rubbish against tree trunks creating temporary dams pushing expanding pools of water toward the road.

Manelin trudged through the mire following the whimper. Cold water hurt his ankles through his boots and mud sucked his feet into bondage. The whimpering escalated into a yelp. A flash of wet golden fur splashed in the water in front of him. Manelin snagged the squirming animal with his staff and pulled it toward him. Frantic paws paddled against the flow, splashing Manelin as he dragged the pup close enough to grip the skin on the scruff of the neck. He yanked the squirming dog from the sweeping current.

The trembling puppy stopped struggling and settled in Manelin's arms as he waded up the incline. He tucked the pup into his poncho using his body heat to warm the shivering ball of fur. It nestled beside his heartbeat and fell asleep. "Poor little pup, you're sopping wet. Wonder what happened to your mom."

Manelin scanned the horizon for any sign of another dog. "I guess it's you and me, Sop. Grandfather won't have you, but the goats will be thrilled to have you around. You can help protect them."

Sunshine reached through the clouds clustered along the horizon, burning away the pastels of dawn as Manelin came upon his flock in the Valley of Rocks. A group of kids frolicked while a black and white nanny stood watch. Males and females grazed together. Manelin planned to move the herd to higher ground before the males drifted into groups to prepare for the next mating season. Early yellow flowers and black pods of the spring gorse would provide nutrients lacking during the winter in the valley.

Sop wriggled free from beneath the loose fitting poncho and hopped to the ground. The skittish goats eyed the intruder. Vahe sniffed the air, his horns curving gently away from his black head. The others waited for his determination of the furry newcomer. As the strongest goat in the flock, he served as protector and followed at the back of the pack where predators attacked. He pranced toward the dog, but the puppy wagged its tail not recognizing the threat.

Manelin crouched beside Sop and pushed her back end to the ground.

"It's okay, Vahe." The goat paused, fidgeted a bit, but after a few moments went back to feeding while cautiously eyeing the puppy. Lush spring grass and new growth on the scrubby brush lured them to gorge their insatiable appetites.

Nubs marked the kids' heads in the days since Manelin had been away from the flock. They'd grown enough to keep up with the herd as he moved into the foothills for shearing. There, caves and clefts in the rocks provided shelter for the shorn goats.

Aja ambled to Manelin's side. The gentlest nanny in the flock, she brushed up against his leg and stopped.

"What's the matter, Aja? Feeling a little left out?" He patted the goat's head. His heart ached for the doe, her kid stolen by a large wolf the week before. "I need you to look after Sop."

Sop sat, clumsily scratched behind her ear and fell over. She sprang to her feet and ran into the mix of kids scattering them in all directions. The nanny overseer darted from Manelin's side and lunged at the yapping pup.

"Aja, come girl." He whistled two shrill notes and all the goats stopped feeding and watched. Vahe trotted to Aja's side and the dog stopped in front of one of the kids and lay in the dirt panting.

Aja bleated. Her brown eyes trained on the little misfit.

"Sop, here girl."

Aja stepped toward the golden ball of fur. They sniffed each other, and the goat licked the dog's nose. Sop flinched, barked and ran in a circle.

Manelin laughed. The kiddless goat ran her tongue along Sop's back. The puppy settled into the grass, rolled to her back letting the nanny's tongue work along her belly. Aja stepped over the dog, full udders hanging just above Sop's snout. Sop sniffed and licked the spotted teat. Aja bleated, and the dog suckled.

"That takes care of that problem," Manelin announced to himself. He looked out over his flock spread across the grazing land. Kids bounced in a circle and two chased each other around the scrubby meadow.

Manelin glanced over his shoulder toward the rising river in the distance. He sat in the grass and pulled the large wedge of cheese from his pouch. The pungent aroma made his mouth water for the salty flavor. He carefully unwrapped the crumbly chunk. *I think we'll move to higher ground today.* He studied the hills around him. The Valley of Rocks would soon be green again, as spring chased winter away for good.

Sop finished suckling, wandered to Manelin's side and sniffed his hand. She licked Manelin's fingers, climbed into his lap and nibbled salty crumbles clinging to his hand. Manelin wrapped the remaining cheese in the cloth and stashed it in his pouch. The puppy wanted to tug on the cheesecloth. Manelin played halfheartedly while his attention turned to the river.

"I don't like the looks of that, Sop." He stopped tugging and raked his fingers through Sop's thick puppy fur. Goats would swim if they had to, but they didn't like it. They hated water in their faces.

"Let's get your new mama and her friends to a safer place." Sop's soft pink tongue swiped Manelin's cheek and repeatedly lapped his face. Manelin laughed; his eyes squinting shut."That's enough." He put his hand on the dog's snout and the puppy settled down.

It's great to be out here. Manelin took in a lung full of fresh air and stroked Sop's damp fur. The dog helped keep his mind off of the questions swirling around in his thoughts.

"Welcome to the Valley of Rocks, Sop. We'll be heading up there." He pointed to the foothills. "I don't need to take a chance of you getting near that river again."

With Sop tucked under one arm, he reached into his pouch, pulled out his flute and strung its strap around his neck. The smooth oval fit into his palm like it belonged there. He played a few notes and the goats' ears perked. Vahe chewed and waited for the others as one by one they fell into line to follow their goatherd into the uplands. Aja led the string, while Vahe guarded the rear of the line.

Manelin rested Sop's paws on the ground. The dog would have to find her place among the flock. He'd leave them to feed at the base of the hills tonight, and make the more dangerous part of the trek refreshed the following day. Sop chased to the head of the line and fell into place behind Aja. The dog jumped at her as if to play, but the goat nipped the pup lightly and she settled down.

Manelin veered to the left at Two Fingers Rock and headed toward the Western Foothills. The melody of his flute made the time pass quickly. Late morning shadows stretched across the valley floor toward the large granite plateau known as Potent's Table.

We'll stop between the plateau and the foothills, Manelin decided as he hit a high note. Sop broke rank and ran off across the flat, scrubby hardpan. A large brown and white nanny cried out. Her warning tipped off Manelin that a young one had wandered off. She'd accepted the dog as part of the flock.

"Sop!" Manelin's flute fell against his chest, bouncing as he ran after the dog. The goats behind him stopped to feed. "Sop!"

Zareb bleated her concern as Manelin sprinted after the dog. The blur of fur ran as if chasing a rabbit. How did such a young pup have this endurance and speed? Her golden color stood out among the dark green spiny plants and low growing heather as she tore across the field toward the granite wall reaching skyward toward the flat plateau. The puppy turned, barked, spun around and disappeared into the shadows stretching between Manelin and the sheer rock wall.

Manelin stopped, out of breath, at the huge landmark. "Sop?" Where had the dog disappeared? He searched the low growing shrubs along the base of the rock bulwark. Thorny brambles scratched his forearms. His goats would love these shrubs.

"Sop!" He rubbed a fresh scrape raking the underside of his arm. "Where'd that dog go?" He wiped sweat gathering on his brow and turned to check the goats. They'd spread out. The males headed to the thorny bushes and tree bark while the females fed on the ivy and grass.

A soft whimper grabbed his attention. He whistled two sharp trills. "Sop?" The dog yapped, a hollow echoing bark. Manelin stooped to search for an opening in the rock. The dog barked again leading Manelin to a hole hidden in the rocky bulwark behind prickly shrubs."Sop!" he called into the crevice.

Thorns snagged his trousers as he crouched to peek into the darkness. Sop's barking turned to whining. *What have you gotten yourself into?* Manelin tucked his flute inside his shirt and pressed flat on the ground scooting through the small opening on his stomach. He pushed his sack to his back squeezing through the narrow passage. "Sop!" The tunnel smothered his voice. Fear of getting stuck in the small space paralyzed him. The dog yapped again. She couldn't be far. Manelin pushed forward.

His hands groped into the darkness dragging his weight forward. Dread closed in on him. *What if I get stuck? No one will know where I am.* A burning sensation spread across his shoulder reminding him of the mark. His fingers patted the floor in front of him to avoid falling into a hole headfirst. A hint of light up ahead lured him onward. *Light? Inside this big rock?* The formidable granite formation stood out in the middle of the valley, as a convenient landmark.

The body-hugging tunnel spilled into a dimly lit room carved into the heart of Potent's Table. Manelin pulled his body free and stood staring in awe. Dust stirred in the opaque rays of light highlighting the first six steps of a circular staircase disappearing into the darkness of a silo shaped structure to his right. Dim light reflected off a pool of water at the opposite side of the room. Manelin didn't move, listening for signs of the dog's whereabouts. Where had Sop gone?

Across the room, he stopped to admire the tower-like structure housing the circular staircase. His fingers explored chisel marks in the stone. He tested the first stair while staring up into the darkness. The stair treads reminded him of the slabs used for the Sacred Stairway he and Philander climbed the day before. Manelin brushed dirt from the front of his poncho squinting into the shadows for signs of movement.

Sop barked from somewhere above him. Manelin stepped onto the first slab. It held his weight. Stagnant air tickled his nose. He sneezed. The sound bounced around the chamber echoing up the staircase. Sop answered with a bark.

Chapter 15
Visions

The scene melded within the haze of color and refocused on the stone in the hand
of a different young woman wearing a crown. The woman turned.
Blood red eyes stared back at Manelin and Jalil

Manelin hurried up the stairs. A surreal inky twilight swallowed him
and slowed his pace. His fingers brushed the stone and mortar lining the
interior wall to help keep his footing if an uneven step threw him into a
tumble. His eyes adjusted. Light leaked through tiny crevices overhead.
"Sop?"

The dog answered with one yelp. Manelin jumped. The dog's yap
sounded close, almost next to him. He squinted. Sop sat in the shadows
beside a door on a narrow landing connected to the staircase by a tapered
walkway. Manelin stood in the archway peeking into the cavern below.
The slightest misstep would find him splattered below. If the dog hadn't
barked, his life could have ended in a flash. Dizziness washed over him.
He didn't like heights.

He sucked in a calming breath. "Sop, come here girl," he whispered.

Manelin didn't look down, fearing the dog would fall in a burst of
excitement. "Come, Sop." He patted his thigh.

Sop padded obediently across the disintegrating stone bridge. Her
right rear leg slipped from the crumbling walkway scattering loose stone
into the dim recesses. The dog stepped through the archway into the
tower wagging her tail, sitting at Manelin's feet. He scooped her into the
safety of his arms and hugged her against his chest. "Good girl," he said
as he scratched the thick fur on the back of the dog's neck. He backed
into the cistern shaped stairwell and resumed his climb. Where would it
lead? His free hand explored the uneven wall to increase the chance he
might find an opening before his eyes could detect it. He inched his way
higher into the tower. The stone slabs wound around the bend.

Sop nestled in his arms. Manelin paused, turning to look behind him.

"Don't look down." He covered the dog's eyes, and focused on the stairs before him. How much further did he have to go? Maybe he should turn around and try that door. *That must be the way in and out of here.* In his mind he considered all the times he'd walked past this landmark and never noticed it to be anything more than a big rock. Curiosity encouraged him to keep climbing. He'd see where these stairs led before he moved back to the door.

The stairs spilled onto planks propped against a narrow ledge. Manelin clutched the dog. Dim light offered enough detail to make out an ordinary wooden door on the other side.

"What do you think, Sop?" He tested the plank with his boot. It didn't move. He put the dog down beside him. "Wait here," he said as if the dog understood. Planting one foot in front of the other, he rushed across the plank to the door and tested the latch.

To his surprise, the door opened without much complaint. He squinted, holding his forearm to shield his eyes to the light. The air smelled fresh compared to the stairwell. Stunned, he stood at the threshold absorbing the fact that this place existed. A spacious sunlit room furnished with a table, stools and shelves proved others had been here before him. But who? Just below the ceiling, rectangular holes a little bigger than his fist lined the walls to his right and left. An odd sense of déjà vu played with his mind.

He turned to call the dog, but she had disappeared. "Sop?"

The dog barked from inside the room. Manelin spun around, his heart slamming in his chest. "Sop!" The dog sat in the center of the room. She must have slipped in behind him. He patted her head and looked around in awe.

Shadows danced across walls covered with petrographs. Clay jars littered the small table and filled a shelf on the far wall.

"Where are we Sop?" He picked up the dog to be sure of her whereabouts.

Walking to the table he lifted the lid to one of the jars. Scrolls. His mind flashed back to the Stygian scrolls he and his grandfather hid along the unused goatherd trail. Sop squirmed from his arms and landed with a thud on the smooth surface, kicking up a cloud of dust.

"How long has it been since someone was here?" He waved at the dust hanging in the sunbeams and gently put the lid in place. His attention drifted to the shelves at the far end of the room. More clay jars, each housing individual scrolls.

Two painted jars stood out from the rest, marked with unfamiliar symbols. The jar on the left bore a series of three symbols. On the bottom right, a vertical line touched by an acute angle. He reached out and touched the clear gem embedded at the center. What did this mean? His eyes drifted to the highest symbol of the three. A vertical line ran through the middle of an acute angle. A small chip of green sparkled from the triangle formed by the merger of the two symbols. At the bottom right side a small downward arrow pointed to a red chip.

He lifted the lid, setting it carefully on the shelf and pulled out the scroll. His fingers worked carefully to unroll it. Nothing but a blank page. "Strange." He stuffed it back into the jar when from his peripheral the painting of the second jar caught his attention.

A simple circle painted around two dissecting double-sided arrows covered the side of the jar. Each arrow tip pointed in a different direction. Where had he seen that?

He dusted his palms and walked across the room to study the petrographs decorating the eastern wall. His grandfather would find this place fascinating.

"Look at this!" he said to himself.

His fingers brushed the image of a female and stopped on the clear detail. A twisted foot. "A bumble foot." The same as the drawing in his Grandfather's book, including the circle of eight animals surrounding her. He'd never heard of a bumble foot until this week and now this. His thoughts returned to Jalil and the unpleasant experience at the shrine. "I wonder what she'd think of this place and this—"

"Manelin?"

Jalil's voice startled him. His breath caught in his throat as he spun around to face her.

Sunlight played across her golden curls as she looked left and right. "Where are we?"

Her blue eyes settled on Manelin, drifted to the table and wandered up to the holes where sunlight leaked into this long forgotten place.

Sop wagged her tail, galloping over to the girl. Jalil stooped to stroke the eager pup.

"Jalil?" Manelin scratched his head. "How did you get in here?"

Jalil shrugged and limped toward Manelin. Her pink lips tightened into a thin line. "Promise not to tell others of these meetings." She stopped beside Manelin and used the wall to steady her balance. "If my father heard of this, I'm afraid he'd think me crazy and send me away like my mother."

Manelin took in a deep breath. "My grandfather knows. I told him about what happened at the shrine."

Jalil's mouth fell open; her blue eyes grew wide. "You told him?"

Manelin raised his hands to calm her. "It's okay. We talk about everything. He doesn't think I'm crazy. In fact, he pulled out some old book his ancestors wrote and started reading to me." He shrugged. "I never even knew he had that book until the night before I met you at the shrine." He paused searching for the right words.

"What exactly did happen at the shrine? And how did you get here? I thought that might be a dream, but this...?" His arm swept in front of him encompassing the large room. "I couldn't use my legs in the shrine. Here," he stomped his boot against the floor, "I can walk."

Jalil stared at the wall; her eyes fixed on the petrograph of the bumble foot woman. "I've never been here, like this." She pointed to the floor. "But, I knew it existed. I don't understand. It scares me." Tears spilled along her cheeks. "Look around. This is where we met the last time. Only now we see the details clearly." Her fingers brushed the picture on the wall.

"I want to go home. I want a normal life." She leaned against the wall and stared at Manelin.

He backed up a step raising his hands in surrender. "Don't look at me like that. I don't know how you got here! I was just looking at these pictures on the wall, saw this one," he rested his finger on the petrograph of the bumble foot, "and thought about what happened at the shrine. Now you're here." He jabbed his finger toward the floor. "And I don't like this." He waved his hand back and forth in the air. "The way you sneak up out of nowhere."

Tears spilled from her cheek, trickled to her chin and dropped to the floor painting wet blotches in the dust. "You don't understand what I'm going through. Until we left Tehya, I'd never been outside the village walls. In fact, I rarely stepped outside our home. My parents hid me." Her cheeks flushed and she looked away. "I'm not supposed to be alive."

Her lip quivered. "The trip to Chock—seeing the mountains and new rock formations—I was excited, happy to be alive. When we arrived in Chock, I thought it would be the same." Her shoulders slumped. "Papa hides my condition well. People don't know I'm a bumble foot. He tells them I was injured during the move. If the queen learns I'm a bumble foot, she will have me killed and probably my father too."

The reality of the law stunned Manelin.

Jalil let out a deep sigh. "I don't know how this is happening. I don't even know you!" She thrust her finger toward his chest. "I never had anything like this happen to me until I heard you calling me to the shrine. Now, I have dreams, and, and … I've heard a voice I don't know."

Manelin crossed his arms in front of his chest. "But, I didn't call you. I felt sorry for you. You know," he raised his palms toward the ceiling and shrugged, "I saw you left behind and felt bad that you had to miss the journey. I only *thought* of you." He shook his head. "I never…" He paused.

Jalil wiped tears across her cheek with the back of her hand. "What?" She sniffled.

"I thought of you." He grabbed her shoulders. "I thought of you when I saw you in the crowd, and I thought of you when I saw this picture." He gestured with his head toward the petrograph.

Her blue eyes narrowed and her face tightened into a slight scowl.

Manelin released his grip. "But, I didn't think of you when I was at the shrine." A rush of air brushed past his lips as he exhaled. His shoulders stooped. "I was unconscious."

Jalil nervously bit the corner of her lip. "I thought of you."

She looked at the floor and peeked at Manelin, keeping her chin tucked against her chest. "After finding myself in the crowd at the halfway point on the Sacred Stairway, I wondered how that happened. How did I get there? I hardly had time to think about it and I found myself back home in our apartment. It scared me. I thought of my mother and wondered if I might be going crazy. I sat to do my spinning to take my mind off of the experience, but I thought about the fact that you accepted me like I am. The next thing I knew, I stood within the grotto. Well, not stood, but floated. You lay on the ground. I didn't understand. I still don't understand. What's going on?"

Dust drifted quietly in the beams of light slicing between the two of them. They stared at each other. Manelin rubbed an imaginary itch from his nose. "You … you don't know how it is that you arrived here?"

He patted his leg, gesturing for Sop to come to his side. The puppy's gangly legs bounded upwards. She propped her front paws on Manelin's thighs. Her tail brushed the floor in quick wags, sweeping dust to each side.

Jalil bent to pet the dog. "I didn't know you had a dog." She glanced from the dog to Manelin. Sop whined, dropped her paws to the floor and spun chasing her tail. "He's cute." She smiled and stared into the Manelin's eyes.

"She," Manelin corrected, "I just found her today. Her name is Sop." Manelin returned Jalil's smile. His back to the wall, he slid to the floor with the puppy in his lap.

Jalil's attention drifted to the wall behind Manelin. "Look at this." She straightened and hobbled toward the petrograph. Defused sunlight filtered through the holes in the west wall and spread enough light onto the ancient images to see a touch of color. "How old do you think these are?"

"I'm not sure." Manelin cradled Sop in his arms and stood. "What do you think they mean?"

"Well," her fingers traced the dark haired woman with the twisted foot, "I think they tell a story." Her fingertip stopped on the amulet hanging around the image's neck, then fingered the leather strap around her neck.

Manelin stood. Gritty soil crunched beneath his soles as he stood beside the girl. Her finger moved from the picture of the bumble foot to the circle of animals surrounding the image. "I wonder what the significance of these animals might be."

Manelin's attention rested on the owl and his shoulder tingled. He thought back to his experience with the owl and the same image in his grandfather's journal. Maybe this was a dream. He glanced at the fair-haired girl and wondered.

"She's the reason I'm here," Jalil said.

Manelin blinked at the picture and turned to look at Jalil. "What do you mean?"

"Her name is Ojal."

"Ojal?" This was a bit more bizarre than Manelin cared to deal with. "Has she talked to you in your dreams?" Manelin waggled his eyebrows and wiggled his fingers in front of her face. "Ooooooooooooo."

"Stop it." She pushed her palm flat against his chest. "It's not funny." Her eyes drifted to the puppy. "I just know." She crossed her arms, turned to lean against the wall and shrugged her right shoulder.

Sop ran off to explore the room.

Jalil bit her thumbnail. "What will my father do when he finds I've left our apartment?" She limped toward the middle of the room and glanced at the holes overhead. "I need to go home."

A clatter from the far end of the room swallowed the silence.

Sop lumbered toward Jalil carrying a twisted walking stick in her jaws. Jalil closed her eyes bracing for impact as the dog pounced toward her. Sop balanced on her hind legs, the staff clenched firmly in her teeth. Her front paws pushed against Jalil's skirts. The girl's arms windmilled fighting to keep her balance. Manelin leaped to her side and grabbed her upper arm to break her fall.

"Sop, down!" The puppy jumped again. Manelin grabbed her by the scruff while holding Jalil upright.

"I'm sorry." He gently released his grip on Jalil's arm.

"Don't be. I'm fine." Her delicate cheeks brightened.

Was she angry with the dog or just embarrassed?

The squirming dog dangled from his left hand and barked once. The walking stick clattered against the floor. He rested Sop's paws on the floor and scolded her. "No jumping."

"Hey," Manelin picked up the walking stick, "look at this." He walked over to the wall and compared it to the staff clutched in the petrograph's hand. "This is the walking stick in the picture."

Jalil stood like a statue. "It seems like I know about this, but I can't remember." She tapped her forehead with her fist.

Manelin carried the staff to Jalil in the center of the room. "Here, use it to steady your steps."

He propped the staff before her with one hand.

She reached out and rested her hand on his. A whirlwind of color blurred around them. A sound like running waters filled the room. Images appeared faster than Manelin could take them in. He caught a glimpse of his grandfather, but it blurred with the others. The sound of rushing waters slowed, becoming a clear female voice.

Manelin's shoulder burned.

"Born on a moonless night, Arich to the people. Gird yourself for action. When the star rests beneath the crescent moon, you will rise to power. The eye that sees marks your position. Claim it. Lives of many rest on your insight and leadership."

Scenes of ships on the great sea blurred and refocused showing ships burning and scuttled in the harbor. An old woman's intense dark eyes stared briefly from the whirl of color, her face painted, and light glinting against her necklace. Her hand shoved a blank scroll toward them and the scene changed.

A dark haired woman talked with a pregnant Jonnick woman seated near a campfire. They focused on the white stone in her palm. The scene melded within the haze of color and refocused on the stone in the hand of a different young woman wearing a crown. The woman turned. Blood red eyes stared back at Manelin and Jalil.

Jalil let out a gasp. Manelin wrapped his arm across her shoulder as the vision changed. An old humpbacked man played a small oval flute like Manelin's, but the image dissolved and Philander came into focus hiding the Stygian manuscripts in the cave. Images smeared from one to another, blurring with visions of dark haired people, a young couple holding a child. The surreal images paused long enough to clearly snatch a detail before they melded into the swirling colors.

The voice continued. "Privileged to guide the Arich. Augur with a heart of love, stand at his side, together destined to unite the people at the great gathering. The Oracle of Ojal written for your eyes. Read it; open your mind; pass on wisdom from ages past. Serve him well."

Images spun in a tightening whirlpool of revelation. A woman sitting on a cot in a desolate room flashed before them.

"Mother," Jalil cried out. Her hand lifted from the walking stick, reaching to touch the apparition.

The whirl of colors spinning from the head of the walking stick abruptly shut down.

Awkwardness washed over Manelin. His arm around Jalil, she turned to look at him. He felt drawn to her.

Jalil lifted her forearm to her head. "What—what was that?"

"I don't know." He looked at his feet. A delicate yellow flower sat in the dust among their footprints. He handed the flower to Jail. "Are you all right?"

She smoothed her skirt and avoided touching the walking stick. She accepted the flower. "I think I need to sit down." She shuffled across the floor to the wall, glancing at the petrographs as she crouched to take a seat.

Manelin propped the walking stick against the wall and joined her on the floor. "Did you see what I saw?"

Chapter 16
Mysteries Within the Fortress of Stone

*Jalil stared at the painted symbols and held her necklace
out in front of her chest. "They're the same."*

Jalil stared at the painted symbols and held her necklace out in front
of her chest. "They're the same."

Jalil drew her legs to her chest, wrapped her arms around her shins
and spread the hem of her full skirt to hide her feet. "I saw my mother."
She rested her forehead on her knees. "I miss her."

"Your mother?"

Jalil's face grew determined as she looked at Manelin. "My father put
her in the asylum. She hasn't been well since I was young, but I love her.
She lived in a … another world. I thought it was the strain of keeping me
hidden. She'd sit in her chair humming, and even talk from time to time,
just like this." She gestured with her hand from Manelin to herself. "My
father hopes they will heal her, but the longer she's gone the more I think
I'll never see her again. She's been in there for two years."

"At least you remember her. My grandfather's brother has been in
the queen's dungeon for about fourteen years. Grandfather doesn't even
know if he's alive."

Jalil blotted her damp face with her sleeve. "That's awful. What did
he do?"

"They say he murdered an old woman. Grandfather said he'd never
take a life. As a Healer, he traveled from village to village. Someone
pointed the blame for the murder on him because he visited the woman.
I only have vague memories of him, but I remember missing him when
they first took him away. He taught me a song on the flute."

"What can you do?"

"Nothing. Grandfather says if we draw attention to ourselves, we'll
find more trouble than we can wrestle. Truthfully, if I had a brother, I
couldn't imagine leaving him in that place. "Manelin rubbed his shoulder.

"This all means something. It's no accident that I found this place and that you somehow," his hand moved in a circular motion with his index finger pointed, "arrived here." He combed his fingers through his hair. "But what do the visions mean?"

Jalil shook her head. "You know what I think? My mother would understand. This is the 'other world' she told me about." At the back of her head, she nervously wound a strand of blond hair around her finger, let it loose and wound it again. "Did you hear the voice?" She stopped twisting her hair and waited. Her blue eyes stared into his.

He nodded. "Without a doubt."

She chewed the corner of her lip. "I've heard that voice in a dream." Her shoulders lifted and dropped. "I think it was a dream." She cast a sideward glance at him.

"I'm sorry I made fun of you." He picked a dog hair from his tunic and glanced back at her. "I really am sorry. Go ahead. Tell me more."

A half smile tugged at the corner of her mouth. "I understand. I don't really want to believe it's real, but after this," she held up the flower and pointed to the twisted walking stick, "I know it's real. We can't be having the same dream. And look," she lifted his arm. "You're bleeding."

Manelin glanced at the raw scrape on his forearm. "You're right. I ran into some nasty thorns outside looking for Sop. It smarts. If it was a dream, I guess I wouldn't feel it."

"We should find something to wrap it." With the aid of the wall, she shimmied to her feet and hobbled toward the table in the center of the room. "Maybe we can find something over here."

She lifted the lid to one of the clay pots and stared at the scrolls. "What do you think these are?"

Manelin stepped to her side sliding one of the scrolls from the collection. His eyes scanned the words as he unrolled the papyrus. "That's what I thought." His arms relaxed, letting the scroll dip toward the floor. "Stygian tellings. This place is Stygian."

"Tellings?"

Manelin nodded, wary of offering too much information.

Jalil reached for his arm. "Be careful, you'll drip blood on it if you're not careful." Her fingers brushed his skin sending a tingling sensation shooting throughout his arm. A blinding light flashed. Her hand jerked. The two of them blinked. "What was that?"

"My arm!" Still clutching the scroll in his hand, Manelin lifted his forearm, not a mark on it. He threw the scroll onto the table. "I'm not sure what's happening here, but it's not natural."

"Obviously." She leaned on the table for support. Her curls shimmered as she tossed her hair over her shoulder. "What does the scroll say? Let's sit over there on the floor with Sop." She pointed to the napping dog.

Manelin shrugged one shoulder. "Do you want me to help you walk over there?"

Jalil's mouth tightened. "No, thank you." She picked up her skirts, straightened her posture and limped toward the wall of Petrographs. Sop lifted her head and wagged her tail as the girl sat beside her.

Manelin read the scroll as he walked toward Jalil. "I remember my Grandfather reading these when I was young." Fear gripped him. He'd promised never to mention the scrolls.

"What's wrong?" Jalil's face tensed with fear. "Is it something dreadful?" The palm of her hand rested against her chest.

"No," he sat on the floor beside her, "I just broke a promise, and I don't take it lightly."

"A promise?"

"Never mind. Talking about it will only make it worse."

Jalil leaned against the wall giving him a sideward glance. "Fine." She stretched her legs out in front of her and tilted her head back against the wall closing her eyes. "I almost wish I could go back and live in the cellar."

"Look." Manelin tapped her shoulder.

"What?" She opened her eyes.

Manelin pointed. "A dragonfly."

Its iridescent wings shimmered in the sunlight. The out-of-place insect landed on Jalil's toe.

"Look at that!" Manelin didn't move.

Jalil stared at the delicate creature decorating her misshapen foot. "A creature of the winds."

"What?" Manelin glanced from the insect to Jalil and back again.

"Represents tricking of the senses. Change is on the way." She pointed without lifting her hand. "See the color on its wings?"

Manelin nodded.

"My mother taught me to read signs. When she talked, that's the kind of things she'd tell me about. My father thought she was crazy." She let out a deep breath. "She said dragonflies represent magical times." Jalil glanced around her strange surroundings.

Manelin looked over his shoulder and back at Jalil. "It sounds like something in my grandfather's journal. The owl—"

"You know of the owl? The eagle of the night." Her face beamed but faded quickly to little worry lines gathering across her forehead. "I've never talked to anyone of these things other than my mother."

Manelin took in a deep breath. "I've never mentioned the tellings to another." A hunger stirred within him, more than curiosity. He longed to hear more. "What's happening in this place is definitely magical."

The dragonfly flitted from her foot and lazily zigzagged through the air and out one of the narrow rectangular openings.

"I want to know more."

Jalil raised one brow. "You won't laugh at me?"

"I said I was sorry," Manelin shrugged, "what else can I do?"

Jalil tucked the yellow flower behind her ear, sat up straight and smiled. "You can admit you were wrong."

Sop walked over and settled with her head on Manelin's lap. Her brown eyes looked up at him. Manelin stroked her soft golden fur and nodded. "I was wrong."

Jalil relaxed. "Mother used to tell me stories to pass the time. I'd listen to the same stories over and over. Before she was put away, she swore to me that the stories were true. I didn't know what to think. Walking on wind, feeling people's presence, strange things. I've never told anyone, because I don't want to end up in the asylum. Especially stories about the queen."

Queasiness rumbled in the pit of Manelin's stomach. "The queen?"

Jalil pointed toward the center of the room where they'd experienced the whirl of images. "Did you see her in the visions?"

"Was that the queen?"

"Of course," little lines crinkled Jalil's nose, "who else wears the crown of Ranaan?"

Manelin's mind settled on the unpleasant things his grandfather had to say about the queen. "What about her?"

"Did you see her eyes? My mother was right. She's not crazy." Jalil bit her bottom lip.

"Tell me," he grabbed Jalil's shoulders and shook her lightly, "what? My grandfather dislikes her, but he won't speak of her."

"You have to promise not to speak of this. It can put my mother in grave danger."

"I promise."

"My mother is ... was a Windwalker."

"Windwalker?"

Jalil let out a breath. She sighed. "Papa forbids me to speak of it at all. My mother had hidden it from him until she was injured. He has a strong dislike for the Stygian…"

Manelin winced.

"What?"

"My grandfather lost the sight of his left eye because he wouldn't agree to hate the Stygian and live with the queen."

"Lost … his … sight?"

Manelin nodded.

"Papa doesn't even want to talk about them." Her fingers reached to the leather strap around her neck. "That old woman in the whirlwind of visions, the one with the painted face. Did you see her?"

The fresh memory flashed to the forefront of Manelin's mind. "Yes."

"Look at this." Jalil tugged the necklace from inside her blouse. "Do you recognize it?"

Manelin's mouth fell open. He reached out and held it in the palm of his hand, studying the symbols. "I've never seen anything like it, until today. It's the same necklace isn't it?"

"I'm not sure. It might be one just like it; I don't know."

Manelin took Jalil by the hand and pulled her to her feet. "Come here," he dragged her toward the shelves at the far end of the room, "you're not going to believe this."

Jalil struggled to keep up, while Manelin half lifted and half pulled her to the far end of the hall. He stopped in front of the shelf holding the painted jars. His chest heaved as he pointed. "Look at that."

Jalil stared at the painted symbols and held her necklace out in front of her chest. "They're the same."

"What can it mean?"

"I know the meaning of the symbols." She clutched the necklace in her fist. "Mother used to draw symbols in the dirt of the cellar floor to teach me to read the ancient language. She used to joke that Jonnick females were not allowed to read Ranaan, but what could they do about a Jonnick no one knew existed reading a language they've done their best to wipe out?"

Manelin rested his hands on his hips. "So, my dear Jonnick, Stygian reader, what does it say?"

* * * *

Nilenam wrapped the poultice against Riona's wound. "It might help if you told me how you injured yourself," he said.

Riona's eyes flashed with anger. "Don't forget your place, Nilenam."

He fought a smile. She called him Nilenam. It was progress. Over time he hoped to draw her back to the girl he once knew. Perhaps even give her the opportunity to join them in the new land.

He glanced at the opulence surrounding her and back at her hardened, cold face. Her symptoms were physical, but the cause...

Riona pushed his hand away. "Enough."

Nilenam inched his stooped body to a standing position. His bent frame bowed forward, gathered his herbs and bag and walked away without a word. He'd grown use to the routine. Only hope for the future helped him endure life in the dungeon. Outside the throne room he lingered in the warmth of the sunshine pouring through the high overhead windows.

Without hesitating too long, he pushed himself to head to the dungeon. The guards had grown accustomed to his routine. He'd heard them talk about the 'old Healer.' The more they considered him harmless the better it would be in the future.

Chapter 17
The Great Hall

"It tells us it's time to shed established customs." She held the necklace thoughtfully. "A time to change," she shrugged, "start new projects."

Manelin and Jalil stood beside the dusty shelves eyeing the painted jars. Jalil grasped the necklace and lifted it for Manelin to see. With her free hand, she pointed to the three symbols etched in silver. Each bore a tiny chip of precious stone matching those on the clay jar. Her fingertip rested on the vertical line touching an acute angle. "This line represents the path of life." She traced the line. "The way it touches this angle indicates a good habit." She paused and let out a deep breath. "It encourages a person to continue with their work and even extend it."

"What about this?" Manelin pointed to the clear gem on the jar.

"It stands for order. The clear color equals the number one. We read that first." She glanced up and her eyes met his. A smile flickered across her lips.

Manelin's heart raced.

She looked down at the second symbol, and Manelin inhaled the fragrance of her hair.

"See the vertical line here at the top of the circle and how it runs through this angle?"

"Mmm hmm."

"It tells us it's time to shed established customs." She held the necklace thoughtfully. "A time to change," she shrugged, "start new projects."

"Mother used to tell me this makes growth possible."

Manelin glanced around the room. "We've made a good start shedding established customs. I'm talking to you about things I've been taught to keep to myself."

Jalil nodded. "Me too. It's kind of scary. I've dreamed of having a friend someday, but never imagined something like this."

She lifted her hair and tossed it over her shoulder. "Manelin, I don't have any friends." She glanced at her fingers nervously twisting the necklace, before looking back at him. "If I went to school, I'd have friends. If I could read, it would give me a way to pass time." Her eyes darted left and right and back at Manelin, "I'm trapped in our apartment most of the time." She shook her head. "I'm not complaining. It's better than living in a small room under our home in Tehya."

Manelin connected on a new level with the girl. Now *this* scared him. "It's your turn. Do you promise not to talk about this stuff with your father?" He reached down and patted Sop's head. "Or, anyone else?"

She nodded and looked away. A rosy hue colored her cheeks.

"I didn't have friends in school." Manelin flinched. His voice suddenly sounded as if he were yelling from a mountaintop. He cleared his throat. "I'm the only child in our village, in fact the only person in the village, with brown eyes! They called me Stygian … and other names." Anger rekindled in his gut. "Grandfather decided to teach me at home, and that's been fine. He's a good teacher, but I miss having…" He drew in a deep breath and released it slowly. "I miss having someone my age to talk to."

Jalil twiddled the necklace in her fingers and nodded. "You're right. My father doesn't trust you." She glanced up at him. "Because of the color of your eyes."

Manelin swallowed hard. "People have no control over the color of their eyes. No more than you can help that you have a bumble foot."

Jalil smiled. "So, let's be friends. The bumble foot and the brown-eyed boy." Her giggle echoed within the hall of Petrographs.

The muscles in Manelin's back relaxed. "I'd be honored." He cradled her hand in his and kissed her knuckles. Her hand opened like a flower at his touch. The necklace fell against her chest.

"What's the last symbol mean?"

"Promise not to laugh?"

"I think we're beyond that." He lifted the jar from the shelf to study the symbols. "We're friends." His thumb rested on the green gem sparkling from the triangle formed by the merger of a small arrow pointing downward. Its tip touched the red gem.

"It indicates a spiritual person with prophetic talent."

Manelin's dirty fingers brushed the surface of the jar. "Prophetic, huh?"

Jalil lifted one shoulder and let it fall. She nodded.

"Want to test it?"

First signs of a frown crawled across her face. She crossed her arms. "Like what?"

He lifted the lid from the jar pulled the blank scroll into view. "Look at this and tell me what you think."

She accepted the scroll and shuffled over to the table to sit.

Manelin felt guilty. He meant it as a joke. She'd probably be angry with him. He hurried to push her stool up to the table. "Never mind."

His hand reached in a flash and grabbed the scroll, but she snatched it from his grasp.

"There's nothing to read."

"Let me see it." She slapped it onto the table and unrolled it. "What are you trying to hide?" Her eyes scanned back and forth as if she was reading.

What was she doing? Manelin stared at the blank parchment. He figured it out. She was turning the joke on him. "Okay, I'm sorry."

Jalil looked up from the scroll, "It's the Oracle of Ojal," her face drained of color. "I can read it."

* * * *

Hoof-beats clattered along the cobbled street as Delaine trotted toward the metalsmith's shop. Since Senta disappeared, his father proved to be nothing more than a coward. His father might prove to be a liability. He pushed the thought from his mind as he saw the burly smith step from his shop slopping a bucket into the street.

A smile stretched across Delaine's face as he reined his steed to a standstill. "Good day, Adish." He tipped his red uniform hat. The horse sidestepped and shook his head.

Adish propped his hands on his hips. "Hello, Delaine. You're a bit early aren't you? Remember, between the Dawn of the Beginnings and Jalil's birthday, I won't make another delivery until the end of next week."

"I'm not here for the report." Delaine patted the stallion's neck. "Sheridan threw a shoe. I was wondering if you could help me out." The horse bobbed its head and shook its dark mane.

"I won't have time today. You could leave Sheridan here and take one of our horses until tomorrow."

Delaine flashed a smile and dismounted. He tucked his hat under his arm and ran his fingers through his blonde hair. "May I ask you a personal question, Sir?"

Adish scratched the back of his neck. "Why not? You want to come in?"

"Let me ask you first." He studied the shine on his boots and glanced up at Adish. "I wanted to ask your permission to see your daughter."

Adish didn't move. "See my daughter?" He stroked his beard. "You mean court her?"

Delaine stood a little straighter and nodded. "Yes, Sir."

"You know she's got a crippled foot. We didn't have a Healer and—"

"Sir, I know about that. It's my job to know of anyone with a crippled foot. You know it's the law to report such an injury."

Adish stepped toward the door. "No, I didn't realize it. Guess I can report it to you then?" He gestured for Delaine to follow him into the shop. "Bring Sheridan in here and let's have a look."

Delaine followed Adish into the shop. The musky smell of horses and straw mingled with the smoldering kiln.

Adish checked the horse's foot. "I can take care of this tonight if you'd like. It shouldn't take that long."

Delaine stepped toward the older man. "And what about Jalil?"

Adish straightened his back. "I don't mean to speak for her. You can stay for dinner if you'd like and we'll let things sort themselves out."

"Fair enough, Sir."

* * * *

Jalil opened her eyes, still grasping the walking stick. "Amazing." A moment ago, she thought of home and now she stood in the tiny apartment above the blacksmith shop. It worked like the scroll said it would.

Sunlight filtering through the two windows told her that she'd been gone for a good part of the day. Instead of feeling happy to be home, she felt let down. Had she really been with Manelin in that—that hall? Or, did she so desperately want a friend that her imagination filled her dreams with a make-believe friend in some exotic place? Was she crazy like her mother?

Her eyes settled on the twisted walking stick in her hand. Fear squeezed her chest. She threw it down like a snake, lost her balance and tumbled onto the floor. What would she tell her father? Panic made it hard to catch her breath. She stared at the walking stick as it rolled and came to a stop beside the couch.

"Perfect." She scuttled across the floor on her hands and knees and stashed it beneath the couch. For the first time in her life she felt so alive, and couldn't speak a word of it to her father.

Her everyday world crashed in on her. How could she have dinner ready in time?

Groceries scattered across the shelf warned her that her father had come into the apartment. What would he think?

A part of her longed to return to the secret room and devour the information written on the scroll. She could read! For the first time in her life, she had the ability to look at a scroll and know what it said, yet the words filled her with trepidation. For now, she set her mind to the mundane task of preparing dinner while she pondered the flood of experiences she shared with Manelin and the information contained on the scroll.

According to the Oracle of Ojal, Jalil was an Augur—whatever that meant, it didn't sound mundane. Her life had been anything but boring since Manelin came into her life. She thought back to the whirl of visions. What did the voice say?

"An Augur with a heart of love would stand at the Arich's side." Her mind drifted to Manelin. The sign on his shoulder clearly marked him as this Arich. The oracle placed her at his side. It flattered her to have a title, but disappointment colored her feelings. Manelin saw himself as nothing more than a goatherd. He'd rather tend his goats than "gird himself for action."

What did it all mean? With the aid of the walking stick, she possessed a sense of control. She looked forward to learning how to bridle the power. Tomorrow, she'd return to study the scroll. According to the oracle, she belonged to the order of Windwalkers. The instructions on the scroll brought her home. Tomorrow, she'd do the same in reverse.

A short golden hair on her skirt caught her attention in the sunlight. "Sop." She picked it from the fabric and pinched it between her thumb and forefinger. Her foot dragged along the floor as she moved to the window to let it go. It would be best to avoid her father's eye for detail.

In the street below, her father spoke to that freckle-faced lad in a uniform. Jalil nervously chewed the inside of her cheek and stepped away from the window. She turned to look at the vegetables. Would Papa wonder where she'd been? What would she say? Most days if she stepped out the door she sat on the bench outside the shop.

She poured water from the ceramic pitcher into the bowl and picked up a turnip. Her mind drifted to her mother as her hands took to the chore of scrubbing. If only she could talk to her mother, tell her about the brown-eyed boy. It was so nice to have someone near her age to talk to. And, he didn't make fun of her. She propped against the counter and stood on one leg working the blade of the knife through the spicy pulp.

The image of the bumble foot on the wall flashed into her head. Ojal held a special place in history, and she foretold that Jalil would stand at Manelin's side. What did that mean?" She thought of Manelin's warm touch and the reflection of light in his brown eyes. Perhaps people would learn to accept brown eyes. She dreamed of a world where people looked beyond the color of eyes or hair.

She slipped her necklace into the collar of her blouse, thinking again of the story the symbols told. "What does it mean?"

"Who are you talking to?"

Jalil jumped. The knife clattered to the floor. She grabbed onto the corner of the table to keep her balance. Her free hand flew to her breast. "Papa," she blinked, "I didn't hear you come in." She laughed.

He chuckled. "I noticed. What are you doing, Daughter? Talking to your imaginary friend like when you were a child?" His brow wrinkled. "It's time to put such things behind you. You're almost of age to be betrothed." He rested his hands on his hips.

His words stung. She'd never be betrothed and they both knew it.

The corners of her lips quivered and lifted into a smile. She pushed the thought to the back of her mind. "I was just thinking out loud." Her skirts brushed the wooden floor as she turned to face the table. Heat spread across her cheeks.

"Are you feeling well?" Adish walked up behind his daughter. His bulk towered over her petite frame. "I haven't seen you much today."

Jalil balked. She yanked the greens from the top of the turnips and glanced at her father from the corner of her eye as he stepped beside her.

"I haven't seen you much either." She smiled and turned her attention to running the blade of the knife across the surface of one of the purplish vegetables, removing most of the skin.

"I hope you don't mind turnips again." She shrugged. The excitement of the day, and making a new friend wiped away her appetite.

Talking about food usually sidetracked the conversation. One of her father's few loves in the world, besides his work, was food. From the look on his face, he regretted making the remark about betrothal. They both knew he would be saddled with a bumble foot spinster daughter.

Her mind wrapped around the image of the dragonfly, and for the first time in her life hope of change allowed her to dream beyond her physical limitations. Maybe someday a man would seek her hand in betrothal.

"I know; it's your favorite," he said pointing to the turnips.

Her life was so predictable. He always asked the same question and in the end tried to cheer her with food.

Her father's ample belly shook as he laughed. "I have a surprise for you."

"Really?" She plucked an apple from the collection of produce and cut it in half. "Oh, Papa, tell me." Her heart longed to share her new dream. She'd walked on the wind today, and she cherished the kindness of the brown-eyed boy and his puppy. Big plans awaited her. She swallowed the dream and held it close to her heart. Now was not the time.

"We have a dinner guest."

The blade in her hand stopped. "A guest?"

"He's the young fellow that comes by twice a month to check on deliveries for the queen." He rested his hand on hers. "He's asked to court you."

Jalil blinked. A few days ago, she would have been flattered, but now she didn't relish the thought of spending time with someone from the ranks of the queen's army.

"He's down in the shop."

"What!"

He patted her hand. "Don't worry. He's captivated with your beauty. How long until dinner?"

Her breath caught in her throat as he waited for an answer.

* * * *

Jalil climbed into bed exhausted. Mixed emotions battled within her. Delaine treated her like a queen, and her father enjoyed his company very much, yet something didn't seem quite right. She couldn't place her finger on it.

Her thoughts lingered on Papa. His excitement over a prospective beau opened her eyes. Did this mean he hoped to have her out of the house like her mother? *Mother, I wish I could talk with you. You could help me...*

The memorable flash of light enveloped her and deposited her in a dank place so dark she couldn't see. Moonlight filtered through a small window. Her eyes adjusted. Enough light leaked into the room to make out shapes. Jalil didn't move. Where was she and why was she here?

"Who's there?" a woman's voice asked from across the room.

"Mother?" Jalil spoke without thinking.

A shadowy form sat up. "Jalil? Is it really you?"

Jalil scuffled across the floor to her mother's arms and the two held each other as if they'd never let go.

Chapter 18
Protection

From a distance, the dog's eyes locked with hers.
This dog possessed hidden strength. A force more
powerful than anything she'd experienced in her lifetime.

Manelin moved the flock into the foothills to a grassy mesa with an adequate supply of shrubs, grass and thorny flowers. Sop slept quietly against Aja's side after feeding and Manelin quietly stepped away to head toward the village. Grandfather would wonder what delayed him. His mind turned over the words from the old book.

The Jonnick risked everything. That dreadful sickness ... he'd never heard of such a thing. It chased them from their homes and onto ships filled with dead people. A shudder ran down his spine. *I wonder what it was like when they first arrived here.*

He'd lived in the same place all his life and couldn't imagine leaving this village. For the first time, he considered the possibility. *Had Grandfather lived in Chock all his life?*

Jalil lived in another town before coming here. Her face flashed into his mind. He loved her smile. Time with Jalil intensified his interest in learning more. He wasn't sure if it was the excitement of unraveling the mysteries held within that room or spending time with Jalil, but he looked forward to tomorrow. They'd meet within the Potent's Table to discuss the whirling visions.

He pulled his flute from the collar of his tunic and pressed it to his lips. One note filled the air and died as he cupped the flute in his hand, studying the markings in the diminishing light. Light reflected the faint outline of a circle, the paint worn, and inside the circle the markings rubbed away with the exception of four tiny triangles.

His mind shot back to the second painted jar. The circle with the dissecting arrows! He hadn't even opened the jar. So much had happened so quickly. He couldn't wait to tell Jalil.

Sop yapped from behind him. Manelin turned. The dog's panting tongue draped from the side of her mouth. How had she followed without him hearing her?

"Come on." Manelin patted his knee. "You can't come home with me, girl."

The dog bounded forward. Manelin tucked the flute inside his shirt so the dog wouldn't chew it and stooped to scoop her into his arms. She licked his face and squealed with short whines of delight.

Manelin laughed, scratching the dog's head. "I have to figure out how to tell Grandfather you'll be living with us." He hugged the dog against his body and headed toward the bridge to cross the swollen river. Late afternoon sun cast petals of color on the ripples of the rapidly moving water. The current climbed the banks a little higher. He'd be able to cross tomorrow without a problem, but beyond that it was hard to say. He played with the idea of traveling through space between home and tending the herd. *If I could travel like Jalil it would never be a problem.*

From the corner of his eye, movement caught Manelin's attention. He stopped and searched the shadows. "What was that, girl?"

Sop growled.

The sound struck a chord of fear in Manelin. He scratched the dog's head, aware of the shadowy form. Clutching the puppy to his chest, he hurried across the bridge, checking over his shoulder.

* * * *

Riona's essence streamed from her body and took shape. She glanced from her large paws to her sleeping form on the bed. Instinct dictated her outward appearance. Her imperceptive footsteps whispered from her bedchamber down the stairwell and into the throne room. More at home in this body than any other, she stopped to admire her sleek muscular bulk. Golden eyes stared back at her in the mirror and flashed red. She turned to gaze at her other side and cursed the Stygian wench that haunted her today with this festering wound. Tomorrow, she'd have the old Healer treat it one more time. He'd proven more useful than she had imagined.

No one questioned the presence of a large cat in the foothills or Valley of Rocks. She wandered the more rural areas of her kingdom faithfully. If anyone planned to build a "fortress of stone," they'd quarry there. It was one more preventative measure to guard against the takeover of Ranaan. No one would stand between her and her rightful inheritance.

In the process, she purified Ranaan by feeding on Stygian half-breeds.

She walked the outskirts of Chock and stopped to drink at the river. Her long pink tongue lapped the rushing water. The scent of Stygian wafted on the breeze. She raised her head.

Freezing the Stygian within the mountain beyond the Nefarious Forest left her hunger unsatisfied. She crouched and waited.

A dog barked. She recoiled and cursed to herself. A blond young man slipped into view trailed by a golden puppy. The man lifted the dog. It filled his arms. Her inner alarm told her not to move. From a distance, the dog's eyes locked with hers. This dog possessed hidden strength. A force more powerful than anything she'd experienced in her lifetime. She thanked the stars for her special insight.

The boy stared into the shadows.

Riona's heart thumped. In one fell swoop, she could rid Ranaan of one more adulteration.

The dog growled.

Hair on the nap of her neck stood on end. A shield of unseen power protected the boy. Curious. Riona licked her whiskers. Tonight the boy lived, but if he ventured this way often, she'd find him a tasty morsel.

The dog was another matter, worthy of her attention. A formidable power. Who was it? Another Mage?

* * * *

Manelin entered the gates of the village with the dog in his arms. A few people nodded toward him. The older he became, the less friendly the villagers grew. Jalil's voice echoed in his mind, *"The bumble foot and the brown-eyed boy."* For the first time in his life, he didn't feel alone. He had a real friend.

The warmth of Sop against his chest filled him with a sense of belonging.

Manelin set the puppy outside the door. "I need to break the news of your arrival."

The dog cocked her head and scratched behind her ear. "Here," he picked the dog up and walked around the side of the house to the orchard out back, "you stay." He lowered his hand slowly toward the ground and whispered. "Stay."

Sop barked and wagged her tail.

Manelin pressed his finger to his lips and glanced toward the house. "Sop, please." He pulled the remnants of cheese from his pouch and spread the cloth on the ground. Sop stuck her snout to the ground and lapped up every crumble as Manelin headed into the house.

"Grandfather?" The house sounded unusually quiet. "Grandfather?"

He stepped from the main living area and peeked into the bedroom. Grandfather sat slumped over his desk, his face resting on the book of his ancestors.

"Grandfather!"

Manelin rushed into the room. The old man's eyelids fluttered. He sat up stiffly. His bushy white eyebrows lifted and his eyes opened. "I'm sorry." He rubbed his good eye. "I must have dozed off."

"I see you were reading the old book again?"

Philander nodded. "After reading that bit last night, it stirred memories of when I was a child. I hungered to know what it said. I wanted to know the history of my family." He straightened his crooked back and stretched. "I wanted to read it again." His jaw lingered in a wide yawn. "There's things in here I've forgotten, and other things I never knew." He hung his head. "I should have never put it away." He shrugged his shoulders. "Some of it I wanted to forget."

"Like what?" Manelin slipped the pouch from his shoulder and hung it on a peg next to the bedroom door.

"Well," Philander rubbed his neck. "When our ancestors reached these shores they were in bad shape. The Stygian people helped them. They healed some and helped bury others."

"The Stygian?" Manelin's nose wrinkled.

Philander raised his hand to stop the protest. "I know, I know. We're not to speak of them." His blue eye looked directly into Manelin's eyes. "It's time for you to know."

Manelin slumped onto his grandfather's bed. "Know what?"

His grandfather closed the worn leather cover of the book. "This book tells the story of history. The past and the future."

"The future?"

Philander nodded. "But, to understand the future you must study the past."

"Here," Philander licked his finger and thumbed through the book. "Here it is. Look at this." His index finger rested on the yellowed page.

Manelin blinked at the image of an eye staring at him from the page. His hand moved to his shoulder. "I can't stop thinking about it."

His grandfather turned the book toward him. "Look what it says."

Manelin perched on the edge of the bed and leaned forward. Faded ink scrolled beneath the sketch in large letters filling most of the page. "The eye will guide the one who wants to see." Manelin looked up from the page and searched his grandfather's eyes. "What does that mean? I'm one who wants to see?"

Philander nodded. "Yes, and it also means it's time for us to learn the history in this book." He closed the cover and let his palm rest upon it. "We'll study it each night, and someday the book will belong to you. You'll hand it down to your children and their children."

Scratching sounds from the living room drew Manelin's attention to the present.

"What's that?" Philander scowled.

"I found a puppy." Manelin stood holding up his hands. "Before you say no, listen to me."

"The river is swollen with the spring thaw. I stopped to get a drink and heard the pup splashing and crying. I saved her."

Philander stood and walked into the living room without a word. Manelin pushed around him and hurried to the door. "I couldn't just leave her to die." He opened the door and the puppy bounded into the close quarters and jumped landing with her front paws against Philander's trousers.

Manelin picked the dog up by the scruff of the neck and cradled her in his arms. "Her name is Sop." He smiled.

Philander let out a deep breath and nodded. "Look at the size of those paws. She's going to be a big one." He reached out and stroked the dog's head. Sop settled down and cuddled against Manelin's chest. "She's a young one, probably not weaned yet."

Manelin nodded. "She suckled on Aja's teat today. I'll bring her with me tomorrow. I tried to leave her with the flock but she followed me. I knew you'd worry if I was too late." He gently bent to deposit the dog onto the floor, and brushed stray hairs from his chest.

"Get cleaned up, put the dog out, and I'll start dinner," Philander said. "We'll read the book later."

* * * *

After dinner, Manelin fidgeted with nervous energy. He wondered what else he might learn from the old book and if it would shed light on what he found inside the Potent's Table.

Philander lit the lantern and rested it on the edge of his desk in their bedroom. Manelin sat on his grandfather's cot and watched the old man turn to the first pages in the journal.

18th Yeppa, 1529

Donnel led a small group of us to the shipyard under the cover of night. The stench of death fills our streets, and rotting bodies littered the ships. We threw corpses overboard. No one pays attention. Grief consumes those spared the sickness. Part of me doesn't care to escape. I look at Donnel with Amelia. The hope that burns within them keeps me going. New life awaits us beyond these borders on the other side of the sea. Tomorrow we set sail for the shores of Ranaan.

Unused food in the hold of the ships makes preparation less stressful. Grain and dried meat found on three of the ships will feed us. Donnel announced today that we will leave earlier than planned. We'll meet with the others in the morning to discuss the new plan and choose captains for each ship.

Donnel plans to leave ahead of schedule in hopes of catching his mother-in-law off guard. Her threat to pass on the power of the Mage to Amelia fills him with fear. It would end his marriage. Amelia is not privy to the change and is a bit suspicious of Donnel sneaking about like a thief.

Evan Davis

Philander rubbed his eyes. "I can't imagine what they went through. I used to dream of it as a child."

"What were your dreams like, Grandfather?" Manelin thought of his experience with Jalil at the shrine.

Philander sat back in the chair. "My dreams were very real. I saw dead bodies strewn in the streets. Only it was the streets here in the village. That's one of the reasons I didn't want to read the book to you. I had trouble sleeping. Dead people groped my clothes and asked me to help them." He shuddered and turned the page. "I think it was the business about the power of the Mage. When I was a child, I remember hearing only one can defeat a Mage. A Windwalker." Philander marked the new entry with his finger.

Manelin thought of Jalil. Did this mean she was in danger? Did the power of the Mage arrive on that ship?

25th Yeppa, 1529

High seas toss our ships like corks. Seasickness ravages most of us as we wander the decks retching over the rail. I'm useless to help run the ship. Perhaps we've made a mistake. I don't say a word to Donnel because it is too late to change our course.

To make matters worse, the sickness followed us aboard the Vanya. Donnel quarantined those showing signs of the malady in an effort to hold the ravages of the disease at bay. Fear twists my gut, making me more nauseous than the rolling seas. One day I may be past the seasickness to find myself wandering among the condemned on the decks of the quarantine ship.

I strive to wipe such images from my mind. The clear horizon leads me to hope in tomorrow.

Evan Davis

Philander blinked back tears and glanced at his grandson.

Manelin nodded. "I see why you had those dreams. That's awful. But," he tapped his index finger to his chin, "if we have the book, and you and I are here, then he made it."

Philander smiled. "You're much more logical than me. Perhaps if I had thought like that I would have slept a little better."

"Keep reading," Manelin urged. After his experience at the Potent's Table he wanted to know everything he could about his ancestors. Perhaps something hidden within those pages would help him to understand what was happening to him. He rubbed his shoulder. He'd ask questions later, for now he'd absorb all he could. It might help him better grasp the meaning of the whirring visions.

21st Tirtius, 1529

We arrived on the shores of Ranaan three days ago. Natives helped carry the sick from our ships. Those well enough threw our stores overboard before we burned the ships and the dead with them. More than half our people have died.

Donnel passed with Amelia's name on his lips. It saddens me to know that he'll never meet the child she carries. I promised him I'd take care of her, and honestly don't know where to begin.

The Stygian care for our sick, give us food and a place to lay our heads. One woman named Salus nursed Donnel until he died and now has taken Amelia under her care. I'm concerned for Amelia. Her heart is broken with the loss of Donnel. I'm not sure if it is because she is great with child or lost the will to go on. She's not herself. Her hand clings to that white stone as if her mother's magic could bring him back to life. Only time can heal her loss. I pray she has the time.

Evan Davis

Manelin stretched. "It's strange. I feel like I know these people. Maybe because they are my ancestors." The vision of ships scuttled in the harbor made it more real.

Philander massaged the bridge of his nose with his thumb and forefinger. "It may be because you are getting to know our history. What happened to them touches our lives today. Just as the spring thaw sends tiny rivulets of water from the mountain, as they collect and join the river it becomes swollen. Sometimes it overflows the banks and becomes swift enough to alter the landscape around it. It is the same with our history. Each action we take alters the future."

Manelin exhaled. "I never thought about that. I wonder if Amelia had her baby."

Philander lifted a finger. "Your answer is here."

27th Tirtius, 1529

I'm learning my way around this beautiful land. A young boy named Izzi has picked up our language quickly. He works at learning our language unlike Salus' special ability as an interpreter. He's taken me to the place where his father first saw our ships. His father Kynan heads the tribe. I believe Salus is his sister.

Izzi teaches me what plants to eat, and tells me they will be moving on for the hunt. A hunt sounds good. I haven't eaten meat since we touched these shores.

Amelia lies in a small cave. It's more like a hole in the rocky mountainside. She's lost the sparkle in her eyes. I hope when the baby arrives that she'll regain the will to go on and make a life here in Ranaan. Izzi tells me that they would normally move on at this time before the river floods, but they don't want to move Amelia in her condition.

"The river is flooding now," Manelin said. "Do you know if her baby lives?"

"Yes, I know."

"Well?" Manelin's eyebrows arched with expectation.

"We'll read to find out. Each word written in this book is here for a reason. If you hadn't heard this first part you would not care about the child. We'll read each passage."

Manelin's shoulders slumped. "Okay, I just want to know the whole story."

His grandfather chuckled. "We'll read for a little longer."

Sop whined from outside the window. Manelin looked into his grandfather's eye, "Please, just tonight can she be with us? Tomorrow, I'll leave her with Aja."

Philander fought the smile tugging his lips. "Just this one night. Go get her. She's probably hungry."

Manelin hurried to the door and called the puppy into the house. He went to the cupboard and sliced a chunk of goat cheese carrying it into the bedroom and setting it on the floor. She sniffed it, licked and gnawed the salty wedge it into small chunks with her fine teeth. "Okay," Manelin said, "Let's read the next entry."

4th Quade, 1529

Izzi's father and I sat down to talk of plans for our people. The sickness has taken another 23 of the crew and a few of the natives as well. They held a great mourning ceremony for an old woman known as Ojal the Ancient. Izzi says she had magical powers. These people are as superstitious as the Jonnick, but without their kindness, I would not have survived.

Spring rains fall steadily and the Potent says it is time to move his people to higher ground. I'm not ready to move Amelia. Kynan tried to explain how they would carry her, but I'm not going. I'll not be responsible for the loss of Donnel's child and my only living relation. The remnants of our crew agree we will not be moving on. This valley is lush and provides a great place to settle. I don't want to put Amelia at risk.

5th Quade, 1529

Kynan promises to return when the weather warms and the river is safe. It surprised me to learn that those symbols he's been drawing is their written language. Izzi read a bit of it to me in his broken speech. I don't begin to understand their strange customs, but I'm thankful for their warm hospitality.

Kynan tells me the old woman that died knew we were coming. She even told them of the disease and that one ship was lost at sea. I find it hard to believe, but remain perplexed. I never said anything about the fourth ship. Perhaps Donnel said something before he died. If they really knew of the sickness, why would they help us?

Tomorrow, life will change. The Stygian set out for the hunt. Kynan is allowing Salus and a few others to stay with us. Izzi begged to stay, but his father ordered his participation in the hunt. I'll miss the boy's companionship and the tunes he plays on that little instrument he carries. I considered traveling with them, but I cannot ask Amelia to make the journey. Donnel's child shall arrive any day.

Evan Davis

"The Stygian just left them?" Manelin frowned. "Amelia's sick, and the baby is about to deliver. I wouldn't do that to a goat."

Little lines formed between Philander's brows. "If your entire flock was in danger, would you stay because one pregnant doe couldn't make it?"

"Well," Manelin blinked, "No, but I'd find a way to bring her along."

"Kynan offered to bring Amelia along, but Evan refused." Shadows from the flickering lantern danced across Philander's stern expression. "You can't control what others do. You can only control yourself. Kynan made a choice and Evan made a choice. Even Donnel made a choice."

Manelin nodded. "Just like we made a choice to read."

"Yes." The light reflected in his wet eyes. "Something we should have done sooner. A poor choice on my part. We can learn from history." He knuckled a tear gathering in the corner of his eye.

Manelin rested his palm on his grandfather's age-spotted hand. "What's wrong, Grandfather?"

Philander closed his eyes, drew in a deep breath and let it out slowly. "Times change. I hear Evan Davis' words and realize he had hopes and dreams. Donnel Brophy had hopes and dreams. Amelia Brophy's life changed when Donnel died."

"Does the baby live?" Manelin asked.

A smile tugged at the corner of Philander's mouth. "Such a sensitive boy you are. Life does not always treat us the way we would like, but the child ... well let's read one more passage."

* * * *

Manelin climbed into bed wondering about the magic of the white stone Amelia clutched in her hand. She must have been the pregnant woman in the whirring visions.

The vision of the stone in the Queen's palm, the look on her face, those red eyes.... A shiver ran down his spine. Uneasiness settled over him until the bed lurched. Sop's warmth filled the bed beside him squeezing him next to the wall. Manelin didn't mind. He wrapped his arm across the dog and fell asleep with plans to visit the Forbidden Cave in the morning.

Chapter 19
Within the Forbidden Cave

She says she's been visited by Ojal the Ancient

Riona collapsed onto her throne and settled her jeweled crown in her lap. Morning did nothing to ease her discomfort. The festering wound beneath her royal silk gown mustered thoughts of the old Healer. Could she control him enough to trust that he'd do his best to heal her?

She studied the glittering gems. Senta's untimely decision to take the stone from her hand was regrettable. Not only had he interrupted her need to feed, but of all times.... She slapped her hand against the arm of her throne. The Dawn of the Beginnings was the best place to harvest the essence of Windwalkers. He robbed her of that opportunity and his punishment left her unsatisfied.

All of life left her discontented. Loneliness clawed at her core.

Her fingers lingered on the impressive colors imbedded in her crown as she wondered how many of the people she'd stripped of their essence still lived. The tip of her finger snagged on the chipped gem rekindling the question. Haunting laughter filled her mind. The incomplete transference of the Windwalker's essence troubled her every time she thought of it. What did it mean? She had swallowed the woman whole. How could any trace of her escape?

Drastic measures were called for. She eased from her throne, holding her side and walked to the door. Waiting at the threshold, two guards stood at attention. "Go to the dungeon and bring me the Healer."

* * * *

Nilenam stood at the threshold of the queen's throne room dressed in a new gray tunic. The guards had taken him to the garden to bathe in a small pond. While ignoring the insulting taunts of the guards who mocked his disfigurement, he treasured the few moments of freedom. All the insults in the world didn't do a thing to change the hump on his back, but sunshine and a clean body refreshed his spirit.

Why did Riona want to see him? His heart slammed against his ribcage. He feared the woman Riona had become; yet part of him cared deeply for her. Beyond the hard shell she'd crafted over the years, he believed the girl he knew as a young man still existed. The girl that rejected him for his brother.

"Come in, Nilenam."

He stepped across the marble floor without a sound, stopped before the throne, bowing his head and acknowledging her position, but then looked directly at her. Her icy blue eyes met his. He admired her beauty and youth while pity stirred his compassion.

"You called for me, my Queen."

Riona let out a breath. "I let you rot in that cell and that's all you have to say?"

"It's your kingdom. I'm here to serve you."

Her eyes squeezed into slits of suspicion. "What of your brother?"

"What brother? The one who hasn't seen fit to pay one visit since I arrived here?"

Her head cocked to the right as she rubbed her finger across her chin. "Very well." Her index finger tapped just below her bottom lip. "As a murderer, I cannot free you, but because you've proven to be a loyal subject, and a Healer when I've needed you, I'd like to commission you as my personal Healer."

Nilenam folded his hands and nodded. "I'd be most grateful to serve as the Queen's Healer." His mind raced toward possibilities. The stars had placed him here. "I would need an herb garden and a few supplies."

He wanted to kick his heels and scream, but his bent body settled for the satisfaction of knowing he'd have time out of that rancid cell. Perhaps over time, he could find a way to really heal her.

* * * *

Manelin followed the unfamiliar trail down the uneven mountainside. Sop wandered along the path close to his side. The fragrance of sagebrush wafted on the spring breeze as the sun disappeared behind white feathery clouds edged with gray. The spring rains would start any day. He planned to grab the Stygian tellings and read them with Jalil once the flooded river prevented his return home.

Pebbles skittered and bounced from the trail and spilled along the steep slope as Manelin skidded to a stop in front of the waxy broad-leafed bushes. Delicate yellow flowers dotted the mountainside above the shrubs. Manelin rummaged through the brush searching for the mouth of the small cave. Red ripe berries filled the thorny plants, littering the ground with pungent fermenting fruit. He lifted the branch carefully between his thumb and forefinger and moved it to the side. Sop ran through the bramble and into the cave.

"Sop, you have to stop doing this." Manelin stooped and walked into the darkness. Inch long thorns lining the rubbery limbs snagged his trousers as he eased through the tangle of undergrowth.

He paused, staring into the inky interior of the cool, damp tunnel. Wind whistled overhead through scattered openings. His eyes adjusted to the limited light filtering into the inner chamber.

"Manelin?" a soft female voice called from within the cavern.

"Jalil?" He rushed into the refreshing coolness. How things had changed since yesterday. Not only did he recognize her voice, but it didn't surprise him to hear her in this secret place. "What are you doing here?" he called ahead.

The short narrow tunnel curved to the right and dead-ended. He slid to a stop and stared at the vision. Direct sunlight cut through the darkness spotlighting Jalil. It reminded him of the vision at the shrine. He advanced one step and gave her a sideward glance. "Are you really here?"

She looked up at him. "Manelin, so much has happened since I saw you yesterday."

He rushed to her side. "I've learned some new things as well." Manelin crouched beside her. "What are you doing here?" His eyes searched the confined enclosure. A small table made of two planks of wood and four logs sat low to the ground. A bit of sadness washed over him as he pictured his grandfather and uncle playing in this place as children.

Jalil gazed into his eyes. Tiny lines etched her delicate forehead.

"What's wrong?" Manelin took her hand in his.

"Manelin, I'm in danger. I needed a place to go. My mother said to follow the visions, to learn from them."

Manelin held up his hand and settled on the cold floor beside her. "What do you mean danger?"

She expounded on Delaine's visit almost tripping over her words. "I don't trust him, Manelin. He's up to something." She reached out and grabbed his forearm. "I felt trapped. Papa is so excited that I have a suitor that he didn't even stop to ask me how I feel. Before dinner, he said it would be up to me, but as the last bite passed our lips he'd made arrangements for Delaine to check on me while he travels. I couldn't sleep.

My mind revisited the hall of petrographs, the whirl of visions, finding
the Oracle of Ojal. Those things," she threw her hands up, "those things
are good." She wrapped her knuckles against her chest just below her
necklace. "I know it here. Last night at the table with Delaine and Papa,"
she shrugged one shoulder, "I can't explain it, but I sensed an evil. All
my thoughts jumbled. The more I tried to sort it out the more confused I
felt. I longed for my mother's companionship and advice."

Manelin sat beside her on the dirt floor and drew his knees to his
chest. "I came here to get the tellings. I figured we could read them while
I'm on the other side of the river. The spring floods will be here soon and
I'll be trapped on the other side with my flock."

Jalil sighed. "What am I going to do? I have to let Papa know I'm
safe, but my mother says for now I need to stay away. She says the great
awakening draws near."

"I thought you said your mother was in the asylum."

Jalil nodded. "I visited her. If I hadn't experienced our time together
yesterday, I'd think her crazy. She says Ojal the Ancient has visited her.
It's helped her to understand things that confused her."

"Ojal? The old bumble foot?"

A frown scrunched Jalil's delicate features. "The Augur."

Manelin's face heated. "I'm sorry." He rested his forehead against his
knees. "So what are you going to do?"

"Follow the visions. That's why I'm here."

Manelin nodded. "The vision of Grandfather hiding the tellings
here."

"That's right. I arrived at first light." She put her hand on his forearm.
"Manelin, the tellings scare me. I barely understand the power of
Windwalking, and the Augur's staff allows me to hear people's thoughts.
When I was in the Asylum, the mental anguish was almost more than I
could bear. The people there aren't crazy; they've been robbed of their
essence. It's the part of them that connects one part of life to another.
Most of them are Windwalkers. Their experiences are all the same. Some
large animal attacked them as they walked on the wind."

Manelin's shoulder burned. "Is that what happened to your
mother?"

Jalil nodded. "Papa didn't know of her Windwalking. She'd given it up
because of his strong feelings about the Stygian, but when I was born she
knew," Jalil touched the bodice of her high-waisted dress over her heart,
"in here that she would be called to walk on the wind. When she heard

the old Healer had been arrested, her spirit compelled her to see him."

Manelin stretched his legs out and crossed them at the ankle. "The old Healer? My grandfather's brother?"

"Yes! I'd forgotten. My mother knew him. I can tell by the way she talked that they were friends. He used to play the Joining Song on his flute for her when she was expecting me." Jalil blinked teary eyes. "Last night she hummed it as I lay beside her on her cot. She used to do that when I was young."

"Jalil, I don't mean to rush you, but what about this stealing of the essence? What does that mean?"

"It sounds frightful. Mother said three strong blasts of freezing power knocked her from the sky as she walked the wind. She found herself within the Nefarious Forest. A huge ghost-like snake slithered in the air. The earth shook and trees shattered in its wake. As fate would have it, Mother landed near a hollow tree and hid inside."

As Manelin listened, his jaw dropped.

"That's not the worst of it." Jalil swallowed hard and stared into Manelin's eyes. "She witnessed the snake eat the old woman ... but she didn't die without a fight. Mother says the old woman buried a stake of wood from one of the splintered trees into the snake's underbelly."

"Did it die?"

Jalil shook her head. "No, it ate the woman in two gulps."

"What does it all mean?"

Jalil shrugged. "I'm not sure, but Mother said the old woman called the snake Riona." Jalil paused and looked at Manelin from her peripheral vision.

"Riona?" Manelin's forehead gathered a series of worry wrinkles. "You mean Queen Riona?"

* * * *

Adish stared at the layer of coke and tuyere surrounding the heart of the firepot while dragging the circular rake across the new layer of coal. "What should I do?" he asked himself.

Why, why, why did he allow Delaine into his personal life? Now, Jalil had run away and what could he do to help her? Anything he could do would only draw attention to her. He shoved the rake at the fire bed sending sparks into the air. If something happened to her, his life was over.

His responsibility to the queen pressed in on him. This month's delivery to the God-forsaken caves and tunnels on the other side of the Nefarious Forest was already late. If he didn't fulfill his duty .... He shuddered. Jalil would be alone.

He drew in a deep breath and let it out slowly. His eyes searched the shop. Success was meaningless. If only the sanitarium had cured Estel as he hoped. They'd be living in the mountains away from all this. Family meant everything.

Family. He'd go talk to Laul. If he could trust anyone, it would be his brother. He'd load the mule and be on his way before Delaine stopped by.

* * * *

Ojal listened to the conversation between the Arich and Augur. Their innocence and pure hearts were all that the tellings said they would be.

"You can come home with me," Manelin said.

Jalil's blue eyes grew wide. "No! I can't return to Chock. Ojal told my mother that I must flee. The face of Chock will change. We won't recognize it." She squeezed his arm. "Stay here with me."

Manelin shook his head. "I have to go home. My grandfather," he raked his fingers through his hair, "I can't just leave. I wouldn't want to cause him worry." He held up his index finger. "But tomorrow, I leave for the sheering. He'll not expect me home for two or three weeks. I'll meet you here tomorrow and we'll travel together."

Her eyes shimmered with disappointment as she nodded.

"I'll leave Sop here to keep you company."

A smile flickered on her lips.

Chapter 20
The Quest

"The time of the awakening is near."

Manelin sat across from Philander at the dinner table, his thoughts anchored in the Forbidden Cave. He wished he hadn't left Jalil alone. His grandfather ate in silence pondering all Manelin had told him.

"Grandfather?"

Philander glanced up from his plate with his good eye. "Yes?"

"I wish we could go back to the way things were."

Philander nodded. "I used to have this conversation with my brother." He pushed his half-eaten food to the center of the table. "Many over the centuries have felt the same way. We need to look beyond ourselves, and what we want. Focus on what is to come. The new land, You'll usher in the life many have longed for. It will be well."

Manelin stretched his arms over his head. "I'm exhausted. All this thinking wearies my mind."

His grandfather smiled. "Now you know how I feel."

"Do I have to wash my hair tonight?"

"No," Philander stroked his white beard. "There's no need."

Manelin sat back in his chair. Things really had changed. Melancholy washed over him and left him longing for the familiar. His shoulder radiated the heat he recognized as a forewarning of something otherworldly on the horizon. Would he sleep tonight, or be whisked away by some vision?

"I'm going to bed," he said. "I'll need my rest."

He climbed into his empty bunk and wished Sop was here. Funny how attached he'd become to the pup. He played a quiet tune on his flute. His eyes grew heavy and exhaustion claimed him within minutes.

* * * *

"Manelin!" Someone shook him. "Wake up!"

"Grandfather?"

Manelin opened his eyes to an eerie orange glow seeping through the window from the street. Was he dreaming? Shadows played tricks on his eyes, but the fear on his grandfather's face almost caused him to hit his head on the ceiling as he bolted upright.

He jumped from his bunk. "What grandfather? What's wrong?" Manelin rushed into the living room to the only window in the house facing the street. A huge fire burned down near the candle maker's shop. "What is that?"

"Take this and run." Philander shoved the worn book into a sack. "Now!" He pushed the bag into the young man's hands. "Don't come back. Your time in Chock is finished. Hurry!" His hand shook while his bent finger pointed to the rear window facing the forked tree. "Go."

"But, grandfather what about you?" Manelin sat perched on the windowsill. One leg dangled inside while the other hung along the outer wall. The owl hooted from the branches of the forked tree. Firelight lit up its golden eyes.

"Follow the eagle of the night." Philander embraced him. "I love you, Manelin."

"Grandfather, I don't understand. Why can't I stay, or you come with me?" He grabbed a fist full of his grandfather's nightshirt. "I don't want to leave you here."

"No, Manelin. I can't go. I'd slow you down and they wouldn't stop looking for us until they found me." He pulled Manelin's hand from his shirt. "Many things I should have told you, but I didn't know where to begin. I love you like a son, but I'm not your real grandfather. I promised your parents..."

Pounding at the front door made the old man jump. His eyes filled with tears and spilled onto his beard. "Hurry, go and don't come back. Don't let them take the book."

With his palm against Manelin's shoulder, Philander pushed him out the window. "Go!" The sound of the door breaking called his grandfather from the window. The swoosh of the owl's wings flapped overhead. Manelin trained his eyes on the shadow of the large bird. He crouched outside the window and listened. Maybe they were searching for Jalil.

Angry voices shouted. They had come to collect books containing Stygian writings. Manelin hugged the sack to his chest. Books fueled the fire in the street! His grandfather protested.

Panic sent Manelin's thoughts skipping like a stone across the river. He ran through the orchard. The fresh scent of apple blossoms mingled with smoke. His eyes strained to see in the pale moonlight. He didn't want to leave; yet he couldn't stay. His heart raced. Heat radiated across his shoulder as he headed through the trees toward the back trail.

When he reached the gate, he turned toward the radiance on the horizon. Smoke curled through the branches and followed him up the mountain. *What gave them the right to do this?*

His bare feet slowed his progress. He'd have to find something to wear. What would he do? Where would he go? Would it be safe to return to the herd? He thanked the stars that he kept an extra change of clothes in the field in case he fell into the river, or had an accident with one of the kids.

The nippy mountain breeze clawed at his skin. He clutched the sack his grandfather—or whoever he was—thrust at him. *He's not my grandfather.* The reality of Philander's words hurt. Manelin felt betrayed.

Instinct warned him to leave the trail. Branches snagged the loose fitting fabric of his nightshirt as he pulled himself up the side of the mountain. Small trees provided handholds to steady his frenzied pace while he clutched the book to his chest. He climbed in the dark until he found a cliff, a small alcove. He backed into it and watched the fire burn in the village. Muffled shouts worked up the mountain but he couldn't understand the words. Shadows of men on horseback moved through the cobblestone streets.Only the queen's army and the very wealthy rode horses. *Delaine's probably down there.* The thought of that arrogant freckle-faced blight mistreating his grandfather fueled his hatred. If he went down to the village he'd be caught. He'd have to take his time, make a plan.

He'd hide here for the night and figure out what to do when the light of dawn made travel a bit easier. Knees to his chest, Manelin wrapped his nightshirt tightly around his body. Tears stung his eyes. *What do I do now?* The owl hooted somewhere in the darkness outside. He felt like an animal burrowed into the earth for safety.

Grandfather's words echoed in his mind as he pictured the night they read from the worn book about the symbol of the forked tree. It meant so much more now that division ripped him from his home and the man he'd lived with all his life.

Who are my parents? It wasn't a new question, but one that plagued his thoughts many a day out in the field when he had time for thinking. Now he yearned to understand. *Why did they leave me?*

His mind drifted to Jalil. Her mother had been taken from her, left to rot in that dreadful asylum. Her father had put Jalil in an awful spot with Delaine, but at least she knew her parents. She had memories. *Jalil, can you hear me?*

"Manelin?"

He heard her voice as if she sat outside the large hole in the rocky cliff.

"Jalil?"

"I'm here," she answered. "Where are we?"

He crawled to the small opening. "I'm in here," he said. "Grandfather warned me to run and never come back. Look at the fire." He slipped out onto the ledge.

Jalil clutched the walking stick tighter, closing her eyes. Muted light from the raging fire flickered across her face. "The queen's army goes from door to door ridding the village of Stygian influence. Delaine rides his steed through the streets barking orders. His arrogance gains strength."

She gasped.

"What?" Manelin tugged on her arm. "What is it?"

"They've taken your grandfather." Her eyes widened with panic. "Delaine condemns him for harboring Stygian beliefs like the old Healer."

"What does that mean?"

Jalil wiped her hand across her forehead brushing away wisps of hair blowing in her face. "Oh Manelin, he's being taken to the queen's dungeon."

* * * *

The owl swooped to the ground in front of the tiny alcove. Manelin's shoulder burned. He pushed himself between Jalil and the large bird. "Don't move."

In the eerie blush of the raging fire burning in the street below, the bird changed shape. Wings and clawed talons gave way to four legs and golden fur. Manelin stared at his beloved dog in disbelief.

"Sop?" Fear paralyzed him. He stepped back and bumped Jalil. "What is this?"

"Manelin, it's alright." Jalil put her arm around him. "Place your hand with mine." She extended the walking stick. "Listen."

"The time of the awakening is near." The voice of the whirring visions sounded flat.

Jalil spoke. "It's Ojal, Manelin. Sop is part of her metot. Remember?

The animal symbols on the wall. She's here to help us."

Ojal's voice continued. "The Arich stands poised on the cusp of change. Intense trials and training prepare his way. His answers are found within the Yoke of Inspiration."

Manelin's hand dropped to his side. "How can I be the Arich if I don't even know where to find the Yoke of Inspiration? I can't do this." He spun and crawled into his hiding place.

Jalil appeared beside him. Eerie shadows danced across the wall of stone. Suddenly a white light brightened the confined space. Manelin glanced at Jalil. The strange light emanated from her necklace.

"What is that?" He reached out to touch the surreal radiance. A shock zapped his hand, and for a moment, he saw images of dark haired people frozen like statutes. His hand snapped back. The light went out.

He shook his hands, exercising his fingers. "What was that?"

A quiet moan escaped Jalil's lips. "What happened?"

"I ... I saw something. People. A lot of people posed as if frozen in a moment, all gathered in tiny groups." He rubbed his eyes.

Jalil moved beside him adjusting her position. "I didn't see anything."

* * * *

Manelin opened his eyes. His body ached with cold. His stiff joints complained as he crawled outside. Smoke lingered in the sky above the Village of Chock. Tears welled up and leaked from the corner of his eyes. He no longer belonged there. Light wispy clouds stretched along the horizon as the sun burned its way into a new day. *I don't belong anywhere.*

"Manelin?" Jalil called from behind him. "What are you doing?"

"I'm going to go get something to wear."

Sop lifted her head and watched Jalil shuffle outside to stand beside Manelin.

He glanced over his shoulder. "Come with me."

Jalil shook her head. "Manelin, we each have a purpose. Ojal has helped me see I have much work to do. I'll meet you after you reach the Yoke of Inspiration." She brushed her fingers against his cheek.

He recoiled at her touch. Fury boiled within him. "I don't even know what or where to find this—this Yoke of Inspiration. I thought you were supposed to help me."

Jalil's lips pressed into a fine line. "I cannot tell you because I don't know. I must wait for you to invite me there, just like you invited me to the Sacred Stairway and the Fortress of Stone."

He sucked in a calming breath and stared out at the village below. "I didn't ask for any of this."

She rested her hand on his shoulder. "I didn't ask to be born a bumble foot, or to be given the responsibility to serve as Augur. We must leave behind what we want. Others depend on us, including your grandfather."

* * * *

Adish stood at Laul's door. He glanced behind him at the mule, turned to the door and knocked.

"Adish?" Laul blinked in disbelief. "Come in, come in," he opened the door wide. "What brings you here?" He rushed to the table and pulled out a chair. "I can't believe it. It's been ages. What brings you here?"

"We have to talk." Adish lumbered to the table and sank into the chair.

"What is it?" Laul hurried to sit across from him. "Is something wrong?"

"Laul, there's something you need to know. Something I've hidden for years."

Laul's face paled.

"My child—"

"You mean the one who died?"

Adish held up his hand and nodded. "Let me talk." He stared at the table. "The baby was born a bumble foot."

Laul sat speechless.

"She lives."

"What? You let her live? But … but…"

"I'm sorry Laul. Estel and I waited for so many years. I just couldn't. We decided to say she died and hide her."

Laul pushed to his feet, sending his chair skittering across the floor. "Do you know what this means?

"It means a lot of things, Laul."

"You don't understand. I killed Yram to keep the secret."

Adish shot to his feet, hands pressed flat on the table. "You what!" He slammed the table top with both hands. "You … you killed Yram?" He rubbed the back of his neck without looking at his brother.

"I did it for our family, Adish. When she told me the baby was a bumble foot, I realized what that meant for our family. When you walked out and said the baby died, I thought you had done what the law said you were to do. Kill it." Spittle sprayed from his lips.

"Laul, listen to me. Jalil is missing."

"Jalil? You named it?"

"Laul, she's my daughter. I'm here to ask for your help."

Laul backed toward the door. "I'll have no part of helping a bumble foot conceived in fornication." He pointed toward the door. "Nor, any part of a brother that would allow it to live." He pointed to the door. "If the queen gets wind of this, I'll not back you."

Adish walked to the door and stopped face to face with his brother. "I didn't know I was trying to protect a murderer all these years. And you, the one who blamed the Healer for Yram's murder."

Laul sneered. "That," he smiled, "was the queen's idea."

* * * *

Manelin reached the apple grove. Using the trees for cover, he pressed against one of the larger trees at the middle of the grove and waited. Birds called to one another in the early morning light. Not a sound from the house. He glanced at the chimney. No smoke. Fearing Jalil might be right, he wanted to turn and flee.

Manelin scurried to the back window. He flattened his back against the outer wall of the house and waited. His heart hammered in his chest. Not a sound in the bedroom. Not a snore or familiar clatter of dishes. He twisted to peek inside. Grandfather's empty bunk and the overturned desk filled him with horror.

He eased through the window without a sound and grabbed his poncho from the peg near the door. From the threshold of his bedroom door, he stared at the fireplace. It offered no light or heat as the last embers fought to stay alive. His grandfather was gone. The front door hung open revealing the smoldering pile of ash in the middle of the street near the center of the village.

He crept back to the bedroom and dressed. It felt good to be warm. His heart longed to stay, to awaken from this nightmare, to fight with Grandfather about washing his hair, or spending time reading the old book. Manelin grabbed a wheel of cheese and the stale bread from last night's dinner and shoved them into the pouch, slinging it over his shoulder.

He slipped out the back window and through the orchard.

What should he do now? Jalil was deserting him to carry out her 'responsibilities' and Sop was no longer his dog, but some old woman from the past, Grandfather was being held in the Queen's dungeon and he was suppose to find something called the Yoke of Inspiration to save people he didn't know. Frustration and anger simmered as he followed the trail out of town and headed toward the river. He decided to spend time with his flock until he figured out what to do next.

His mind drifted to the empty bunk and ransacked room. *Grandfather knew. That's why he warned me to run.*

He reached into the pouch and pulled out the old book. He flipped through the pages as he walked. The script of men long dead covered most of them. Near the back of the book, illustrations filled the pages. Looking at the book slowed his pace. He snapped it shut; he'd read it once he reached safe haven. Perhaps it would help him find the Yoke of Inspiration.

After stuffing the book into his jute sack, his thoughts returned to last night with Jalil. Her necklace bore Stygian symbols. It had belonged to her mother. It befuddled him. Jalil's father hated the Stygian.

Visions of his grandfather telling him to take the book and run crowded his thoughts. Tears brimmed at the memory. His mind relived the great fire—the pile of burning books in the town square. *Will I ever see Grandfather again? Or, Jalil?* He looked to the horizon. Resentment colored his feelings. Somehow, he had to find this Yoke of Inspiration without any help.

* * * *

Nilenam awoke to shouts and scuffling in the dank dungeon. He pretended to be asleep. The creek of hinges, a body slamming against the floor of the cell beside him and the sickening slam of the door and click of the lock told him he had company.

"I don't know why the queen bothers to keep these old Stygian lovers alive," one guard said to the other.

"Ours is not to question, but obey."

"Yeah, yeah, well Delaine has other plans."

The door at the end of the corridor banged shut behind them. Nilenam sat up on his cot and stared at the crumpled body on the floor. He longed to rush and help the poor soul but his joints didn't let him move quickly. "Are you all right?"

The body struggled to sit up. "Nilenam?"

"Philander!"

Chapter 21
The Yoke of Inspiration

"The answer you seek is here. Enter with a pure heart.
Be one with the Land and with the people of the Land."

Manelin eyed the Fortress of Stone in the distance as he headed into the foothills. It was hard to believe such secrets existed in the middle of the Valley of Rocks. A pebble in his boot slowed his progress. He stopped and emptied the nuisance. The tiny stone bounced on the ground, rolled and came to a rest in the print of a horseshoe.

No one ever wandered out this way. What was someone on a horse doing on this little traveled route?

A falcon circled in the sunny blue sky and cried out a mournful call. Manelin ran, following the foreign tracks. He stuck to the narrowing trail, which spilled into the grotto where he skidded to a halt. Bodies of his beloved flock littered the area. Manelin fell to his knees. "No."

After he cried himself out, Manelin walked the area hoping to find any sign of life. He knelt beside Aja's cold body. Her lifeless brown eyes ripped at his heart. Why would anyone kill these poor animals? They didn't even take their hides. Vahe's neck twisted at a grotesque angle. Manelin reached down and pulled a patch of cloth from the goat's mouth. Dried blood coated his horns.

"You didn't give up without a fight, boy." Manelin stood studying the scrap of cloth. A shiny gold button clung to the center of the fragment. A familiar gold button. His mind shot back to Delaine's spittle landing on his uniform jacket as he mocked Philander. "Delaine." He squeezed the proof in his fist and took in the deceptively peaceful grotto with resolve for revenge.

Manelin buried the bodies of his beloved flock under mounds of stone. With each stone piled on the graves, he vowed to get even.

That night, he sat before the fire emotionally naked. The queen's men had ripped all he ever cared about from him. He pulled the old book from his pouch. For his grandfather, he would do this. He flipped through the illustrations, searching for the Yoke of Inspiration while feasting on stale bread and cheese.

* * * *

After days of traveling north, Manelin headed into the Nefarious Forest with a bit of apprehension. Cold, damp wind whistled through the lofty pines. He jumped over the jagged remains of a moss-covered stump. Pinpoints of sunlight sliced through the shade of the majestic trees. Each tiny beam fought the retreating layer of frost painted on every surface and chased it into the swirling mist gathering about his ankles where the legs on his trousers wicked moisture to the knee. A chill ran down his spine as he climbed over a fallen tree.

He straddled the fallen pine and marveled at the velvety green moss covering the crumbly bark. How could it grow in this climate? He scraped it with his dagger, tasted the musty flavor and added it to the tidbits he had collected. His bread gone, he had to plan ahead.

No one would dare follow him here; many had lost their lives in the forest. Jalil's story of the ghostly serpent filtered through his thoughts, keeping him on edge.

Manelin struggled to sort out his jumbled emotions. Philander had warned him to run. He paused and searched his surroundings. "Run to where, Grandfather?" he asked. He watched the vapors of his breath blossom and die in the chilled air. According to the map of Ranaan in the journal, the series of tunnels and caves known as the Yoke of Inspiration lay on the other side of this forest. If it wasn't there he had no idea what else to do.

He grasped the downed tree for balance and leaned to scoop a frost-covered pinecone from the ground, adding it to the jute bag slung across his shoulder. Light and easy to carry, he might need them to build a fire. Sticky pine scent clung to his stiff fingers. He pulled his collar toward his ears, staving the bite of the frosty chill on the back of his neck. If he hoped to see Jalil again, he had to press forward.

Thunder rumbled in the distance, but didn't subside. Manelin paused and listened. Dark gray clouds swirled low in the sky, almost touching the treetops. He sheathed his dagger. Tree branches swayed in slow rhythmic movements. A vibration inched across the bog, causing the earth to tremble beneath his feet. Branches overhead moved one direction and twisted another, faster with more fury. The roar of the storm drew nearer. His heart pounded. Could it be the monster Jalil's mother witnessed?

Manelin glanced at the devastated trees around him and sprinted away from the brewing tempest. Gusts twisted and tore branches, throwing them to the ground. He cut between majestic pines swallowed by the fog. The sound of trees snapping like twigs in the distance pushed him to run faster. His breath shot out in sporadic vaporous balloons as he darted amid gnarled roots with the grace of a deer.

* * * *

Frigid winds blew across glacial rivers, and stirred stiff spiny-leafed plants sparsely scattered about the sculpted mountains of the frozen tundra. Riona's power swooped into the treeless valley of ice, up the walls of the canyon and tore into the cold, marshy pine forest to the south. Trees splintered into brittle shards in her path. One purpose drove her forward.

Nilenam's treatments had done miracles for her energy and well-being though he could not heal her totally. *Nilenam.* She'd forgotten to send word to him to cancel their session. He'd see she wasn't there and return to his cell and check on her later in the day. If he foolishly entered her bedchamber, she'd regret his demise on a base level, but he could be replaced. Thoughts of the humped-back Healer vanished as she picked up the Stygian scent.

Rushing above the Nefarious Forest, devastation crashed in her wake, the sounds and scents reminded her of the day she'd trapped the Stygian within the ice forever. Her keen eyes searched for her prey. At the edge of forest where it blended with the foothills, she lost the scent. Her tongue slithered, probing for the taste of Stygian in the air. Deadly heat generated from the cavern. The same cavern the Stygian clans used to try and escape their fate. It didn't work then and it wouldn't help the Stygian brat now.

Tepid currents of air held her at bay. Her beastly form lingered but the warmth from the cave forced her to move on. She would return home to regain her strength. When his scent filled the wind once again it would mark his arrival on the other side of the mountain. Riona's serpent form turned on the wind. Tomorrow, she'd position herself as guardian above the Valley of Blades.

* * * *

Manelin relaxed against the wall of the cave as he watched the ashen beast slither off through the air. Warmth caressed his stiff fingers as he slid to the ground like melted wax. He rested his hands against the tepid stone beneath him. His fingers stung as heat restored movement to his joints. Something moved to his right. Panic rushed through him. He wasn't alone. Manelin crouched with his dagger drawn, squinting into the shadows. A small animal—a fox. Its long bushy tail twitched and settled across its nose. Its ribcage rose and fell in a steady rhythm. Dim light seeped through recesses overhead. Markings on the wall above the slumbering animal caught Manelin's attention. More petrographs? He crawled across the floor and stared at the image on the wall.

A map! The floor rumbled beneath him. Dust rained from above. He closed his eyes and held his breath. Was that monster still chasing him? The tremor subsided. He opened his eyes, glanced at the map and stumbled to his feet to get a better look.

"The vernal season draws near; the divine has arrived as foretold. The time of silence will end." The voice of the whirring visions sliced though the stillness.

Manelin looked left and right. "Who said that?"

"I did," the fox replied.

Manelin searched his memory for what Jalil said of the fox metot. "Are you here to guide me?" he asked.

The fox stood and stretched. "It's time for action, my young Arich, but I can only guide you if you are willing to learn and move forward. I sense you harbor something within your heart that does not have a place on this journey. When you are ready to let it go and move forward, I'll be here to show you the way."

Manelin slumped to the floor. Why couldn't things be clear? Just tell him what to do.

The fox scurried into a side passage and disappeared.

Manelin pulled the old book from his bag and flipped to the page explaining the purpose of the owl. He turned the leaf. The image of the dog brought him back to Sop and his time with his flock. If Sop had really been his dog and stayed with the flock, they might be alive today. He forced himself to stop thinking of what might have been. It changed nothing and frustrated him more. One day, Delaine would pay for all he'd done.

On the next page, he found what he was looking for. *The fox teaches the concept of unity.* What did the fox mean when it said he was harboring something within his heart? Did this mean he had to let go of the hatred for Delaine, or perhaps the queen for ruining his life? Grandfather had told him to hate the action but not to harbor ill will against the person, but that wasn't easy.

"Use this knowledge wisely," the fox called from the darkness.

Manelin admitted to himself that he did hate the actions. Delaine's mistreatment of people and animals always bothered him. He had taught his goats to trust and look what happened to them. The queen was no better. She made unfair laws and now his grandfather sat in her dungeon. Manelin didn't even know if he was still alive. He rubbed the burn on his shoulder. "I don't hate them," he said.

No response.

Manelin glanced around the cave. His body ached as his attention drifted to the map. The burn radiating from his shoulder intensified. "I've seen that before." He flipped to the back pages of his grandfather's journal. The smell of the old pages carried memories of sitting across the table from the gentle old man. Raw emotion clawed at his innards. He longed to return home to his simple life and times gone forever. Tears blurred his vision as he eagerly searched the yellowed pages. Grandfather's life could depend on him. Salty droplets trickled to his lips. He stopped and smeared the smell of pine across his cheek as he wiped his face. "I won't let you down, Grandfather."

Manelin slipped the strap of his sack from his shoulder and emptied the contents onto the floor of the cave. Pinecones skittered across the floor in the dimming light. The end of another day drew near. He flipped through the worn book, tasting the bitterness of pinesap as he licked his thumb to turn the page.

"Here it is," he pressed his palm across the page, "A map of Ranaan."

Daylight grew faint. Manelin rested the book across his chest. He was too tired to play his flute. His eyelids grew heavy. Exhaustion dragged him into a fitful sleep. Visions of the fox running through the cave entertained his mind while subconsciously he sought understanding of the dream.

"You've reached the Yoke of Inspiration," the fox said. "The answer you seek is here. Enter with a pure heart. Be one with the Land and with the people of the Land."

Manelin stretched his hand toward the small creature. "I want to be one. What can I do? I'm only one person."

"The coming of the Arich has long been expected. Before your birth, the ancients chose you. It's not a matter of superiority. Instead, it is your ancestry and timing of your birth. Today you come to age. You can fulfill your destiny or allow yourself to wallow in self-centered pity. Choices rest upon your shoulders."

* * * *

Nilenam returned to his cell and collapsed on his cot across from his brother. "Riona didn't want to see me. She wasn't in the throne room."

Philander sat up. "Didn't want to? Are you sure she's here?"

"What do you expect me to do? She missed her treatment yesterday. I thought for sure she'd be waiting for me today." He rested his face in his hands and rubbed his eyes. I stood at the threshold of the bedchamber but she didn't summon me. I am not allowed to enter without her permission.

"Nilenam, the time for fulfillment is upon us. We must find that Magestone."

Nilenam cast his attention to the floor and folded his hands. He nodded. "Very well. I'll go. If I don't return, you know what happened to me."

"Be careful," Philander said. "Whatever you do, don't touch it."

Nilenam stroked his beard, averting his eyes to the small window overhead. "If something happens … if I don't come back; don't hesitate to leave me behind."

Philander rested his hand on his brother's shoulder. "I doubt we've come this far for you to be left behind. It's no coincidence that we are reunited. We'll enter the new land together."

A smile flickered across Nilenam's thin lips. "You've always had amazing faith."

* * * *

Sunlight peeked into the mouth of the cave. Manelin wiped sleep from his eyes and stretched his stiff back. The journal, opened to the map, fell to the floor. He glanced at the details, comparing it to the map on the wall. The diagram etched in stone differed from the map in the journal. It detailed the Yoke of Inspiration. From what he could determine, he stood at one end of the yoke.

Manelin's stomach rumbled. He longed for a hot meal.

He stood brushing dirt from the seat of his trousers and walked to the map. His fingers traced the etching. Stygian symbols of the metot animals framed the map, resembling the petrographs in the great hall of stone. "The fox." He nodded and looked toward the dark passageway where the small animal had disappeared. A decorative line at the bottom of the map turned upward and curved in toward the map on each end. Manelin recognized the symbol. Within the Fortress of Stone, Jalil had taught him that it represented a dream.

He glanced over his shoulder toward the mouth of the cave. A shudder shimmied up his back at the thought of going out to find fuel for a torch. Eyes closed, his fingertips brushed the warm stony surface to take in the map's detail.

A flash of light filled his vision. Laughter and chattering of far away voices echoed in his head. The swish of his heartbeat filled his ears. His weightless body floated like a lazy summer day on the mountain lake. He opened his eyes. Dark haired, Stygian milled about the cavern beneath him. Children sat in a circle, playing a game, while adults gathered in clusters speaking in hushed tones. His attention focused on a man comforting a woman near the mouth of the cave.

"I couldn't save her." She brushed a tear from her cheek. "She didn't care, and now she's put a curse on The Land. We'll never see our son again."

"Don't say that, Awena. Have faith in the Arich." He stroked her head as if comforting a child.

She pulled away. "Stop saying that! We don't know that our son is the Arich, and you didn't see the look on Trinak's face. She's brought trouble to The Land, a curse. There may be no healing."

Warmth lulled Manelin's muscles to relax as he surveyed his safe haven filled with Stygian. His mind raced. His heart ached for their safety. A transparent image of the blue fox appeared at the mouth of the passageway. "Are you ready?" the fox asked.

The mark on Manelin's shoulder burned. He glanced around at the crowded cavern. *I wish I could stay and be with them. Help them.*

"They are not here," the fox answered. "What you witness are reflections of things that have been. Within the Yoke of Inspiration you will possess the ability to see many things, past, present and things to come."

"And what is this?" Manelin pointed to the couple near the mouth of the cave.

The fox's eyes glowed like golden orbs. "Things past."

"Why do I see these things?"

"The power of the map of dreams activates the aura of the one reading it. The things you see take place in your lifetime. Beyond that you will not see."

"You mean the Stygian people were here during my lifetime?"

"Consider what you know."

Manelin floated above the families huddled in the cave. A sudden rush of wind gusted into the cave. Parents scooped up their children and moved to the back of the cavern. The couple near the mouth of the cave joined the others. "It's the curse," the woman said. "It's cut us off from the rest of The Land. No one will find us. We'll enter the cycle of death forever."

The man put his finger on the woman's lips. "Hush, Awena. Don't let the others hear you. Your lack of faith will breed despair. Trust me. We've done the right thing."

The woman leaned her head on the man's chest and apologized.

A bat flew from the ceiling beside him and into the passage where the fox had disappeared. *The symbol of the bat*, he searched his memory. Jalil had mentioned something about a bat flying through your dreams. *What did that mean?*

Rebirth. The bat symbolized rebirth. She had said that if one flew through your dream, it offered the opportunity to leave behind part of yourself. That was exactly what he needed to move on.

Manelin opened his eyes. He stood with his fingertips above the map, resting on the image of the bat. The cave around him seemed empty and still. He walked away from the map of dreams, wondering what part of himself he needed to leave behind.

He rummaged through his pouch, found a piece of moss clinging to one of the pinecones and slipped it onto his tongue. The earthy flavor made his mouth water but sent a shiver down his spine. Eating like this while out with the goats was one thing. Back then, he knew a hot meal awaited him when he arrived home. *Home.* Tears stung his eyes, but he forced them back. He no longer had anything resembling a home. Grandfather had taught him not to dwell in the past. In his honor, he would move forward. His shoulders slumped. Loneliness crashed in on him as he sat on the floor, resting against the wall of the cave. He used his empty sack as a pillow.

"I'm not going out there." He stared out at the swath of destruction leading to the cave. "And according to that thing," he turned his head to look at the map of dreams, "I'm not going anywhere in here until I figure out what part of me I need to leave behind."

A lump formed in his throat. He closed his eyes and wished for sleep. It provided his only escape from the loneliness. He buried his desires and embraced the challenge ahead. It was clear. People's lives depended on him. He was their Arich.

"This way," the fox called to him.

Manelin stumbled along the uneven surface of the cramped passageway. His toe caught a ridge in the floor, sending him skipping on his knees. "Wait," Manelin cried out. "Don't go so fast. I can't see where I'm going." Sparks lit up the passageway for a brief second. Something like stacked logs of wood crowded the corridor to his right. Manelin pushed to his feet and moved forward. "Where am I?"

"The map will tell you."

"I thought I couldn't come this way until I left part of myself behind."

"You did."

Manelin steadied himself against one of the piles of wood. He reached out and used the opposite wall to guide him. "I did?"

"Selfishness and bitterness feeds the ashen serpent. It consumes those harboring division in their heart."

"What is that—" Manelin tripped and bounced onto a smooth flat surface, "noise?"

The splashing of water raised his hopes of quenching his thirst. He blinked, straining to see into the darkness. "Does it have to be so dark?" His words returned to him three times.

"No, it does not."

Manelin listened. It was more a rush of water, like a waterfall. The image of the map of dreams flashed into his mind. A pool of water marked the center of the Yoke of Inspiration. He crawled toward the sound, feeling ahead as he moved. It reminded him of the day he followed Sop into the Potent's Table. That day changed his life forever.

A fine mist coated his skin. His palm slapped the surface of the Waters of Nen. He lifted wet fingers to his nose. It smelled clean. He touched his finger to his tongue. The refreshing taste invited him to drink. The water soothed his parched throat and hit his empty stomach. Growls of hunger echoed his need for more. Dim light filtered into the area. Manelin squinted into the low light and searched for the source of illumination but found none. He scooped another drink. The light brightened.

"Welcome to Sharis Havyn."

Manelin's eyes adjusted. Water spilled into the emerald pool from the darkness above. "How is it light in here?"

"You are no longer blinded by your lack of faith. Drink, eat and be filled, for your journey is difficult. You'll need your strength."

"Eat?" Manelin looked around the empty cave. "Eat what?"

"Be patient. Feed your soul."

"Where are you?" Manelin asked.

"I am with you."

Manelin let out a sigh. He bent over the pool of water to wash his face and stared at his reflection. He'd changed so much since the last time he'd seen himself. Ebony hair framed his sun-darkened face. No wonder Grandfather insisted he wash his hair every night. His fingers brushed his cheek, testing the reality of the image.

"I'm Stygian," he admitted to himself.

His thoughts drifted to times he and Jalil talked of the Stygian people. What would she think of him now if she knew? Her father hated the Stygian.

A flash of movement cut through the water into the air. Manelin fell backward, his rear bouncing against the hard surface. A twitching weight slammed against his torso and knocked him flat. His chest heaved. He skittered to his feet in a crouch, hand readied on the hilt of his dagger, eyes searching the murkiness. Beside him, gills of a large orange fish sucked air. Food! Real food. He picked up the ample meal wishing he could share it with others as hungry.

A strong fishy odor wafted within the confined area. Manelin stopped breathing through his nose. He wasn't sure which smelled worse, him or the fish. A smile tugged at the corner of his mouth. No contest. He'd eat, take a bath and get some sleep.

"I've got the food, but I need fire." He waited for the fox to answer. Nothing. "Why would you provide food without giving me a way to cook it?" The splash of the water was his only answer. He waited. His life had become a series of run and wait.

For the first time since he fled the Village of Chock, Manelin considered the other people living there. His grandfather was missing, but was he the only one? What of the Healer? Had he died in the queen's dungeon? Feelings of inadequacy pressed in on him.

Manelin eased his tired feet into the refreshing pool. All those years Philander fussed about washing his hair. "I hated the smell of that stuff," he said to himself. His nose scrunched at the memory. His shoulders slumped. Philander's hand of protection had rested on him. "As long as I have breath, I vow to find you, Grandfather."

Images of the night he fled filled his mind while emotions swelled to his throat. He pushed them into submission. This was not the time for private struggles to ambush his mission. He would never be able to help his grandfather if he did not save his people first; that is, if he was truly the Arich.

Manelin leaned to grab his journal. Philander was Jonnick, yet he treated him with the love of a father. The familiar musty smell of the parchment comforted him in a strange way.

The enormity of the task flooded him with apprehension. *I can't do this.*

Manelin's thoughts rested on Jalil. Her beautiful blonde curls shined in the sunshine of his memory. "I thought Jalil would be at my side," Manelin called out to the fox, "if she is my Augur."

"Manelin," Jalil beckoned from the recesses of his mind. "Manelin, where are you?"

Manelin closed his mind. As much as he longed for her company, he couldn't allow her to come into this dangerous situation. First, he wanted to investigate, then he'd invite her in. Steam spouted through a crack in the floor. Manelin skittered backwards like a crab from the plume spraying from the unexpected vent.

"That's it!" He hurried to plop the fish over the vent. As the flesh steamed, he broke off portions and ate his fill. Warm and filled, Manelin stripped off his dirty clothes and bathed in the bottomless Waters of Nen.

Chapter 22
Cage of Ice

Flames shot from the lizard's mouth.
Manelin squeezed his eyes closed.
Heat washed across his body followed by a rush of cold air.

The temperature in the narrow tunnel dropped as Manelin moved further from the Waters of Nen. He pulled his goat hair poncho close to his body. His ability to see in the dark stayed with him as he walked away from the source of the power. Another wave of frigid air blasted around the bend. Would this power to see in the dark wear off? He hurried. Too bad it couldn't help him to see where he was going. Why couldn't the visions be clear and tell him exactly what to do?

Icy floors slowed his precarious steps. The floor sloped down a hair and he lost his footing. Tumbling forward, he landed on his stomach, cascading along the icy floor and spilling into a larger cavern. He stood while picturing the map in his mind. This was the other side of the yoke.

Colors of light refracted across the Cavern of Ice. Irregular spikes of crystal-like ice hung from the ceiling reaching toward a steamy layer of fog covering the floor. Manelin dipped his hand into the fog and pressed his palm to the warm floor. *A lava tunnel must run close enough to keep the floor warm.*

Manelin stepped to the mouth of the cave, shielding his eyes from the bright sunlight. Wind whipped under his poncho and picked at his skin. His body fit between the shafts of ice blocking the mouth of the cave. He tucked his head and walked into the stiff breeze, stopping at the edge of a snow-covered cliff. Below, a valley filled with jagged icy formations stretched between this mountain and the smoldering ice-capped mountain across the way. A dead end. What should he do? He scanned for anything resembling a Cage of Ice. How could he rescue people from the Cage of Ice if he couldn't find it?

He turned and studied the cavern entrance. The thick icicles almost looked like bars to hold people in, but they were too wide apart. He'd slipped right through them.

Manelin turned his attention to the mountain across the way. Tiny frozen specks stung his face as a gust rushed down the mountain. A narrow ridge of ice and snow joined the two mountains. It ran along a glacial wall of frozen chunks, piled like a giant child's tumbled blocks, spilled into a mountainous pile. He hugged the wall to block the wind and tested the ledge with his boot. Snow crunched beneath his boot as he clung to the uneven surface of the frozen wall. He inched away from the Yoke of Inspiration along the narrow ridge.

White drifts of snow deepened, slowing his progress. Wind tore from the slope above, buffeting his body and playing tricks with his footing. He paused, waiting for the gust to subside. Across the gorge, numerous openings pocked the side of the mountain. Manelin's fingers numbed. He glanced back at the cavern behind him. *Halfway.* The vision of Stygian people depending on him pushed him onward.

Snow swallowed Manelin's feet up to his calves. Ice beneath the snow slanted toward the Valley of Blades. Wind gusted and pummeled his body. Manelin groped for a handhold with stiff fingers. His feet skidded from beneath him, slamming him face first into the glacial wall, and hitting his ribs against the ledge leaving him teetering perilously above the jagged ice below. His fingernails clawed the frozen surface. If he didn't fall and die, he'd freeze to death.

A shadow eclipsed the sun. Manelin struggled to cling to the frozen surface. His white knuckles slipped. Another inch and he knew it was over.

A loud whip-like snap close to his ear startled him. His hands lost the battle to hold on. It almost seemed like a dream. Falling backwards toward the Valley of Blades, his feet kicked and his hands groped air. He closed his eyes waiting for the bone crushing impact. The whip-cracking sound shot through the air again. Something warm wrapped around Manelin's wrist and jerked him to a stop.

Manelin opened one eye and then the second. A rope-like blue tail pulled him into the sky. He glanced at the mountains and up at the scales on the underbelly of a large flying lizard. Manelin's emotions collided. Relief as the jagged blades of ice moved further away gave way to fear that he would be the monster's next meal.

Manelin stopped struggling and grabbed the unlikely safety line with his free hand. Sunlight glinted like gems from the serrated blades of ice reaching from the valley floor. Warmth from the sun fought the icy fingers penetrating Manelin's clothing. Dangling above the frozen tundra gave him a unique perspective. The Valley of Blades merged with the Valley of Rocks. Across the mountains and into the valley he saw the Village of Chock, the Potent's Table, and the foothills where his goats had died.

Manelin's mind returned to the hours he and Jalil spent putting pieces into place while reading the scrolls. They had joked calling them Stygian puzzles as they gathered information a piece at a time. Without Jalil, he'd never have the courage to look for a Cage of Ice. A sense of helplessness washed over him.

Wispy tendrils of smoke from the mountain across the way drifted on the stiff breeze, stinging his eyes. Wind whooshed from beneath the lizard's large rubbery wings carrying Manelin toward the smoldering mountain. Sunlight bounced like a beacon off the mirror-like surface of a large sheet of ice embedded in a large crag like a setting in a ring. Manelin's shoulder burned.

"The Cage of Ice." If he paid attention, the mark on his shoulder helped him see. If only it could help him know how to get in. From this vantage, the sheer mountain wall offered no help. For now, it didn't matter. The lizard soared higher and away from the Cage of Ice.

Gray clouds scuttled across the sky, cutting the glare of the sun. Manelin glanced at the yellow underside of the giant lizard and down at its shadow, darting along the frozen landscape. The cold numbed his ears and nose. His hand felt blue from lack of circulation.

They circled the mountain, descending into a semi-circular depression on the western side. Was this the dragon's lair? Walls of stone and ice enclosed three fourths of the crater while the other fourth overlooked the Valley of Blades.

The lizard's tail released its hold. Manelin dropped, rolled in a tumble and popped to his feet. He dashed away from the jaws of the dragon and crouched behind a small outcropping of ice beside the wall of stone. Flames shot from the lizard's mouth. Manelin squeezed his eyes closed. Heat washed across his body followed by a rush of cold air. He peeked. His hiding place had melted. The dragon belched another furious ball of flame but it missed, hitting the back of the semi-circle. Jagged icicles diminished to tiny dripping fingers, pointing to a passageway large enough for him to stand. If he could get to it, he'd be safer.

Manelin bolted toward the safe haven. The mountain beneath his feet shook, knocking him to the ground. Behind him, the dragon lumbered toward him. Panic sent him skittering backwards. His hands frantically searched for a stone or chunk of ice to throw; finally, he wrapped his fingers around a rock. It wouldn't budge. He thrust his hand into his sack pulling out a pinecone. He stared at the unlikely weapon for a moment, almost feeling foolish.

The dragon cried out. Its golden eyes pinned; its irises kaleidoscoping. Manelin threw the pinecone. It bounced against the dragon's leathery hide and ricocheted to the ground. The reptile's long blue tongue slithered, snatching the pinecone and tossing it into its jaws with a snap.

Manelin pushed to his feet, glancing over his shoulder at the safety of the small cave.

The dragon squealed. The ground shook from the impact of the monster's weight as it walked toward him. Manelin's arms windmilled. He slipped backwards, landing with a thump onto his seat. The dragon's clawed feet cut into the icy surface without a problem. Manelin grabbed another pinecone, whipping it high overhead. The dragon lunged into the air toward the tiny morsel, flapping its rubbery wings for lift. It reminded Manelin of playing with Sop.

Manelin moved cautiously toward the passage but stopped when the dragon eyed him. He flipped another treat into the air. The lizard's tongue sucked it into its vicious jaws. A howling shriek pierced the frozen atmosphere, sprinkling snow along the mouth of the passageway.

Manelin dropped to his knees and covered his ears.

The echoing scream launched a cascade of cracking and snapping of ice overhead. He needed to get into the passageway. One more scream would bury him in an avalanche. The monster swooped toward him. Talons opened to snatch him. He turned and ran toward the tunnel. The mountain rumbled. Large sheets of ice broke loose, crashing toward the valley.

Fire shot from the monster's maw toward the massive chunk. The enormous mass dissolved to the size of a small boulder, crashing into the ponding runoff. For the first time, Manelin noticed the sound of running water trickling along the slope, gathering into streams, spilling in to the Valley of Blades like a waterfall. Manelin peered over the edge amazed at the flood of water partially submerging the fingers of ice. Layers of steam collected over the waters swirling in the mountain winds.

* * * *

Riona paused on the balcony sensing a strong Stygian presence. She had sent for the healer. His treatment would help her gain the strength that had dwindled after chasing the Stygian brat in the Nefarious forest, the strength needed to complete her purpose. A touch of fear tempered her hatred. This Stygian scent was different, a Windwalker for sure, but powerful. The Augur? The thought threatened everything she held dear. She had no time to wait for the Healer. Her footsteps clattered against the marble flooring as she fled through the throne room toward her bedchamber. Soon, she wouldn't need healing. She'd cleanse Ranaan of the Stygian filth.

Her royal robes fluttered behind her as she slipped into her bedchamber. Once she completed her quest, the power of the Mage offered a new beginning, but she had to earn it. She grasped the powerful stone in her fist, hurrying to the bed to lie atop the satin. Her crown rested on the pillow as she closed her eyes to concentrate.

* * * *

The sun disappeared behind the clouds. Manelin stood trapped with his back against the wall of the crater, near the edge overlooking the fog-filled Valley of Blades. Gloom settled over the surreal situation. The beast turned. A red-hot ball of fire shot through the ominous sky and spread in a flash of heat against the side of the mountain across the way.

A barrage of large raindrops plopped from the sky. This was no time for the spring rains to set in. Manelin's breath stretched out in white vaporous puffs. Below him mountains of ice floated. Through breaks in the fog, he noticed large chunks of ice and debris lodging against one another forming a dam where the Valley of Blades connected to the Valley of Rocks. If that thing broke, a flood would wash away every town he knew.

Before he could think to do anything about warning the Jonnick in the valley, he had to get away from the dragon. Manelin displayed his empty palms. "No more pinecones," he said as if the monster would understand.

He backed toward the tunnel. The sour smell of the dirty beast filled the air as its thin blue tongue reached out and dragged its rough texture against his hand. A cry of disappointment screamed across the rainy sky. Stiff gusts of wind blew icy grit across his wet face as the large wings lifted the dragon. Manelin protected his eyes with his forearm, watching the beast lift and veer toward the mountaintops.

Vibrations tickled the bottoms of Manelin's feet. Cracking and shattering overhead warned him to run for cover. He scrambled toward the passageway, slipping and sliding on the wet icy surface as he sprinted toward safety. Shards plunked into the standing water. Furious crushing of ice and snow combined into a thunderous response to the animal's shrieking. Sheets of ice pulled loose, followed by walls of frozen debris.

Manelin ducked into the sanctuary of the narrow passage, tripped and landed on his back, knocking the breath from him. He leaned on his elbows and stared at the ice and frozen debris blocking the way out. It formed a barricade between him and the monster. Intense heat rushed across his body; chased away the chill for a brief moment until the warmth retreated into frigid gusts and dissipated. The blockade of ice melted under another of the dragon's fiery blasts. Still on his back, Manelin propelled backwards using his elbows. His body picked up momentum, sliding headlong on his back into the inky unknown. Down, down, scraping against the stony chute, he tried to slow his speed with his arms and feet to no avail. He curled into a ball to protect his limbs. Like a cannon ball, he shot into daylight and landed with a thud. He stared at the hole in the ceiling of the large cavern. One thing was clear. He wouldn't leave the same way he arrived.

"Where am I now?" he wondered out loud rubbing the ache from his shoulder as he stood.

Light filtered into the cavern through thick sheets of ice, working like windows. His breath spread into frosty balloons while he tucked his fingers under his arms trying to warm them. He stepped up to the largest sheet of ice amazed he could see through it so clearly. Through it, he watched the lizard circle between the two mountains. A piercing shriek pushed Manelin's hands to cover his ears. A ball of fire shot toward him. He ducked, but the orange-red glow bounced off the window of ice, melting a hole the size of his head in the barrier.

Fear pinned Manelin to the spot. A ghostly white serpent slithered through the rolling storm clouds. It was equal in size to the dragon. The large lizard discharged a wall of flame, thwarting the serpent's advance. It slipped into the clouds. Manelin thought of Jalil's story of the ashen serpent and found himself rooting for the dragon to win. The snake's head popped from a cloudbank, jaws snapped open, fangs dripping as a vaporous cloud shot from its mouth, immobilizing the dragon's left wing. Its right wing beat the air frantically while its body spiraled toward the foggy lake forming below.

Manelin backed away from the melted window of ice, searching for a place to hide. Columns of ice offered plenty of hiding places. His feet slipped on the icy floor and skidded along a slight downward slope. His body picked up speed and he slammed into the wall. His shoulder burned. He rubbed the mark, wondering what it meant for him this time.

Shadowy forms on the other side caught his attention. What was that behind the wall of ice?

He rubbed his sleeve in a circular motion to see clearly. People! He spun to look around the cavern. Tiny rooms lined the perimeter. Now, looking hard he could see the people trapped behind the ice. He pounded the wall with no result other than the throb in his hand.

"What am I to do?" The cavern was void of any materials to build a fire. He stepped back to the half-melted window of ice, drawing his stiff fingers through his tangled wet hair.

Bolts of lightning streaked the dark sky. The dragon had regained partial use of its wing, but the mass of the ethereal serpent coiled around its prey. The pair plummeted. Fire billowed from the dragon's snout and spread across the mountainside above Manelin. An avalanche of ice and melted snow thundered past his window, following the pair into the Valley of Blades. The dragon broke free and gained altitude, but the serpent caught its tail. It responded with another shot of fire diving head first at the snake. The pair slammed into the side of the mountain, frozen debris plummeted breaking the window of ice and clogging it with rubble. Light leaked through tiny crevices in the frozen blockade. Instead of rescuing the Stygian, he found himself trapped with them.

The mountain around him rumbled. The roar of rock, ice and mud slid outside the cave. An explosion overhead shook the cavern, sprinkling shards of ice across the floor around him.

"The volcano!" Manelin pounded his shoulder against the debris again and again without effect. He collapsed to sit on the floor wrapping his arms around his shivering body. "So much for being the Arich."

The symbol of the eye burned his shoulder. He wanted to cut it out with his dagger for the help it was. His hand rubbed the spot while his mind thought back to the day he received the unique mark. "Jalil," he hung his head, "I've failed."

* * * *

Adish stuffed the banded cluster of explosion logs into the mouth of the secondary passageway off the Crystal Cavern. The floor shook. That mountain across the valley threatened to blow. One quick blast of fire and this whole mountain and all its Stygian sacred places would disappear along with the threat of the Arich. None of that mattered right now. His daughter was missing and he squandered his time planting explosives that may never be used.

He wedged the blasting logs into place and walked into the larger cavern. The frozen beauty mesmerized him. This place actually appealed to him, quiet, beautiful and a good place to think. Queen Riona would reward him handsomely as always. The thought left him empty. He'd give it all up to have his family together. Estel had left him long ago in her own way, and now Laul…. If he didn't find Jalil, what really mattered?

He peered between the thick icicles at the mouth of the cave, looking toward the rumbling mountain. Wind whipped across the Valley of Blades, carrying the faint scent of smoke. Dark skies threatened rain. Adish pulled his heavy cloak tight. Frost gathered on his reddish-blond beard above his top lip. By the time he returned home, he'd be soaked to the bone.

His donkey brayed behind him, acting a bit skittish. A large shadow circled in the stormy sky. Adish grabbed the reigns of his pack mule. "What by the stars is that?" He pressed his face against the ice staring at the beast.

Its shadow glided between the two mountains. A flash of bright light and an explosion threw him to the floor. Pain shot through his leg. He stared beyond the sword of ice impaling his leg. "The blasting logs!" He struggled to free himself before another ball of fire shot his way.

Movement in the sky grabbed his attention. Two monsters clashed in the sky. If he lived through this, people would think him crazy. *Like Estel.* He yanked the spear of ice from his leg, vowing to free his wife. Blood spurted across the wall.

"Jagger, come here, girl." The donkey took two tentative steps toward him. Adish pushed to his feet. Pain shot through his leg. He hoisted his bulk over the mule's bony back. "Get me out of here, girl."

Fire shot into the room as the donkey slipped into the passageway filled with blasting logs. Adish was too weak to fight with her to cut straight to the center of the yoke. A creature of habit, it would take more work for him to change the donkey's direction than to let her go the path she knew so well. Adish only hoped the fire didn't find its way to the blasting logs while he was anywhere near.

* * * *

Jalil blinked. Her eyes adjusted to the dimness. "Manelin?" She clutched her walking stick in her right hand while rubbing the cold from her arm with her free hand. Where had he called her to this time? High-pitched shrieks hurt her ears. "Manelin?" she called louder.

Manelin scurried along the frigid ground like a crab moving away from her. He stopped, half hidden in the shadows. "Jalil?"

"Oh, Manelin, I was worried about you." She bent to touch his cheek. "You're so cold." Her fingers lingered against his face. "Where are we?"

"Jalil," he grabbed her upper arms and pulled her close. "We're in the Cage of Ice! I found it, but I don't know how to free them. The Stygian … they're in here. The dragon battles an ashen serpent outside. They've blocked the way. I'm trapped."

"Manelin," dim light reflected in her wide eyes, "The serpent is the guardian of the queen's power."

Manelin drew her to him. "Jalil, there's something I must tell you."

She strained to see his face.

"Jalil, I'm … I'm…" The earth rumbled and threw them to the ground. Chunks of ice crashed around them. Dim rays of light broke through the blockage at the mouth of the cave, highlighting Jalil's blond hair pulled back from her fair face. Manelin hugged the shadows. "I'm not what you think I am," he said quietly. Heat warmed the cavern.

"Don't worry," Jalil took his hand. "I stayed within the Fortress of Stone, hoping to find you there. I used the time to study. My understanding of Stygian history has deepened."

"I've learned a bit of Stygian history myself." Manelin stepped into the light. "I know why my eyes are brown." He offered a half smile. "I'm Stygian."

Chapter 23
The Arich, Augur and Ancient

"We've got to have faith," he repeated her words.
"This is the time of rebirth. It's a true new beginning."

"I'm here to treat the queen," Nilenam said to the guards.

"Now?" one guard said to the second.

"Don't be long," the second guard said, "I hope to get home before the rain."

Nilenam waved off their concern. "You can't rush an old man. Why don't you go? The queen will be sleeping. I'll see myself back to the dungeon like always."

"We can't do that, just hurry."

Nilenam shuffled a few steps. "I'll do my best. Shouldn't be more than a couple of hours." He stepped into the throne room and paused.

"A couple of hours?" the second guard said to the first. "Think we can trust him?"

"What's he going to do? He's so old if he runs he'll die from the exertion."

The first guard chuckled as Nilenam trundled through the throne room and up the stairs to the queen's bed chamber. If she caught him here uninvited, he'd die for sure. He pushed his fear aside. Philander's insights usually proved right. He thought back to the moonless night when the Arich was born. That one prophetic episode gave him faith to find the Magestone.

At the top of the stairwell, Nilenam paused outside the gold plated door. Who but Riona would waste gold in such a way? No one came up here. He lifted the latch and peeked in. Her still form rested upon red satin at the center of the room. Bed curtains stirred in the breeze from the open window. Statues cluttered the outskirts of the room. Strange statues with grotesque faces.

Nilenam trained his eyes on the queen. Her chest rose and fell. He stepped to the side of the bed, staring at the Magestone resting in her palm. His brother's warning rang in his head. How could he get rid of it if he didn't touch it?

He could only think of one way.

* * * *

Jalil's smile reached her crystal blue eyes. Her face had grown lovelier in the days since he'd seen her last. "I don't know what you think of me," she said, "but I love you for who you are...the real you. It doesn't matter Jonnick or Stygian." She stroked his dark hair. "It's a matter of heart. I know your heart." She rested her palm against his chest. "You cared for me when I hobbled as a bumble foot. You desired to include me. The heart within you cares without regard to lineage."

His head spun. She loved him. "Jalil." He whispered hoarsely and pulled her to him pressing his lips to hers. "I've missed you."

A loud pop filled the spacious cavern; the floor buckled, ripping them apart. Fractures snapped the icy surface, sending a web of cracks spreading along the length of the cavern. Steam seeped through the hairline fissures.

Jalil stared at the broken floor. "What is that?" Her voice raised an octave.

Manelin clasped her hand in his. He never wanted to let her go. "It's starting to make sense. If I'm the Arich and you are my Augur, the time of rebirth is upon us. A bat flew through my dream."

"You're right." Jalil nodded. "The rebirth is upon us. What do we do now?"

They inched to the mouth of the cave and peered from the underside of water pouring over the opening like a waterfall. "I don't know what we're going to do." He paused. "There's no way out. The dragon carried me here." He draped his arm across her shoulder. "You need to leave. It's too dangerous."

"No, my place is at your side. My gift provides understanding for the symbols and prophecies. Being a Windwalker means I have Stygian blood in my ancestry, but a bumble foot points to Stygian blood on my father's and mother's side. So, I'm not what I appear to be." She smiled shyly. "My father knows, but he would never admit it. I'm thankful he had enough mercy to spare me when I was born."

Manelin's face grew serious. "Come with me." He tugged her hand. She glided above the large crystal-like chunks littering the cavern floor. Steam gushed from cracks in the floor.

"Where are we going?" she screamed over the rumble. Smoke hung in a thick layer above their heads. Manelin slid about three feet and came to a stop. Jalil skidded behind him. "What are you doing?" She blew on her hand and worked her cold fingers.

Misty white puffs marked each breath. Manelin stood in front of the wall of ice. "Come here." He motioned with his hand for her to stand directly next to him. "Look." He wiped frost from the icy barrier with his sleeve. "People in the ice."

"In the ice?" Jalil pressed her face to the glass like surface. She straightened and stared at Manelin. Her jaw dropped. "You're right. It's the Stygian. This is the Cage of Ice?" She glanced to where the wall of ice met the ceiling.

Manelin nodded.

"You really are the one to save them," Jalil said. She wiped away a curl matted to her forehead. "Just like the scrolls predicted. We just didn't realize this is how it would happen."

"How can we get them out of there?"

"Are they alive?" she asked. "After all this time?"

"We've got to have faith," he repeated her words. "This is the time of rebirth. It's a true new beginning."

Manelin turned and studied the flow of water gushing over the opening at the mouth of the cave. The blockage of slush and ice piled there thawed in an instant when flames shot through the small opening. Jalil huddled next to Manelin. Her blue eyes grew wide with fear. She stared at the beast balanced at the edge of the cave. She pointed. "The … the dragon."

* * * *

Riona retreated. Fear gripped her soul. She'd failed. The incurable wound took its toll and the powerful Windwalker's dragon form had taken her by surprise. Since when could Windwalkers shift shape?

Battling the creature robbed her of her strength. She'd never felt so weak. Her pace slowed to a crawl as she headed to the safety of her bedchamber. The Healer could restore her vigor.

* * * *

Melting snow and ice cascaded like a backdrop behind the dragon. Its tongue slithered in and out of its powerful jaws.

"Calm down," Manelin said. "Don't panic. I finally see how this all comes together." Water trickled down the walls of the cavern. Manelin inched toward the monster outside the door. "She's hurt," he said. "We need to help her."

Jalil walked behind Manelin like a shadow. Her voice spoke softly. "The lizard teaches how to use dreams to create a new reality."

Manelin turned to look at her. Her eyes stared blankly as if in a trance.

"It dreams of a situation, and then it is up to the dreamer to decide to continue fueling the circumstances for whether it becomes real or not." She blinked. Her attention drifted from Manelin to the dragon and back again.

Manelin considered the words they had pondered while pouring over the Stygian tellings, the meaning much more explicit. "Thank you for saving us," he said to the monster.

The monster teetered and fell to the ground. Tendrils of smoke curled from its quivering nostrils. Leathery eyelids lifted halfway revealing glazed over dull dark eyes. Manelin glanced at the body for evidence of life. The scaled ribcage didn't move.

Manelin reached out and stroked the snout. For a moment, he thought of Sop. "Come on," he cooed. "Don't give up your dream. The people in here need you. We need a big dream from a big lizard." Scales on the mammoth ribcage reflected the little light leaking into the cavern. "Look!" Manelin pointed. "It's breathing!" He gestured to Jalil to join him. "The dream is alive!"

Jalil knelt beside her friend. "What is the dream, Manelin? You are the one who sees the dream. 'The eye guides the one who wants to see.'"

"Remember how you healed me? That scrape on my arm?"

Jalil nodded.

"Can you do the same for her?" Manelin placed his hand on the dragon's snout. He glanced at the mountain across the valley. Large chucks of icy snow slid in sheets toward the Valley of Blades. The earth rumbled and the lizard lifted its head at Jalil's touch.

"I can't believe it," Jalil said. "A friendly dragon?"

"Remember what we read about the Arich?" Manelin asked. "He unites? Brings the Jonnick and Stygian together?"

Jalil nodded.

"This is a starting point. I'm Stygian and you're Jonnick. We can do this together. You're my Augur and I am your..." He shrugged one shoulder.

"You are the Arich." She tipped her head.

The dragon lurched. Jalil screamed. She put her arms around Manelin's neck and buried her face in his shoulder.

Manelin stroked her hair. Another large sheet of ice crashed outside the cave. The dragon pushed to sit on its haunches like a pet. "I feel connected. Do you feel it?"

"What do you mean?" Jalil asked.

"The dragon." He bent down and tugged at the giant snakeskin under the beast. "Look at this!" He yanked the mammoth skin free, wadding it up and stuffing it into his bag. "Do you remember what we learned about the snakeskin?"

"A sign of rebirth?" She nestled her face against his chest. The fragrance of flowers wafted from her hair.

Manelin nodded. "It's a sign of change." He eased past the bulk of the dragon and peered into the Valley of Blades. "The serpent feeds on hatred. Today the dream crushed the hatred, but if it is fed it will become a threat again."

Water rushed from all directions into the gorge below. Large spears of ice broke and jammed at the far end of the valley adding to the dam. From behind him, a loud crack startled Manelin. He turned to see Jalil walking into the dim recesses.

Outside, across the valley, an explosion from the cavern leading into the Yoke of Inspiration sent boulders flying like cannon balls into the raging waters below. Smoke billowed from the cave, and for a moment Manelin caught a glimpse of movement, a man with reddish blond hair. He swallowed hard. *Could it be Jalil's father? What would he be doing here?*

"Jalil, wait for me." He hurried into the Cage of Ice. *Do I tell her?* He dismissed the idea to avoid worrying her. After all, he wasn't sure.

The frozen sheets blocking the Stygian behind the wall of ice thinned in the steam, cracked and crumbled, creating openings into individual toans. The floor beneath them rumbled as the mountain quaked. Manelin's fingers tingled. It felt good to be warm. He rested his hand against the wall to stay balanced.

Jalil's mouth fell open. "These are the people I've seen in my visions!" She pointed. Men, women and children poised in stiff statue-like positions thawed as the temperatures rose. "Are they ... dead?"

"Remember the snakeskin," Manelin said. "Rebirth," he smiled, "and a sign of change. Can you imagine these Stygian coming back to live in Chock?" His dark eyes smiled, but sadness quickly erased it.

"What's wrong?" Jalil brushed her fingertips along his cheek.

"What do we do now? I've thought about finding them." He pointed to the statue-like natives. "But, I don't know what to do now. Where do we go? How do we get out of here?"

"Find the life." Jalil's tone warned Manelin that she offered another bit of wisdom for him to understand. "You hold the dream."

"Find the life," he repeated. "Sometimes you speak as clearly as the prophecies."

He glanced over his shoulder at the dragon. She carried him here. The ground shook, and rumbling overhead warned that the volcano was active. Not the kind of rebirth he hoped for.

"Do you hear me?"

Manelin turned and looked at Jalil. "What?" he shouted over the noise.

Jalil blinked. "I didn't say anything," she yelled over the cracking and crashing sounds filling the cave.

"*Do you hear me?*" The voice spoke clearly. It was the voice of the whirring visions.

"I heard a voice. It asked if I could hear it. But, I hear it in my head. Does that make sense?"

"That's how I hear you when you think of me! Perhaps someone here is thinking of you." She pointed to the exposed Stygian.

"It's a woman's voice. Could it be another Augur?"

Jalil shrugged. "You know what I know. I'm the one that the writing foretold at the time of the joining, or I thought I was." Her eyes searched the thawing people in front of her. "Perhaps there is another … a pure blooded Stygian."

"Manelin, it's me. Behind you."

He turned and looked at the dragon. "Are you talking to me?"

"*You do not have to speak, but only think the words.*"

"*How? How do I hear you?*"

"Manelin, are you okay?" Jalil waved her hand in front of his face. "Manelin?"

He raised his hand. "I'm fine. The dragon is…" The cavern around him swirled. Foggy mist encompassed him. "*What's happening?*" He wasn't sure if his lips moved or if he only thought the words.

"You are in the world beyond time and space." The dragon sat in front of him. "You've been here before, long ago. I sense it."

"*Where are we?*" Manelin blinked. The odd sensation was strangely familiar.

"*Look closely at your dreams, Manelin. I am here to teach you how to use dreams to create your future reality. Others dreamed the current situation within the Land into existence. Today you hold the power to change the dream, for you are the Arich. Your heart is pure, your desire to unite. Have you seen your future? Your hopes or fears? Let them guide you. Listen to your Augur. As Stygian emerge, the ashen serpent will have opportunity to return if they harbor hatred, for the power of the Mage feeds on hatred. Everything happening springs from your wishes and fears. Do not allow grudges to color your outlook. Go forth and lead."*

Manelin floated in the mist. "My wishes and fears? I don't want this to rest on me. I'm not strong enough."

"That is your fear."

"But, but I just want the Stygian and Jonnick to live together in peace; to learn how to co-exist in the land."

"That is your wish, your dream," the dragon answered. "Look more closely at your dreams. Follow them. Consider your fears. Learn from them."

"Can I ask a question?"

"Of course."

"How do we awaken the Stygian? How does the rebirth happen? What do I do?"

"Learn the lesson of the bat."

Manelin floated between reality and this dream-like realm. *"The bat?"*

"Talk to your Augur. It is her place to guide. I teach how to reach for your dreams to achieve a future reality."

* * * *

"Manelin!" Jalil shouted and shook his shoulders.

He blinked, focusing on her face, marred with smudges of sooty ash.

"Are you all right? What happened to you?"

"You're not going to believe it." He let out a breath, looked at the dragon and back at Jalil. "The dragon brought me to the realm between time and space."

"Where?" Her nose crinkled.

"Remember the first time you transported to meet me? At the shrine, the mist, how we didn't know where we were or how we got there?"

She nodded. "I remember." Her face grew serious. "You were there?"

"Yes." He clasped her upper arms. "Was I here as well?"

She nodded and looked at her feet. "Does this mean you no longer need me?"

"No!" The earth quaked and threw them sideways. "The dragon told me to learn the lesson of the bat." He pushed himself upright. "Do you know this lesson?"

"The bat?" Lines of confusion marked her forehead. "Well, yes. Let me think." Her eyes brightened. "We know it's a symbol of rebirth." She nibbled her thumbnail. "The lesson of the bat is that the person undergoing the initiation has to face his fears and meet his real self." She turned to face Manelin. "This is brought about by tests. They take the participant to mental and physical limits."

"How do I know if this applies to me?" Manelin frowned. "This is all so difficult. I feel like everything rests on me. How do I know what to do? Should I move forward? Do I leave them here?" He thrust his index finger toward the corpse like bodies huddled within the toans.

Jalil's eyes glazed over. "If a bat flies through your dreams," her mouth moved as if controlled by someone else, "it indicates time to take leave of part of yourself." She blinked.

"What does that mean though? I thought I did that back in the Yoke of Inspiration. You're supposed to give me understanding." He squeezed her upper arms. "Not more questions."

"Only you can know what to leave behind." She shrugged. "It's a ritual of death. It's the way you develop further. Are you ready to die?"

Manelin looked over his shoulder at the Stygian frozen in time when the floor shifted and threw him to the ground. Across the gorge, the Crystal Cavern exploded spewing boulders. Panic set in. Had that been Jalil's father in there?

"...vive." Behind him, a male voice spoke one syllable. Manelin turned on his heel recognizing the tall male clutching the female at his side. The Stygian man looked to his left and right bending to pick up his spear. He stared at Manelin. "Is this the great awakening?"

Manelin swallowed. *It's really happening.* "Yes," Manelin picked himself up from the floor. "We need to get the people out of here. The Crystal Cavern has blown; the Valley of Blades is flooded and threatens to flood the Valley of Rocks. Thousands of people ... all of Ranaan will be lost. We must warn them."

The woman beside the man came to life. "The flood would cleanse the land and rid us of the curse."

Jalil stood like a statue. "My father! He's in the village. We must warn him to move into the mountains."

The Stygian man stepped forward. "My name is Cedrick. I'm Potent of this clan. I'll help in any way I can." He pointed to the woman. "This is my wife, Awena."

"This is Jalil," Manelin pointed to his friend, "and my name is Manelin."

"Manelin," the Stygian woman repeated. Her lip trembled. She glanced at her husband. "You were right. Our son is the Arich."

"Son?" Manelin looked from the man to the woman and back to Jalil. "Your son is the Arich?"

"You, Manelin, are our son. Is Philander well?"

Manelin's felt dizzy. "…My parents?"

Chapter 24
The Escape

"If that dam breaks, the Valley of Rocks will be flooded."

Cedrick stepped forward stiffly. "Manelin, I knew it." He turned to his wife and extended his hand. "Awena, we've made it. The cycle of rebirth has begun."

Manelin took in a deep breath as sheets of ice crashed inside the cavern from the ceiling above. Steam swirled as volcanic heat pushed the frozen world to life. It reminded him of the dreamlike world where he met with Jalil and spoke with the dragon. The flutter of wings overhead warned them to duck as the swarm of bats dived toward the mouth of the cave disappearing across the way into the crumbling Crystal Cavern.

"Another sign of rebirth," Jalil said. "But what does this mean for those in the village?"

Manelin rushed to the broken ledge outside the cave. "Manelin," Cedrick stepped from behind him and rested his hand on his shoulder. "I know you have unanswered questions, as do I. We'll have time later to discuss all that has happened and why, but not here. What do we do now?"

Manelin spun and pounded his chest. "You?" His nostrils flared. "You ask me what to do? How should I know? I've fumbled around; trying to learn about the Stygian people when I'd never even heard the word before I was seventeen and everything I ever held dear was ripped from me." He stared directly into Cedrick's dark eyes.

Awena walked behind her husband and leaned on his arm. "I never thought we'd live through this. Manelin." She reached toward her son. "Please forgive us. I thought I'd die when we left you behind, but if we'd brought you with us then you wouldn't have been here to set the awaking in motion."

Manelin sucked in a deep breath and glared at the woman he didn't know. "How can you say that?" He ran his fingers through his hair and yanked it in frustration. "If I'm truly this Arich, don't you think that somehow circumstances would have allowed me to be with my parents and still usher in the awakening?"

"Manelin, don't talk to your mother in such a manner. I had to drag her from you. I entered the cycle of death bearing her anger for leaving you behind. What neither of you understands is that great sacrifice is called for on the part of many. I would have loved nothing more than growing old with my wife and children, and watching my grandchildren come into the world. Instead, I put my faith in the prophecies. We left our only child in the hands of a man whose family we respected. They honored our ways, while most Jonnick despised us."

"How is Philander?" Awena shouted over the brewing tempest. Wind whipped white caps on the floodwaters, slamming the dam of debris below.

Jalil hobbled between Manelin and his parents. "Manelin, let go of the anger. It is misplaced. Your parents follow the path of hope. They love you."

Awena put her hand on Jalil's shoulder. "You must be the Augur." She bowed her head.

Jalil stared at the dark haired woman. "I—well, yes I am. At least, that's what Manelin and I figured. It's only been him and me. My father hates the Stygian. He doesn't even want me to spend time with Manelin because his eyes are brown."

Cedrick placed his palm on Jalil's arm. His brown eyes brimmed with tears. "I see your mother came from the line of Salus. This amulet belonged to her. We had no idea what had become of it."

Awena reached out. Her trembling fingers brushed the necklace. She turned to Cedrick. "I'm sorry I was angry with you. We truly are living in the time of the great awakening. What do we do now?"

"Have you battled the ashen serpent?" Cedrick asked his son.

Manelin nodded. "Actually, the dragon fought the serpent."

"The ashen serpent grows strong as it feeds on hatred among the people." Jalil's trance-like blank stare told Manelin she was again filling the shoes of Augur.

"Look!" Awena pointed across the lake battering the icy dam forming at the other end of the Valley of Blades. "If that dam breaks the Valley of Rocks will be flooded."

"Chock!" Jalil covered her mouth. "My father!"

"And, I don't know where Grandfather is, if he's still alive." Manelin turned toward his mother. "The queen's army took him away. He warned me to flee and I haven't seen him since."

Awena gasped covering her mouth. "Poor Philander."

"He understood the risk and was willing to undertake the raising of the Arich."

"So he knew?" Manelin asked. "All that time he knew?" He glanced into the cavern where the awakened Stygian gathered.

Cedrick nodded. "He hid your heritage well. It was necessary for you to grow up understanding the Jonnick way, for you are the one to unite our two peoples."

"Manelin," Jalil pleaded, "we must warn the people in Chock and Tehya."

"But how?"

"I can return home by the power of the walking stick. It is time to tell my father everything."

Manelin. The female dragon's voice filled Manelin's head. *I will carry your people to safety.* Manelin's head hurt. He rubbed the pain in his right temple. *Do not linger,* the voice warned. *Wasted time will be costly among the Jonnick.*

Manelin turned and looked at all the faces depending on him. "Jalil, the dragon will help transport my people to the Yoke of Inspiration. I'll need you to use the transporting power of the walking stick to lead people to the Fortress of Stone. Go to the villages, the asylum and even the great castle. Those ready for a new beginning will come willingly."

She reached out and squeezed his arm. "I fear for my father."

"Go, take care of your mother. Your father is here within the Yoke of Inspiration."

Her hand flew to her mouth. Fear filled her eyes. "What!"

Manelin held her shoulders. "Listen to me. Many people depend on you. When that dam lets loose, the valley will flood. You can save only those with the faith to accept your instruction. The choice is theirs, not ours. I will care for your father."

"But, he hates you." Jalil glanced at the smoldering cavern across the way, tilted her head to the side and closed her eyes. "I'll meet you in the Fortress of Stone." She leaned to hug him and whispered in his ear. "Please, don't leave him behind."

* * * *

The floor of the dungeon vibrated beneath Philander's bunk and stirred him from dreams of freedom. He sat up, his mind foggy. How long had his brother been gone? The wall behind him marked the days of his captivity. If not for his brother's companionship, he would go crazy. How long had he slept? Where was Nilenam?

Vibrations tickled the soles of his feet. This wasn't a dream. His joints creaked as he pushed the cot under the window overhead, climbed and stretched hoping to take in a glimpse of the commotion. A hint of fresh air brushed across his wrinkled face. His thoughts raced to the fair-haired bumble foot and Manelin, but returned to Nilenam. What had become of him since he went to treat Riona?

Balancing on the edge of the cot, he stretched to look out the window. "Not quite high enough." He cherished the brief view of the limited glimpse of the patch of swirling gray clouds and longed for freedom. Freedom on a stormy day was better than living in this cell in fair weather.

A rolling roar thundered from beyond his view. The bed rocked beneath his feet. Fear squeezed Philander's chest. In his heart, he'd hoped somehow he'd be part of the joining. He glanced at the calculations scratched into the stone. Would he be left behind, rotting in the dungeon of Riona's castle? He stepped from the bunk and looked with despair about his cell. No, he'd not give in to Riona's ways. Nothing would make her happier than breaking his will. Glancing back toward the window, he held onto the hint of hope that he'd once again live in the world beyond the castle walls. A slight hint of movement on the sill caught his attention. Tiny transparent wings shimmered in the natural light. A dragonfly!

Hope surged and renewed his faith. The lesson of the dragonfly tumbled through his thoughts. *Nothing is as it seems.* He glanced around his cell. Did this mean he'd stayed here unnecessarily? Was he blind to the way of escape?

The floor buckled throwing Philander against the wall and onto his bed. He covered his face from falling dirt and dust. When he opened his eyes, Jalil stood before him. He blinked. "Are you real?" His eyes fell to the Augur's staff in her hand.

She smiled. "Philander, we have little time. Manelin will meet you within the Fortress of Stone."

Philander pushed to his feet. "He made it!" He grabbed her shoulders and hugged her like a daughter.

"Place your hand upon the staff, time is short. I've cleared the asylum with my mother's help. Many in Chock refuse help. It's so sad. Delaine's father wanted to come, but Delaine refused my help. He ran his father through with his sword." She stared at the floor. "I wanted to try and heal him, but Delaine held me at bay and slashed at me with his sword. He screamed and ranted like a crazy man. I had no choice but to leave him and others there. From here, I must still go to Tehya."

Philander's gnarled fingers wrapped around the shaft beneath her hand. A sense of weightlessness washed over him. Jalil's blue eyes locked with his.

"The queen's hatred fueled by generations of anger and hatred." They floated inches over the floor. "The force of the Mage is not easily overcome," Jalil said.

Scuffles at the end of the corridor warned them to stay still. "Philander!" Nilenam's breathless voice called out.

"It's my brother," Philander said to Jalil. "Can you free him as well?"

"If he has the faith to join us."

Nilenam dragged the body of an unconscious woman along the floor and stopped before Philander's cell. He rested her head against the bars. "Philander?" Nilenam's face grew pale. He glanced up and down the corridor. "Please tell me I'm not late."

"Let go of the staff and he will see you ... and me."

Philander unwrapped his fingers from the magic of the twisted walking stick. Gravity pulled at his weary bones as his weight returned to normal. "Nilenam, I'm here."

"I've got Riona's body, Philander. The Magestone is in her hand." He lifted her wrapped hand. "I've tied it to her palm so it doesn't fall. I didn't know what else to do."

"Jalil has come to carry us to the Fortress of Stone." He pointed to Riona. "What do we do with her?"

Jalil's image shimmered and coalesced beside Nilenam on the other side of the bars. "Join your hand on the staff with mine."

Stooped and out of breath, Nilenam looked from his brother to Jalil. "We need to bring her with us."

"Riona!" Philander almost shouted. "You can't be serious." He clasped the bars separating the two.

"Brother, I'm a Healer. I can heal her body, but not her soul. Right now, the two are separate. I think it will slow her down if she can't find her physical form when she returns, and it might give me the opportunity to figure out a way to really help her."

Philander's good eye looked from Nilenam to Jalil. She nodded.

Nilenam struggled to drape the queen's body across his shoulder. Her head lay upon the hump on his back like a pillow. Her crown fell to the floor. Jalil snatched the glittering headpiece from the floor, and Nilenam grabbed the head of the staff.

Jalil, Nilenam and Riona vanished reappearing beside Philander within the cell.

"Why not leave Riona here in the cell." Philander gestured toward the cot.

"No," Nilenam shook his head, "I can't leave her to die in the great flood."

Jalil glanced at the face of each brother. "Her essence will return here to unite with her body. If it does not reunite with her, it will look for another host."

Nilenam nodded. "If the Magestone falls from her hand, she'll return sooner. I've tied it into her palm. This way, she won't know we've moved her body until she returns to the castle."

Jalil looked to Philander. He nodded. She glanced at Nilenam who strained under the weight of the queen's body.

"We have no time to waste. Join your hands with mine."

Philander closed his eyes hoping this wasn't a dream. The room around him shook and the four of them drifted toward the window where the sight of deafening floodwaters filling the valley took away his breath. He stared at Jalil in horror. "What of all the people?"

"This is why I must hurry. Each is offered a way of escape." The narrow window before them expanded like a bubble. "But, they must have faith enough to follow it." A bow of transparent colors flickered into existence like a roadway above the flood. "Follow the way. I've others to help." They settled onto the rocky precipice outside the dungeon. Rushing waters crashed and churned below, and the girl vanished.

Philander stared at the bow of translucent colors stretching into the sky. "Are you ready for this, brother?" He closed his eyes and took a step from the rocky ledge outside his cell.

* * * *

Manelin and his father, Cedrick, rode the dragon across the stormy valley. "That valley was filled with life when I last saw it," he shouted over the rush of wind from the great lizard's wings. "The great white serpent's magic altered it, before it turned to freeze us within the Cage of Ice."

"The dragon defeated the serpent today," Manelin said as they landed on the other side. Father and son jumped to the frozen soil. Manelin turned to his father. "The people need someone to ride with them on the dragon's back. It takes some getting use to."

Cedrick smiled and bowed his head. "I shall return and help my ... your people to cross."

Manelin shook his head. "I am of the people, chosen for this time, but you are their Potent."

The dragon lowered its neck and Cedrick climbed aboard.

"Meet me at the Waters of Nen," Manelin shouted. The wind from the dragon's liftoff blew Manelin's hair as he watched them head back to the others.

Manelin watched with fascination for moment. The man and woman in the vision were his parents. He looked forward to getting to know them on the other side of all this mess. He turned and headed into the corridor filled with lingering smoke.

The loop from the Cavern of Ice to the center of the yoke had collapsed leaving the more direct route as the only way. That must have been the explosion he witnessed from the other side. The gift of seeing in the dark worked once again, as Manelin headed into the larger tunnel toward the pool at the center of the underground system. His shoulder started to burn. Water splashed ahead. He knew the answer was here. *If only I can find it before the others join me.* "Fox are you here?"

Only the sound of the waterfall pouring into the Waters of Nen answered him. Up ahead, he saw something beside the pool. A donkey. Manelin approached with caution. The mule's back carried a heavy load. What on earth was a mule doing here?

A low moan stopped him in his tracks. The baggage on the donkey's back moved. It was Jalil's father. He slid from the donkey's back and screamed in pain as he landed beside the pool.

Manelin rushed to his side. His eyes closed; Manelin surveyed his injured leg. He'd lost quite a bit of blood. If only Jalil were here to heal his wound.

Out of nowhere, thick fingers wrapped around Manelin's neck.

"Stygian scum." Jalil's father squeezed Manelin's windpipe. "What have you done?"

"I'm—here—to—help." Manelin struggled to loosen the vice-like grip from his throat.

The donkey balked and hurried down the tunnel toward the Nefarious Forest, leaving the two rolling across the floor. They teetered on the edge of the pool. Adish forced Manelin's head under the water. Manelin pushed

with his legs and propelled the two of them into the pool. Fear gripped
Manelin as they plummeted toward the unknown depths. If they both
drowned, they'd leave Jalil alone to manage unbearable grief. Manelin's
lungs burned. Even with his gift of night sight, the waters dimmed his
perception. His head spun for lack of oxygen.

Adish didn't let go, but his grip weakened. His body went limp.

Manelin welcomed the uncomfortable feeling and looked around in
anticipation. A light appeared in the distance and he pulled the large
man behind him. It seemed a never-ending swim but finally he popped
through the surface, gasping for air. To his surprise, he recognized his
surroundings. The tower within the Potent's Table would lead them up to
the great hall. They'd made it to the pool within the Fortress of Stone.

Manelin climbed from the pool and dragged Adish's body onto the
floor. What should he do? Leave him here and go back? The sound of
water rushing against the walls outside spurred his decision. The dam
had given way. He jumped back into the pool. His father would wonder
what had happened to him.

The swim back was easier. Within a minute, he found his way back
into Sharis Havyn. His head popped through the surface of the Waters
of Nen, surprising a group of Stygian standing off to the side. "Come,"
he motioned with his hand, "this is the way."

His mother stepped forward. "I'm ready."

"Mother, we need as many people as possible to come at once. Time
is short. If you could stay here and let father know. Have weak swimmers
pair with those who swim well. I'll start to take the children."

Awena nodded and pushed two children toward the pool.

"Nooo!" The younger of the two clung to her mother.

"Come with us," Manelin said. He motioned for the mother to join
them. "Hurry. The Valley of Rocks is flooding. We don't have much
time."

The woman grabbed her children and placed them in the water.

"I'll take the boy. You take the girl. Hold onto my poncho so you don't
lose me. Understood?"

"Yes."

They took deep breaths and plunged into the water. At the other
end, Manelin was surprised to see that Jalil's father had disappeared. He
glanced toward the stairway. As much as he loved Jalil, he had to let the
man go. His people depended on him.

He turned to the woman. "The stairs in that tower lead to the Fortress of Stone, but the way is dangerous. Take it slow." He wiped water from his eyes. "Avoid the first door. Go to the top. We'll meet there."

The woman dropped to her knees. "Thank you, Arich. I owe all to you."

"What you owe me is to get your children up to safety. Go!"

He turned and dived into the water.

* * * *

Estel led a string of patients from the asylum across the magical bow of color. "Don't look down. Keep your eyes ahead. Freedom awaits!"

Jalil had told her to follow the ribbon of color to the end. As she approached the large stone formation, she recognized the Potent's Table. Others had gathered atop it, safe from the floodwaters ravaging the Valley of Rocks. The motley group walked in wonder to join the other refugees.

Estel set foot atop the stone structure and helped others make the step from the magical walkway. She glanced over her shoulder at the faces of others standing in the rain, hoping to find one she might recognize.

Adish where are you?

Chapter 25
The New Land

Scraping noises filtered through the thick planks.
Manelin stopped and listened. Far-away voices.
People waited on the other side of the door.

Philander led the way while his brother lugged the weight of Riona's body. The colors of the walkway of light painted a stark contrast against the gray sky.

"Where are we heading?" Nilenam asked.

"You know what I know. What do you think?"

"The Fortress of Stone?"

Philander nodded. "Do you need help carrying Riona?"

"I'll let you know if I do." He paused shifting the dead weight across his shoulder. "I exercised daily during my captivity."

"You?"

Nilenam chuckled. "Not much else to do. I considered it a prudent use of my time in preparing for the future."

The two elderly brothers shuffled along amazed at the ease with which they walked. "Never thought it would be like this," Philander said. "I wonder if I'll see Manelin."

"You'll see him."

"You sound pretty sure of yourself." Philander stopped and peered through the torrent of rain. "There it is, Nilenam! See the people?" He pointed to the Potent's Table protruding from the middle of the flood. People huddled in groups along the top.

Nilenam wiped wet stands of white hair from his face blinking away the rain. "I see them." He adjusted Riona's weight. "My back is about to break, do you mind helping me carry Riona the rest of the way? We're almost there."

* * * *

Riona's essence slithered into the east tower so weak she didn't know if she'd make it to the bed. The dragon had drained her. Almost ... couldn't ... move. She pushed through the door into her chamber and halted above the empty bed. Her essence shimmered. She struggled to pull herself together. Where had her body gone?

She longed to be reunited. If her body were lost what would become of her? Without the stone, the power of the Mage would leave her and without a physical form, she would vanish forever.

Mustering what little strength remained, she pressed into the storm in search of her self.

* * * *

Lightning flashed across the sky. Estel ran through puddles on the roof of the Potent's Table to greet the Healer. "Nilenam! Let me help you." She assisted Philander and Nilenam as they gently placed the woman on the floor. Nilenam collapsed to his knees happy to see them care.

"Thank you."

Estel stared at the woman's familiar face.

"Is this...?" She looked from Riona to Philander. "The queen?" she whispered.

Philander nodded.

"What is she doing here?"

Nilenam crawled across the roof blocking rain from Riona's face. "I couldn't leave her to die. We may be able to help her—free her from the curse of the Mage."

Estel glanced from Nilenam to Philander. "I'm willing to help, but what do we do?" Cold wind whipped sheets of rain across the rooftop. Some women in the crowd cried, and most of the men wore expressions of bewilderment.

"How do we get inside?" Philander asked.

"Inside?" Estel look around. "Inside what?"

Philander stood wrapping his arms around his wet body. "Here," he stomped one foot, "the Fortress of Stone. Manelin and Jalil have been inside. Let's look for the way in."

* * * *

Adish limped up the circular stairwell in the dark dragging his bad leg. He stopped to lean against the wall and collapsed in a wave of pain. If he made it through this experience, he vowed to lose weight. He sat on the stair pondering his life. Why would he want to live? What did he have left?

Voices echoed within the stairwell. Further away, he recognized the voice of the brown-eyed boy saying, "What are you waiting for? Follow me."

"Run your hand along the wall," the boy instructed. "Be careful of the passageway to the right about midway. Keep going until you reach the top of the stairs. Go through the door and wait within the great hall."

A small voice sounded next to Adish's ear. "Do you need help, Sir?"

"My leg," Adish said, "I can't walk. You'll have to go around me."

"The men will carry him," the boy's mother said.

"Can I help?" the child asked in the dark.

"Next time, son," his mother said. "We're holding up the line of people behind us." She lifted the child and patted Adish on the shoulder. "The men will help you."

* * * *

Manelin pulled himself out of the pool into the cavern. Stragglers milled about in water ankle deep. "What are you waiting for?" he asked again. "Follow me."

Mumbles from the crowd varied. People couldn't see. The lack of sunlight on the stormy spring day offered no help. "We need to move up." Manelin spoke loud enough for the entire crowd to hear. "Put your hands on the hips of the person in front of you."

The crowd stirred with chatter and murmurs while Manelin pushed his way to the tower of stairs. "Follow the music." He pulled his flute from the neck of his tunic and blew water from the holes. A few stiff breaths and one flat note sounded. "Once it dries out a bit, it will sound better."

He played while the string of refugees followed him up the staircase. His mind wandered to Jalil wondering if she had found his grandfather. Where were his parents? And what about Jalil's father?

Midway up the stairs, Manelin's shoulder heated. The second door. He never did investigate it. The steady burn told him it was important. For now, he had to lead these people into the great hall and safely beyond the disintegrating walkway heading to the door leading to the unknown.

Manelin reached the top of the stairs and opened the door. Candles and torches flickered shedding light into the stairwell. Sounds of hope and cheers echoed behind him and from the refugees already filling the great hall. Manelin rushed to the far wall, near the shelves of jars, where his father knelt beside Adish.

Cedrick stood and walked over to his son and the two embraced. "The large man wants to see you."

"I can't take the time. Tell him my work is not finished, but I'll return soon and we can talk."

Cedrick let out a long breath. "His leg ... he's lost a bit of blood."

Manelin rested his hand on his father's shoulder. "Take care of him. I'll hurry back."

He headed out the door pressing his back to the wall within the stairwell and inching down the staircase past those climbing to the great hall. In his heart, he thanked Ojal for the gift of seeing in the dark. As his dog, or the fox, bat, owl or great lizard, she'd done much to bring these people back. Things he didn't know or understand, like seeing in the dark.

His enhanced vision allowed him to see the crumbling section of the walkway leading to the door. He jumped and landed easily on two feet. The door opened to a short stairway leading up to a second door overhead. Manelin pushed, but it didn't budge. Scraping noises filtered through the thick planks. Manelin stopped and listened. Far-away voices. People waited on the other side of the door. He reached over his head pounding against the door.

* * * *

Jalil draped her hood over her head to protect from the rain as she appeared in Tehya. She moved from door to door pleading with the people to leave, but most of them laughed or said they were moving to higher ground, putting their faith in the Shrine of the Beginnings.

A sense of happier times washed over her as she passed by her childhood home. The yard had grown thick with weeds and the fence around the small graveyard fell in disrepair. No time to dwell on these things now. She floated to the door of her uncle's house and knocked.

A man that looked very much like her father only younger and thinner answered the door. "Yes?"

"Uncle Laul, I'm Jalil, your brother Adish's daughter."

Laul ran his fingers through his reddish blond hair. "What are you doing here?"

"A great flood is on the way. I have no time to explain. You mean a lot to my father, and I'm offering a way out."

Laul stood wide-eyed staring at the horizon. Jalil turned to see the great wave crashing toward them. "Now," she ordered. In a flash, the bridge of color extended into the sky. "Go! Are there others?"

Laul nodded and climbed to safety.

"Call them, hurry!" Jalil entered the house. "Help!"

Four women hurried to see who caused such a ruckus. Laul called to them from the bow in the sky. "Hurry! Climb."

Three of the girls were a little older than Jalil. Their mother helped them scale the bridge of light. The last of the three reached her father's side as the waters crashed in on their home pulling his wife into the wake.

"No!" Laul pulled the girls to his chest and watched in horror as the waters swept her away.

Jalil shouted over the waters. "Follow the way to the Fortress of Stone. Carry your daughters to safety. I'll try to save your wife."

Stunned and crushed in spirit, Laul turned and wandered the path of light.

* * * *

"Do you hear that pounding noise?" Philander shouted above the roar of the wind. "Sounds like knocking. Someone's looking for us."

Others stood in a circle staring, listening to the noise. "Don't just stand there," Philander scolded. "Look for the way in."

He reached into a puddle in the vicinity of the knocking. His fingers slid across something. A latch! "I found it!" He yanked the rain-swollen bolt. "It's stuck." He stood and kicked it with his heel until it broke loose. The door pushed open, a gust of wind kicked it flat against the roof. Philander stared in disbelief as Manelin poked his head into view.

"Grandfather!" He tripped up the stairs and the two embraced.

"We need to get the people inside," Manelin shouted over the wind and rain, "but it's dangerous. The walkway between the door and the stairs leading into the great hall are in poor condition."

"What do we need to do?" Philander asked.

"Stay to the right, it's dark."

Philander nodded. "I'll tell them on this end; you go inside and help them across the troubled spot."

Manelin stretched his neck searching the crowd. "Grandfather, have you seen Jalil?"

"Not since she rescued me. Don't worry, Son, she'll be back."

Manelin nodded and headed into the dark stairwell with his first group of Jonnick refugees from the asylum. They shuffled through the narrow passage without a word and Manelin actually enjoyed the time of quiet. Once he had all the people into the great hall, what would he do? For now, he pushed the worry aside. It didn't help, but instead put him on edge.

"Did I hear you ask about Jalil?" a woman behind him asked.

Manelin stopped. "Yes, why?"

"I'm her mother!"

"It's nice to meet you," Manelin said, "and good to know she reached you. I'm concerned though. The waters outside rage and she hasn't made it back."

Estel's eyes grew wide. "I can't believe I'm going to lose her again. I just can't."

Manelin reached out in the dark and consoled the woman. "Listen, we're almost there. For now, we have to put our feelings aside. Everyone here has lost something and we need to be strong for each other."

Estel nodded.

Manelin helped the people file beyond the weak point in the walkway. The door at the top of the stairs stayed open offering enough light to guide the refugees.

* * * *

Manelin surveyed the motley crowd gathered within the Fortress of Stone. Seeing Jonnick and Stygian together helping one another seemed like a good end to a bad dream. Beside him, two forms coalesced into existence. Jalil stood drenched, holding a woman beside her.

"Timmon!" Laul ran and helped his wife. "Thank you so much, Jalil." He brushed his niece's cheek. "I'm so sorry."

Laul and Timmon joined their daughters where Timmon collapsed in their embrace.

Manelin hurried to Jalil's side. "Are you alright?"

"I'm very tired." She glanced around the room. "Father!" Instead of using her Augur abilities, she hobbled toward her parents wrapping her arms around each of them.

Adish winced at the pain in his leg. Jalil placed her palm on his thigh. The necklace glowed. Adish stared at his healed leg, back at his daughter and the others who had witnessed his healing. He pushed to his feet, standing straight. "What do we need to do, Manelin?"

Hearing Adish speak his name with respect meant more than anything else he'd experienced this strange day.

Nilenam stood. "Can you heal my friend?" He pointed to the queen.

Jalil floated toward the prone woman. Her palm pressed against the woman's forehead. The necklace glowed. "I'm sorry. Her illness I cannot treat."

Nilenam stared at the floor. His large tears painted dark splotches on the stone floor.

Jalil touched the hump on his back. "The one who can heal her is the Arich's namesake. Use your gift."

Nilenam blinked pressing his palm to his chest, "Me?" He stood straight, no longer impeded by a hump on his back.

Jalil floated over to Manelin and slipped the flute from around his neck and carried it over to the old Healer.

"It's been a long time," he said as he accepted the instrument.

"Play it," Jalil said.

Nilenam caressed each note of the joining song. The sack beside him expanded. He loosened the rope cinching it, and slipped the crown onto the floor. He continued the tune as the bewildered crowd watched. The jewels in the crown popped releasing swirls of color. They filled the room. Some landed on people within the crowd like songbirds resting on their shoulders. Others streaked through the air and joined to form a ball of light.

Nilenam glanced at Riona. Wrinkles etched her once perfect skin. She opened her eyes. "Where am I?"

"You are ready to begin a new life," Nilenam said.

He unwrapped her hand and she stared at the Magestone. "I need to throw it into the sea."

Nilenam looked at Jalil and Manelin. "It's too dangerous. We can't let her go out there."

"There's another way," Manelin said. "Sop, come here girl."

The golden puppy bounded through the door.

"Toss it to her."

Riona flipped the stone. The dog caught it and ran out the door.

* * * *

Manelin searched the faces in the crowd. "The Jonnick gathered here have lost everything they own, but stand here today with their lives."

Adish reached out and took Estel's hand and nodded. Laul huddled in the corner with his three daughters staring blankly. Philander sat on one of the few chairs. His hair had dried to a fine white. His brother bent over the finely dressed woman on the floor.

"The Stygian likewise, have lost everything, but stand here today with their lives," Manelin said.

Cedrick wrapped his arm across Awena's shoulder.

"Some of you have suffered great personal loss, and I grieve for you. However, tonight, we make an important choice. We all want a better way, a new beginning and today it is offered to each of us."

The crowd buzzed with excitement.

"It doesn't matter if you are Stygian or Jonnick or a little of both. What matters is unity." As Nilenam continued to play the flute, a gateway appeared behind Manelin. Beneath the arch, blue skies and rolling green hills made eyes bulge and jaws fall open. "This is the new land." The ball of light hovering overhead burst into individual streaks of color and shot through the gateway.

"Come everyone, new life awaits."

* * * *

Ojal's golden fur bulged as muscular scaled legs clawed at the plateau above the Fortress of Stone as she transformed one more time into the great dragon. Her leathery wings stirred gusts of rain pulling her into the velvet sky. She headed toward the shrine. Her keen vision allowed her to spot the people gathered at the monument, but the flash of movement cutting through the scuttling black clouds drew her attention away from those who had followed Delaine. The power of the Mage lived on as the ashen serpent streaked from the other direction toward the people. Lightning ripped through the sky between them. In the flare of light, the dragon let the Magestone fall from its jaws toward the sea. The serpent screeched, diving toward the stone midair.

The white stone disappeared into the blackness as the illumination dissipated. Howls filled the sky while Ojal's dragon form turned back to the Fortress of Stone. The curse of the Mage no longer had any claim on the queen.

* * * *

Delaine shouted at the sky as the serpent shot from the stormy sea and into the air searching for a new host. Its eyes focused on the hatred and arrogance below. The young man raised his sword as if to ward off the reptile's approach. His pride drew the power of the Mage.

The serpent dropped the stone at his feet and spun away from his blade. People gathered around him calling him a hero as he clutched the stone in his fist overhead. "I am your king!"

He stared at the people around him as they backed away. "I am your king," he repeated. Their wide-eyed response sent him spinning on his heel. The serpent hovered behind him, jaws wide-open. It struck his chest, swallowed his essence and vanished. A king was born. The Mage would rule the land.

Epilogue
The New Land

Adish sat upon a stone in the center of the field. "...through that kindness, I learned to love."

The crowd applauded. Two young children raced after one another. "Grandpa, grandpa, hide me from Izzi." Adish picked up his granddaughter and swung her up over his head and held her at arms length. He jiggled her back and forth. Her giggles were music to his ears. He looked into her big brown eyes and thought of what a different life she knew from that of her own mother's childhood. He rested her feet on the ground and took her hand.

"Grandpa," the child said, "When Mother gave Nilenam Father's flute...?"

"Yes?" Adish smiled. "He played the joining song. It marked the joining of the Jonnick and Stygian and the opening of the gateway to the new land."

"Oh, grandpa I know that part. What I don't understand is that Mother told Nilnam he was the Arich's namesake. That doesn't make sense."

"I didn't understand it myself when it happened," he said. "It's like a riddle. Your father is named after the man that helped deliver him on that moonless night. Your father's parents named their son after the healer, but spelled his name backwards to disguise the Jonnick connection."

"N-i-l-e-n-a-m, backwards is M-a-n...." Her eyes lit up. "I see!"

"Come now and sit on my lap," Adish said. He pointed toward the teaching stone. "It looks like your Grandfather Cedrick is ready to introduce Riona." The old woman sat on the stone. "She once served as queen," Adish said.

The fair-haired girl climbed onto Adish's lap. "What's a queen, Grandpa?" She scrunched her nose and gazed into her grandfather's eyes.

"It's someone that rules the land?"

"That's silly," she said. "Everyone knows the land can take care of itself."

About the Author

Freelance writer and author Donna Sundblad lives in rural Georgia with her husband and flock of pets including five cockatiels and a blue front Amazon named Neelix. Sometimes criticized as a child for her overactive imagination, today that inventiveness serves as a necessary ingredient in the creation process as a fiction writer. Donna shares the joy of storytelling with her grandchildren with a game she created called Sentence With a Twist and her love of writing spreads beyond the pages of her books to workshops and writer's groups. Feel free to contact Donna by email at donna@theinkslinger.net.

About the Cover Artist

Artist, Illustrator, writer, poet, Melissa Landon's creative side is inspired by her Australian heritage with its rainforests, coral reefs and tropical beaches. These days, Florida's natural wonders keep Melissa's brushes primed, where she enjoys hand painting and muraling furniture with scenes that please the eye, along with custom creations, which bring to life her clients ideas. Murals and illustrative book, magazine, poster and T-shirt designs bring variety to her drawing board and keep the brush strokes flowing nicely. She can be contacted via email at coowee2u@yahoo.com.

Afterword
by Jack Herrmann

Deep inside the heart of every intelligent and sensitive reader is a persistent desire to write.

In these individuals, experience, observations and thoughts (gained through the process of living) keep tweaking a wish to make a cultural contribution by means of the written word. All writers have this need. Some writers answer that need successfully. Other writers don't. Unfulfilled writers lack two crucial advantages they must have to gain mastery of the craft: confidence in their own ability, and the necessary training to hone their skills. It is a shame. Every unfulfilled writer continues to merely dream. Every reader loses.

I don't know how many times I've heard, "I've got a story to tell, if I could just write like this." If it is there, inside, it can be brought outside. So, if this is a description of you, what can you do about it? All that needs to be done is to learn that writers write and good writers write better.

As far as skill is concerned, know this: most writers cannot be placed in any sort of genius category.

They all do have this in common, though: 10 percent talent and 90 percent desire. They all can have fun developing their abilities. They all need to know where to find the help.

Where do you go to find that help? Formal scholastic training is costly and time-consuming. Correspondence lessons are similarly expensive and generally do not give benefit of peer group aid, or allow for sudden inspiration, or fun in learning. Face-to face writer's groups have necessary time-scheduling requirements, which can be difficult to maintain within the busy demands of life .

Perhaps you have enjoyed this book. If you have, you should know that this author had similar problems, but found a way to solve them.

Have a look at a web-based site described by Writer's Digest Magazine as one of the best online locales for writers: "Writers' Village University" and its affiliate, "F2K." Both sites were created with specific things in mind: simplicity, effective learning through course study, peer feedback and, most important, emphasis on mind-committing rather than wallet-emptying. Take a look at these.

F2K: A FREE series of six one-week courses designed for beginning writers. Intermediate and advanced writers take this full course as a refresher, or to socialize with and encourage beginning writers. Then, too, F2K is a great way to start writing again and to break writer's block. It is offered six times a year. Check it out by going to:

http://www.wrtersvillage.com

WVU: Writers' Village University is a living, breathing community of support and training curricula, totaling 200+ courses, seminars, study programs and workshops. Each is designed to help bring an aspect of your writing up to higher levels, be it fiction or nonfiction, poetry or literature.

Course scheduling is set so classes can fit into your personal time-slots. To insure this convenience, they are repeated several times each year. You can take what you need, when you need it. No examinations. No cranky teachers, and no impossible assignment demands. Just intelligent guidance and friendly, invaluable student feedback. The cost is, by far, the best value for writers anywhere. Here's where to find more information:

http://www.writersvillage.com

T-Zero – the Writers' Ezine: This is another free service (and also a paying market) offered by WVU bringing you details on:

*Editing
*Writing tips
*Exercises
*Fiction, non-fiction and poetry (Paying Market)
*Hints and practical encouragement

T-Zero has become a premium monthly Webzine designed to keep writers well informed. You can subscribe to it, and check out the current issue and the archives, at:

http://thewritersezine.com

Seize the moment. Become the writer you want to be. Have fun, learn much and. . .

Astonishing luck,

Jack

Order Form for Other ePress Books

IMPORTANT ORDER INFORMATION
ALL BOOKS may be ordered online at **http://www.epress-online. com** or … from the website you may copy the order form and mail it to the address at the bottom of the form.

All ePress books are available as eBooks - price each - $5.00

Some are also available in print, trade paperback - $14.99 plus shipping and handling.

A Sampling of our Books

FICTION
Mystery/Suspense
Absent the Soul - BJ Bourg
A Cobweb on the Soul - Nadene R. Carter
Dancing on the Edge - S.L. Connors
Under a Raging Moon - Frank Zafiro - *eBook only*

Fantasy
A Faerie Ring - Michael Honeth
Death at Dragonthroat - Teel James Glenn
Hierath - Joanne Hall
In Exile - Joanne Hall
Return to UKOO - Don Hurst
Tales of a Warrior Priest - Teel James Glenn
Windwalker - Donna Sundblad

American Historical Fiction
Benning's War - Jeffrey Keenan
Echoes of Silence - Nadene R. Carter

Science Fiction
Needle - L.L. Whitaker

Contemporary Fiction - Short Story Collection
Other People's Lives - Betty Kreier Lubinski

NON-FICTION - Craft of Writing
Pumping Your Muse - Donna Sundblad
The Magic & the Mundane - P. June Diehl
The Shy Writer - C. Hope Clark - *eBook only*